All I Want

All I Want

STELLA STARLING

Contents

Chapter 1

ELLIOTT

"It's Monday, the 21st of November," Nick said, the jolly twinkle in his eye perfectly suited to the role he'd embodied each Christmas at the Chicago Ashby's store since Elliott had been a child. "And we all know what that means, don't we, troops?"

Elliott couldn't suppress the grin that crept onto his face. It curled the corners of his lips up with a cat-like glee and he all but bounced on his toes, already caught up in the spirit of the season that the grandfatherly man addressing them—Elliott's long-time mentor and friend—had been tasked with kicking off.

Ashby's had closed half an hour ago, and the last

customers had finally been whisked through checkout. Apart from the sugary pop songs that played at a low volume through the department store's speaker system, the place was eerily silent as the assembled employees beamed back at Nick.

"Yeah, Nick," Grace piped up from next to Elliott, grinning just as widely as he was. "It means the weekend is too far away."

A snicker ran through the crowd, and Elliott shot a glance Grace's way. She stood at his side, arms crossed casually against her chest, her own excitement betrayed by the sparkle in her eyes. Amidst a sea of natural hair colors, her lilac hair stood out like a beacon.

"Right," Nick answered with a grin, winking at her. "But this Monday is more than that. This Monday is our last Monday before Thanksgiving, and that means that come this time next week, the area we're currently standing in will be decked out for Christmas."

The holiday celebrations at Ashby's were one of Elliott's favorite things about the season. There was something magical about the sparkling red garlands that Ashby's wove around its banisters and the permanence of the fake, glittering snow they set out in the area designated as the "North Pole." Not even the impending chaos that was Black Friday could steal away how special the act of setting the store up for Christmas made Elliott feel. As far as he was concerned, Ashby's North Pole was the highlight of the Christmas season, and Elliott was beyond delighted to be a part of it.

"And Christmas," Nick declared, hands on his hips and chin held high, "means setting up the North Pole and making sure all of us are on our very best behavior."

"Is someone going to give Kevin the memo?" Jose whispered into Elliott's ear, voice raised just enough that it carried to Grace, as well. She snickered from Elliott's other side and took a step closer to the pair, the sound turning into a poorly masked laugh as Kevin, their perpetually cranky coworker, glanced over his shoulder and scowled at them. Jose's jibe had been too low for the man to hear, and Elliott bit back a laugh at Kevin's irritation. Kevin didn't seem to need an excuse to be a sourpuss.

"Don't worry about him," their friend Trevor whispered, catching the exchange. "Every Christmas needs a Grinch. Let's just call him 'ambiance.'"

"Guys, eyes up front," Nick called out.

Elliott stood a little straighter, blushing at being called out, but not even a grump like Kevin could sour the Christmas pep talk Nick gave every year.

"Everyone who works the floor will also be working in the North Pole," Nick reminded them all. "As usual, Ashby's will bring in some temporary workers to help with the holiday rush, and to fill in for you while you're all busy making Christmas magical for the kids who visit us this season."

In any other Ashby's store, the staff Christmas preparations probably would have been coordinated by the department manager. Someone had made the right choice in deferring the role to Nick, though. Martin, a manager who could have given cranky Kevin some competition for the title of Grinch, rolled one of Ashby's iconic red shopping carts in from around the corner, expression as flat and emotionless as always. Even the dour manager couldn't detract from the excitement, though. Inside the cart, stacked high, were folded outfits in bright, cheerful Christmas colors. The reds and greens and golds caught Elliott's eye, and once he saw them, he couldn't look away.

The absolute best thing about working at Ashby's during the Christmas season was the North Pole outfits. It was the one time a year they got to ditch their black slacks, dress shirts, and ties.

"And that means that all of you are going to have to look the part." Nick grinned as Martin brought the cart to a stop beside him. Each of the outfits was sealed in clear plastic and marked with a neon yellow sticky note.

Names.

The lottery happened backstage, but it was always random and always exciting. Last year, Elliott had been an elf. The year before, he'd donned a pair of antlers. Whatever role he'd fill this year, he'd do it with the same enthusiasm of the years prior.

Serving at the North Pole was an honor that Elliott took seriously, and as silly as it was, it was something he looked forward to all year long.

The first outfit on the pile was the Santa suit. Its iconic

reds and whites were unmistakable. Nick plucked it off the top and slipped it under his arm. Ever since Elliott had been a child, Nick had played the role of Santa. That wasn't going to change any time soon. From the booming, but kind, timbre of his voice to his pale blue eyes, he was a great fit. And Elliott knew firsthand that Nick genuinely adored the kids. After all, Nick had been the one who'd made all of Elliott's childhood dreams come true.

"I want to be a sexy elf," Trevor declared.

"Only girls get to be sexy elves, Trevor," Grace shot back. "And there's nothing really sexy about oversized tunics, anyway."

With a wry chuckle, Trevor shook his head. "Hon, *anything* can be sexy. You just need to learn how to work it."

"I hope that I get to fill in as a nutcracker." Jose tried to redirect the conversation. "Elves are fun and all, but nutcrackers are where it's at. You remember last year how Brian and Patrick came up with that whole clockwork routine? And the look on the kids' faces while they watched those two never break character, even once? That's something I want to be a part of."

"Yeah." Excitement stirred in Elliott's chest, and he searched the cart for the red and black nutcracker outfits. They were few, and they were scattered. "That was actually really neat. I'd love to do something like that."

"Heidi," Nick called out, reading the name off the first outfit in the cart. Heidi stepped forward to claim her seasonal wear, then faded back into the crowd. "Jackson.

Jennifer. Florence."

Elves, nutcrackers, and reindeer were distributed, and the longer Elliott watched, the more the excitement burning within him grew.

"Jose," Nick called out. Jose lifted his chin, and Nick tossed him an outfit through the crowd. Martin, who stood by the shopping cart at Nick's side, scowled.

"Nick, don't throw," Martin scolded him. "There are strict policies in place about throwing Ashby's property. This is a verbal warning."

"A reindeer," Grace remarked, rolling her eyes at their sour manager's Scroogism as she poked at Jose's brown outfit through the plastic.

"Could be worse," Jose shrugged. "At least they didn't try to turn me into one of those *sexy elves* this year. I'd call that a victory."

"Carmen. Richard. Grace."

Grace winked at them and stepped through the crowd to collect her prize. Even from a distance, Elliott could see her fate.

Elf.

"*Sexy elf!*" Trevor whispered, thrilled, into Elliott's ear. "You think she'll trade me? We have to be the same size, and if we're not, I'll just skip Thanksgiving and come in on Black Friday to work the weight off."

"I think maybe you should ask her that." Elliott laughed. "But unless you dye your hair lilac, I doubt Martin's going to let you get away with it. Someone'll notice you're not Grace and cause a stink."

"Mm, yeah. *Someone.*" Trevor rested his chin on Elliott's shoulder and glared at Kevin from behind. "Oh well. Always next year, I guess."

"Trevor," Nick called, and Trevor gasped and pulled away from Elliott at once. Elliott saw the outfit at the same time his friend did.

Green.

"*Sexy elf!*" Trevor crowed as he tore his way through the crowd. Last year had been Trevor's first Christmas at Ashby's, and he'd been a reindeer. In a flash of blond hair and solemn Ashby's black, he shot to the front of the crowd to claim his prize.

"At least I'll get to be on Team Elf with Trevor," Grace laughed. Even though she groused from time to time, Elliott knew that she was just as excited as he was. There were few employees who didn't like working at the North Pole, either because they understood the importance of it to the kids who visited, or because they saw it as an escape from working the floors during one of the busiest retail seasons of the year. Elliott's group all appreciated the magic, and he was glad for it.

"Maybe you'll be Team Reindeer with me, and we'll kick it in style," Jose said to Elliott. "There aren't that many nutcracker outfits, and I mean, I know it's a lottery, but there's no way that Nick would have me working without one of you guys to keep me company."

"I don't know. I hope we get to work together." Elliott's

cheeks began to ache from smiling, and he sucked in his cheeks and pushed his mouth from side to side to try to work out some of the soreness. "No matter what, I know we're going to have a good time."

"You got that right," Trevor said as he returned. He'd already torn into the sealed plastic and had shaken free his tunic. "Some black leggings and an accentuating belt, and I'm going to *be* the elf."

"I'll do your makeup," Grace said casually. "Rosy cheeks? Can you work with those?"

Trevor's eyes sparkled. "I will work the *shit* out of them."

All of them laughed.

"Kaleb. Brian. Polly. Elliott."

Elliott lifted his chin and refocused his attention to the front of the crowd, and his heart skipped a beat. In Nick's hand was a red and black outfit.

"Dude, nutcracker duty." Jose slapped Elliott on the back. "Live the dream for me."

"What a loss for Team Elf," Grace lamented. "But a well-deserved win for Team Nutcracker. Get up there and own it."

In a daze, Elliott made his way through the crowd to accept his outfit from Nick.

"Congratulations, kid," Nick said under his breath as he passed the package to Elliott. "Not everyone gets to be a nutcracker, you know?"

"You're just saying that," Elliott replied, but he couldn't chase the smile from his face. Even though his cheeks burned, he couldn't stop himself. "A nutcracker isn't any more special than an elf or a reindeer."

"But a nutcracker gets to act as Santa's official guardian," Nick winked. "And I couldn't have asked for a better one."

Heat bloomed across Elliott's cheeks, and he ducked his head to hide how flattered he was. Nick was like a grandfather to him, and hearing kind words like those left him feeling like he'd really made something of himself.

"Thank you," Elliott whispered.

"See you at the big chair," Nick replied, then clapped his shoulder and let him go.

Stunned, Elliott turned on his heels and made his way back to his group of friends as Nick distributed the rest of the costumes. Grace and Trevor were chatting about effective elf makeup. Jose had opened up the plastic sealing his outfit and taken out the headband with the reindeer horns to turn it this way and that.

"We gotta change into these things, don't we?" Jose asked as Elliott returned to the group. "We're taking pictures for Ashby's yearbook, right?"

"Mmhm," Elliott held his outfit to his chest. The packaging was unbroken, and although the sticky note on the front clearly spelled out his name, he was hesitant to dig in. It still didn't feel real.

Another Christmas was here, and this time he was going to serve it beside the man who'd first instilled in him his own love of Christmas.

"Yeah. We all get changed and take pictures with Santa, and we get to ask him what we want with our bonuses this year," Grace replied. "What are you guys going to ask for? I'm thinking that I want one of those sample sizes of the new Giordani perfume we just got in. The one that's like two hundred dollars for a full-sized bottle? I imagine they make tiny sample sizes that wouldn't cost too much."

"I've got my eye on the new Hadfield line of men's shirts," Trevor declared. "I mean, maybe it's a little expensive to be asking for, but it's not jewelry, at least. Do you remember when that girl Deborah was working here, and she asked for the pink diamond earrings that you'd have to be a Duchess to afford?"

Elliott laughed. Yeah, he remembered. And when she'd opened the pink cubic zirconia knock-offs instead, she'd been convinced they were the real deal, and had bragged about them for months.

"A new frying pan," Jose said.

"What?" Elliott furrowed his brow. "A frying pan?"

"Yeah. I mean, I need one. Might as well take advantage, you know? And I can use a frying pan every day if I wanted to. A new shirt? Not so much."

"Do not diss the Hadfield line," Trevor warned in a mocking tone, lifting a finger to scold Jose. "Fashion serves a function just as much as a frying pan does."

"Eh. Can't cook eggs on a Hadfield shirt."

Trevor broke down laughing, and soon Grace was doubled over as well. Jose shrugged and turned his attention to Elliott. "What about you, dude? You got your eye on something special?"

"I think I've got something," Elliott said slowly. He pursed his lips and thought it through. "But I'm not going to share. Christmas magic only works if you share your wish with Santa and Santa alone."

"You're such a dweeb." Jose laughed. "But it's chill. You do you."

As a child, Elliott's mother had brought him to Ashby's every year so he could visit the North Pole to see Santa, and every year, whatever Elliott wished for while sitting on Santa's lap had come true. Every wish except for one. It was only later in life that Elliott discovered that Nick had been the one pulling the strings to make it happen. Elliott's mother had worked long hours for little pay, and the rent she'd paid on their Chicago apartment had overburdened her. There hadn't been room in the budget for Christmas gifts.

Nick, a total stranger, had kept Christmas alive in Elliott's heart. And, later in life, long after Elliott was too old to visit Santa anymore, Nick had been the one who'd helped him land the job at Ashby's.

But while Nick had seen to it that Elliott's childhood dreams came true, Elliott knew that as an adult, there was little Nick could do for him.

The one thing Elliott wanted was out of his reach.

But maybe, just maybe, the magic of Christmas would work if he whispered his wish in Nick's ear anyway. Even though he knew the man behind the Santa suit wasn't some mystical being, Elliott *believed*. And sometimes, he knew, believing in something was enough to make it happen.

The outfits were distributed, and the Ashby floor staff disbanded to change. By the time they returned, festive and ready to snap some shots for the yearbook, Martin had wheeled out the elaborate chair Santa sat in—the focal point of the North Pole—and Nick was already settled. In his red suit and white beard, he looked every bit the jolly man Elliott remembered from his youth.

Soon enough, Trevor and Jose returned, and Grace joined them just a few moments later. She fiddled with her tunic in an attempt to tame some of the excessive bagginess, but her efforts were wasted. Every year Ashby's gave her the smallest size they carried, and every year it was still too big.

"I've got you," Trevor told her as Grace joined them. "After the meeting's done, give it to me and I'll take it in for you. It'll look great."

"No sequins," Grace warned him. "No low-cut anything, and no other couture fixes."

"Me?" Trevor grinned. "Never."

A few members of the floor staff had already gone up to have their picture taken with Nick, but there wasn't a line just yet. Jose nudged Elliott's shoulder.

"Let's go take a group shot," he said. "All four of us."

Elliott caught Nick's eye and lifted his hand to wave, and Nick looked back and began to lift his arm to wave in return. Before he had lifted it far, his arm drooped and fell back onto the arm of the chair.

What?

Elliott squinted, trying to make out what was going on, and Nick winked at him.

"Nick?" Elliott asked. He broke away from the group as they bickered over the best way to take a group shot with Santa to see what was going on. "Hey, Nick, what are you doing?"

Nick winked again, and then his eyelid fluttered. The corner of his mouth sagged, and half of his face drooped.

Elliott stopped dead in his tracks, heart racing.

"Nick?"

There was no response. Dread laced through Elliott's stomach and squeezed, and he momentarily forgot how to breathe. Something abnormal was happening to Nick.

Something bad.

"E-Everyone," Elliott called out. Typically timid, his voice cut above the chatter and silenced those who had gathered. "Nick needs help right now. Someone go get him some water, and someone go call 911. He needs an ambulance. He's... there's something really wrong."

It looked like Nick was trying to say something, but when he opened his mouth, only half of his face obeyed. The sagging half of his body remained paralyzed and useless, and the sounds that spilled from his lips were jumbled and disjointed.

Terrifying.

Chaos started all at once, and Elliott's coworkers scrambled, some trying to help while others turned into blubbering messes. Elliott wasn't the only one who considered Nick more than just a coworker. In the midst of it, Elliott rushed to Nick's side and laid a hand on his arm. He wasn't sure if Nick even knew he was there, but he liked to think that he did. Sometimes, a calm, familiar presence made all the difference in the face of tragedy.

"It's going to be okay," Elliott promised. "We're going to make sure it's okay. I'm going to stay here with you until the ambulance comes. It's going to be fine."

With all of his heart, Elliott hoped that what he said was true. He had no idea what was happening to Nick, or if he'd pull out of it, but he knew he had to stay strong and keep the faith, just like Nick had done for him all those Christmases ago.

It was the least he could do, but still, it didn't feel like enough.

Elliott knew then that what he wanted for Christmas had changed. If all he got this year was the satisfaction of knowing that Nick would pull through whatever was happening to him, it would be enough for him. The selfish wish he'd harbored in his heart fell by the wayside. Nick was important to him, and Elliott wanted him to pull through more than anything else.

Wishing for someone to love could wait.

Chapter 2

ASH

THE NAME TAG HE'D BEEN GIVEN READ *BEN*, BECAUSE *ASH* was too telling, and the first time Bennett James Ashby had put it on, it had pricked him through his shirt. Now the cold metal bar securing it in place was flush with his skin, and the black Ashby's uniform he wore was hidden beneath a mountain of ridiculous padding and bright red fabric.

And God, was it hot.

Ash pushed at the padding of the Santa suit, disgusted with how it sat on his frame. This was *not* what he'd had in mind for today.

Or for the next week.

Or the two weeks following that.

There was nothing more humiliating than having to wear a getup like this, and Ash was well aware that his father knew it. Worse, the punishment, as far as Ash was concerned, didn't fit his crime. Dressing up to serve as the Santa in their flagship Chicago store when he should be on his way to Aspen to spend the holidays doing what he did best—partying with his friends—was tantamount to torture.

And pretending to be someone he wasn't? Some low-level nobody instead of the heir to the Ashby's fortune? That just made the experience even worse.

To the world, *Ben* was a nobody—a down-on-his-luck retail employee at one of the world's most successful department stores, indistinguishable from any other fresh face on the floor. But *Ash* was far from a nobody. The Ashby name was synonymous with power, prestige, and wealth. There wasn't a person in all of North America who wouldn't know who he was if he casually dropped his surname into conversation. And a good percentage of the world knew his face, too. The media loved him.

Well, the seedier outlets, anyway, but Ash didn't let that get him down.

The fact was, the publicity was good for business. He knew it, and his father knew it, too. The modern world couldn't get enough of the Ashby heir and his antics, and Ash had never been shy about airing his personal life to sate their appetites. Incognito was not his style.

He'd dated celebrities.

He'd dated models.

Hell, from time to time, he'd dated normal men, too, just to keep the world guessing.

None of his relationships ever lasted for long, and some were nothing more than publicized flings, but they scratched an itch and kept the Ashby's name in the lime-light, keeping both Ash and his father happy. Besides, there were better things to do with his time than to fall in love... and there were *certainly* better things to do with his time than to pretend to be Santa at the Ashby's department store right off Lake Shore Drive.

Someone pounded on the door of the staff bathroom.

"Occupied," Ash called out.

"You've been in there for like, fifteen minutes!"

"Right. So then you know it's occupied," he shot back.

Changing into the suit was a time-consuming process, and all the while his new contacts had been bothering him. The telltale turquoise color of his eyes would have been a dead giveaway to anyone with any media savvy, and Ash was supposed to be working undercover as Ben. Drawing attention to himself was off the table, so he'd been given colored contacts.

Stunning turquoise had turned to hazel in seconds.

Bleaching his naturally dark hair to make him into a believable blond had been a more involved process, but Marissa, his personal stylist in New York, had done him justice. It was pale and platinum and didn't look half bad.

"A natural," Marissa had crooned as she'd washed out the bleach. "You're handsome no matter what shade you go with."

But no matter how good the blond looked, it reminded him of what he'd lost. Not just the opportunity to be living it up in Aspen instead of stuck in some ridiculous fat suit, but all the perks that came with the fame and notoriety he normally took for granted.

His father had all but cut him off for the duration of this little adventure into the lives of the not-rich and not-famous.

Ash pulled his white wig on and brushed the thick white curls away from his eyes. The red Santa hat was built into the wig, and it promptly flopped over so that the white pompom at its tip rested on his shoulder. He secured his fake beard over his ears, adjusted it, and turned.

It was time to face the music, he supposed.

Rubbing at his eyes to try to curtail some of the irritation from the unfamiliar contacts, he unlocked the door and pushed it open to find a pissed-off employee waiting on the other side. A little bit on the heavy side, mousy hair kept short, he glared at Ash.

"We're on the clock, you know," the scowling man said.

"Uh." Ash frowned. The name tag on the employee's shirt read *Kevin*. "Are you really going to pick a fight with Santa? 'Cause I'm not really in the mood to get into an argument right now."

"Temp workers," Kevin grumbled. He pushed past Ash and into the bathroom. The door shut a little harder than it should have, and the lock clicked.

Well.

The urge to call it quits grew, but Ash knew the consequences all too well. He had to serve his time, and he *would* serve his time.

Disgruntled Kevins be damned.

Ash made his way out of the staff room and onto the floor, but before he could so much as make it beyond the first rack, a young woman with short, lilac-colored hair stopped him. Her name tag was hidden beneath the green elf outfit she wore.

"Hi," she said, grinning with a level of enthusiasm that Ash thought no minimum wage retail employee should have. "You must be Ben, right? The new Santa?"

To be called Ben was strange. Ash nodded, taken aback.

"Awesome," she said, making it sound like she actually meant it. "I'm Grace, and I'm really excited that you're here. Having a Santa in the store is a big deal, you know? The kids are going to come unglued when you get to the North Pole."

"They're kids," Ash grumbled. "They'd be excited no matter what."

Grace wagged a finger at him, pushing her lips to the side. "There's no room for negativity, Mr. Claus. You'd better get your game face on and hurry up and get to your station. Martin's the manager on duty, and he's a stickler for the rules. If you're late, especially on your first day, he's not going to take it too kindly."

Was that advice, or a warning? Grace was so bubbly and enthusiastic that Ash wasn't sure. Before he could decide how to take her words, though, she winked at him and continued on her way to the staff room.

"Take care, Ben! See you around. It was a pleasure meeting you."

"Likewise?" he asked, but she was already gone.

The place was full of nuts, he decided. Either they were overly grumpy, or way too cheerful for their own good.

This wasn't the place for him.

The staff room was located in the low-traffic area in the junction between bath and kitchen on the ground floor, and Ash stole off into an aisle stocked with bath mats and shower curtains while he wrestled to pull his phone out from his pocket. It was hard to navigate around the Santa suit and the padding he wore to flesh it out, but that just added weight, so to speak, to the realization that had just hit him.

He wasn't cut out for this.

There was no way he could march up the escalator and present himself for duty at the display overhang that housed the North Pole. No way he'd be able to make it through a day of hyper kids crawling all over him, much less the whole Christmas season.

His father was cruel, but he wasn't *that* cruel. He'd have

to understand.

The phone rang in his ear as Ash scrutinized the make of the bath mats on display in front of him and waited for his father to pick up. No customers had wandered over yet, and as far as he knew, he was alone. Still, he couldn't help but speaking in a hushed tone when his father finally answered the call.

"Bennett? What an unexpected surprise."

Douglas Ashby's tone made it clear that it was simply a statement of fact. "Unexpected," rather than "welcome."

"Father, I can't be here," Ash said, not bothering with a greeting. "Let's work out another deal. I'll put in my hours at the board, or work in acquisitions, or *something*. But playing Santa with these... with these people? Just... no." He wove his fingers through one of the shaggier bath mats, silently willing his father to relent. "This isn't teaching me anything. If you're going to make me get more involved with the stores, I'd be better off taking on responsibility at the executive level, don't you think? When will I ever use the training I receive as Santa again?"

There was silence. Ash's father never stuttered or struggled for words. The elder Ashby knew damn well the fear that a brooding silence brought with it, and even though Ash did his best to stand resolute before it, he felt his strength crumbling the longer it went on.

"Father!" he finally prompted, cracking.

"You will do as I've arranged for you to do," came Douglas's firm reply. "As we discussed, you need to start taking this business seriously, Bennett. You've long neglected participating at the executive level, so now I'm giving you the opportunity—" Ash snorted at the euphemism, "—to appreciate it from the ground up."

"I do take it seriously," Ash argued.

"If you took it seriously, you wouldn't have flirted your way through November's board meeting and then taken Christopher McKinnon into a company car to do indecent things to him."

Ash parted his lips, then closed them again. It wasn't as though his spontaneous tryst with their newest board member was that out of character for him.

"The media expects it," Ash argued at last.

"And when the two of you were almost arrested and charged as sex offenders?" his father shot back in a hard voice. "Were they expecting that, too? Because I had to part ways with plenty of money to make sure that didn't happen. Money that we are only in possession of because of Ashby's good name. A certain level of notoriety is good for publicity, but can you imagine what the press would have done to our image if you'd been charged as a sex offender? They're already raking you over the coals for getting taken into the station for indecent exposure."

"We didn't even have our pants off," Ash mumbled, rolling his eyes. The sex offender thing was just vindictive bullshit from a homophobic officer who'd looked positively gleeful at the opportunity to bust someone as high profile as Ash.

"I *don't care*." His father's response was absolute. "The fact of the matter is, if you took the business seriously, you would have exercised better judgment in both location and partner. And so, until you learn to appreciate the life I've laid out for you, you'll have to live without it. That means working in a position fitting of your experience."

Officially, Ash had never worked a day in his life. From time to time, he sat in on board meetings, but very seldom did he participate in them. He'd gone to school because it had been expected, and managed a degree in business even though his grades had been far from stellar. But honestly, it seemed like a waste to devote himself to hard work when his father had already made a fortune large enough for Ash to live off for the rest of his life.

"I have a business degree," Ash tried to argue, but by now his arguments fell flat. His father had never listened to him. Not when he was a child, not when he was a teenager, and certainly not now that he was closing in on twenty-seven.

"A business degree with no experience will get you a menial, entry-level position. And on such short notice? Substitute Santa work is about the best you can expect."

Ash exhaled slowly, trying to keep the emotion out of his voice. His father was on the attack again. Why did it always have to be this way?

"So there's no chance I can come home?"

"No."

"And Aspen?"

Getting away from New York, and from his father, to spend the holiday with his friends was one of the highlights of the year. Money and prestige meant freedom, but that freedom wasn't without its trade-offs. Ash played the media for what it was worth, but being under the spotlight at all times was strenuous.

And paired with a strained home life?

Ash lived on his own in New York, but his father was always nearby, and fame meant that anything Ash did eventually made it back to his old man. Douglas Edward Ashby never cared what Ash did until Ash made a mistake.

Then the gloves came off.

"Bennett, my patience is limited. You are not going to Aspen unless you prove to me you are serious about Ashby's. Ashby's is funding your trip, after all. Not to mention your penthouse, and the clothes you wear, and the food you eat. You will *not* disgrace its name again."

It felt so hypocritical. All of it was bullshit. Ash scrubbed at his face and closed his eyes.

The tightrope his father wanted him to walk between being a focal point in the media while not smearing the brand was a difficult one to tread, and it looked like he'd finally overstepped his boundaries.

"Do what you were born to do, Bennett," Ash's father said in parting. "If you do, perhaps you'll be permitted to visit Aspen this Christmas."

"Fine." Ash's tone was flat. "Goodbye, Father."

The call ended. His father hadn't bothered to say

goodbye.

Ash shoved his phone back into his pocket and fixed his Santa suit. What he'd been born to do was to uphold the Ashby name, not be a loving son. Ash knew it, and his father knew it just as well.

It stung.

Pushing his emotions aside, Ash left the bath section and headed up the escalator to the North Pole on the second floor. A boy, no more than six, stared at him from a few steps above. Wide-eyed and brimming with excitement, he looked like he'd seen a celebrity.

He had. Just not the kind he believed he saw.

What was there to be excited for? Ash didn't understand the appeal. The joy of new toys was short-lived, and after that, there was only bitter disappointment. The holidays brought out the worst in people.

But the little boy's eyes shone.

Ash had to look away.

Several employees in elf costumes waited for him at the top of the escalator, and before Ash could speak, they all started to talk at once, urging him to hurry while whisking him toward the display overhang that was set up as the North Pole. Ash was shown through a freestanding archway decked with fake pine branches and adorned with red baubles and garland and down a red carpet directly to Santa's chair.

It was the same in all Ashby's stores. Oversized and extravagant, every time Ash had always thought the design looked more like a throne. The tall back towered a foot or so higher than necessary, the rounded top lined with golden metallic filigree that, for all its ornate glitter, was most likely just made of plastic. The back was red and plush and made of velvet, accented with rounded golden rivets that drew the eye. The arms curled outward, rounded on top, and boasted the same metallic gold as the top, spilling down the legs of the chair like a magical waterfall. The design was gorgeous. Paired against the fully trimmed Christmas trees and hills of fake snow, it transformed the department store floor into a winter wonderland.

And, for the next three weeks, it would be his.

The elves who'd come to collect him at the top of the escalator were chattering about the details of his job and what to expect, but Ash was lost in his own head. He'd have to spend three weeks sitting in Santa's chair, listening to children drone on about all the material things they thought would make them happy while he sweated up a storm through his fat suit.

Ash settled into his chair and zoned out, studying the grand arch at the entrance to the North Pole. It had been roped off while the elves set up a few last-minute installations, but Ash could already see children peeking in, eager to get to him.

Suddenly, they scattered. Ash furrowed his brow and sat up a little straighter, trying to see what had happened, only to witness an employee in a fitted red-and-black nutcracker outfit jump the rope and scramble to close the distance between them.

His light brown hair was kept short at the sides and longer at the top, and there was a sweetness to his face that drew Ash's eye and kept it trained. The toy soldier uniform he wore was fitted to his body better than the elves Ash had seen so far, and Ash didn't miss how it fit his shoulders just right and amplified the slight taper of his waist.

"I am *so* sorry!" he gasped, halfway down the red carpet. "I didn't mean to be late! I was caught up getting the Giving Tree ready, and time got away from me."

Awkward and sweet. From the very first words, Ash knew exactly what kind of a guy the nutcracker was.

Not his type.

At least... not *Ash's* type. But Ash was currently "Ben," and there was a sparkle in the nutcracker's eye that made Ash reconsider. He was cute in a way that Ash couldn't quite shake.

With a nutcracker like him, three weeks exiled to the North Pole might not be so bad, after all.

Chapter 3

ELLIOTT

CHRISTMAS AT ASHBY'S FELT DIFFERENT WITHOUT NICK. No matter what Elliott had told himself on his long commute in to work, and no matter how he'd tried to talk himself through it in his head, the difference still struck him as soon as he stepped through the familiar doors.

The North Pole was visible immediately upon entering Ashby's. It jutted out from the second floor and was typically closed to clients, serving as a marketing mechanism rather than floorspace. At all other times of the year, the overhang showcased seasonal wear. The transformation that always came the morning after Black Friday had always thrilled Elliott.

Now, it filled him with dread.

Looking up to see the red garland wrapped tightly around the banisters and the staggeringly tall Christmas trees trimmed in beautiful golds and reds and greens made Elliott's heart ache. The happy place he'd come to love was fundamentally changed, because the man who'd always made it special wasn't there to share it with him. Thank God that the doctors said Nick would make a full recovery. Elliott didn't know what he'd do with himself if the older man had passed away.

Nick had suffered from a stroke. The clotting in his brain had shut down his left side and left him partially paralyzed, but with physical therapy, his doctors were confident that he'd regain normal functions... it would just take time. Nick would spend at least two weeks in the hospital as he recovered, and he'd need time off into the new year to heal.

Christmas, for him, was over.

And it was up to Elliott to step up and make sure everything went smoothly at Ashby's.

Part of that meant making sure the Giving Tree was up and running and staffed properly, and while Elliott wasn't the most senior member of the floor staff, he was definitely the most devoted to the Christmas season. He'd taken it upon himself to make sure that the tree was on par with past years.

The Giving Tree was located just outside of the North Pole, tucked around the corner and sequestered off by velvet ropes. On any given shift, two elves were responsible for overseeing it, but today—the first day the North Pole was open—Elliott needed to make sure there weren't any snags along the way.

Apart from visits with Santa, the Giving Tree was Ashby's main attraction. The idea was simple enough. With the help of a parent or guardian, children visiting Ashby's filled out tags listing the things they hoped to receive for Christmas, then strung them up on the Giving Tree. Charitable clients who wanted to make a child's Christmas that much brighter would claim a tag and pay for the present on it. Elliott had made a wish every year during his childhood, and each year, that wish had been granted at the Ashby's Annual Children's Christmas Party, thanks to Nick's generosity.

It only seemed right to pay it forward. To take on the responsibility of making sure that the magic lived on. More so than ever, now that Nick wasn't there.

Elliott hadn't intended to get so wrapped up in last-minute touches that it made him late to his shift at the North Pole, though. Martin was a hardass about being on time, and it wasn't like Elliott to be late. As one of the few nutcrackers, whose purpose was to stand by Santa's side to offer support and run messages to the elves who manned the front arch, he knew his absence wouldn't be overlooked. It was bad.

And what made it worse was that Nick wasn't there to cover for him.

It wasn't far to run, but Elliott ran it anyway and jumped

over the rope blocking off the North Pole from the rest of the store. It was nothing short of a miracle that he made it over without tripping.

"I am so sorry!" Elliott said, adrenaline coursing through him as he got his first glimpse of the new Santa. Being late was not how he'd wanted to make a first impression. Santa was already seated on his chair, the fat suit padding not nearly as authentic on his body as it had been on Nick's. The fake beard masked his face and Elliott couldn't read his expression as he offered a rushed version of his excuse for tardiness. "I didn't mean to be late. I was caught up getting the Giving Tree ready, and time got away from me."

Santa leaned forward in his chair and took a hard look at Elliott, and Elliott skidded to a stop and looked him over in return. There was no telling how old the new Santa was, or what he actually looked like underneath the padding, wig, and beard, but there was something strange about his hazel eyes that caught Elliott's attention.

"It's fine," Santa said. "So, uh, what exactly is it that you're doing here?"

Elliott opened his mouth, then closed it again. He worried his bottom lip. It was short notice to find and train a new Santa, but he'd assumed that the new recruit would have had some understanding of the job.

It looked like he'd been wrong.

"I'm here to stand with you while you work and make sure everything goes smoothly," Elliott said, worried. If the new Santa didn't know that, what more didn't he know?

Elliott had been disappointed that he'd won the role of nutcracker for the one Christmas that Nick wasn't there, but now he was glad. Santa needed his help.

"Oh." Santa cocked his head to the side. "Well. That's great."

"Yeah." What was it that was making his heart race? Elliott shuffled his feet, feeling awkward. He couldn't tell for certain, but the pitch of the new Santa's voice made him think that he was young. Maybe even Elliott's age.

And, as ridiculous as it was to think such a thing about *Santa*, the sound of that voice was hot as hell.

"I'm, um," Elliott murmured, "I'm going to take my post now, okay? The kids'll be coming soon."

"Right." Santa kept looking at him, and Elliott worried his lip again and stepped away to take his place to the right of Santa's chair. Sean, who'd won the other nutcracker costume, made his way down the red carpet and took his place to Santa's left.

"The kids are on their way," Sean announced before he stiffened his shoulders and faced forward. Elliott did the same. The two of them were playing nutcrackers, after all. There was a certain stiffness involved.

But that didn't stop him from sneaking glances at the new Santa out of the corner of his eye.

What was he doing?

It wasn't like Elliott to lust after a guy, and it certainly wasn't like him to be so drawn to a guy he knew nothing about. Even if Santa was his age, and even if he was attractive, there was no way he was gay. And even if he *was* gay, Elliott doubted that Santa would be attracted to him.

He caught himself slumping and tensed against it. The first child had been brought into the North Pole, and he had to refocus his attention.

Christmas was about the kids, not about who may or may not be lurking behind the Santa costume. It wasn't time to daydream.

It was time to work.

Santa was struggling.

"And, uh, who are you?" Santa asked the little girl who'd been brought to see him. Elliott wanted to slap a hand over his face. That *wasn't* the script.

"Um," the girl whispered, shy. "Don't you know, Santa?"

"Oh, uh, yeah, of course I do." Santa's voice was hot, but it wasn't jolly, and he certainly wasn't talking like a Santa ought to. "Why don't you remind me, though? I'm old and forgetful."

The performance was terrible. Who had made the decision to hire this guy? If they were this pressed for talent, Elliott would have volunteered to step in. He'd learned the nuances of the role over the years, and he knew he could have pulled it off.

Since pulling it off was off the table, though, he'd just have to help Santa adjust.

The little girl left, escorted by one of the elves, and

Elliott leaned over to whisper in Santa's ear. "Pretend they're your drunk friends and you're trying to trick them into believing you're actually Santa." A guy with a voice like that had to be the kind to party, right? He hoped he hadn't missed the mark. "Like you've always been friends with them, you know? Just let it go a little bit."

Santa didn't comment—the next child was already on his way down the red carpet—but Elliott saw the improvement immediately, and he beamed on the inside while he remained wooden on the surface. Being a nutcracker was tough, if only because it wasn't so active, but he was already enjoying it.

Knowing that he was directly impacting the Santa experience made all the difference.

The day flew by.

Between offering tips and sharing tricks to help Santa adjust to his new job, Elliott didn't get a moment's rest. There were times when he needed to step in to take care of a child in tears or intervene when one of the older, brasher kids accused their Santa of not being the real deal, but even in those trying moments, Elliott loved what he did.

The fact that he got to witness the new Santa evolve from awkward and static to friendly and almost holiday-appropriate was reward in and of itself.

By the time the last child was escorted down the red carpet to return to his parent waiting at the arch, Elliott was exhausted, but overjoyed. Day one of Christmas festivities at Ashby's was a success, and he felt like he'd held down the fort well in Nick's absence.

Grace and Trevor, who had been manning the Giving Tree, ducked under the rope barricading the section closed and rushed to join Elliott. Trevor's makeup was on point, and he was working his rosy red cheeks like nobody's business.

Elliott grinned.

"Elliott! The first day's done!" Grace cheered. "We rocked it over at the Giving Tree station, and by the looks of the kids coming over after their visit with Santa, it looks like you guys rocked it here, too."

"It went well," Elliott replied. He stepped forward to meet his friends, and out of the corner of his eye he saw the new Santa rise from his chair and stretch. "It was a little rocky at first but we smoothed things over quickly enough."

"Come out for drinks with us," Trevor insisted. "I already texted Jose and he's in. Sean, you in, too?"

"Yeah." Sean wandered over to join them. "Elliott was on fire today. He really kept our new Santa on the right track."

"I'm in for drinks," Elliott said. "What about you, Santa?"

He turned to look over his shoulder, heart unaccountably racing in anticipation, but the new Santa was already gone.

"Don't worry about him." Grace waved him off. "He's got this weird vibe going on. I tried to talk to him this morning and he didn't want anything to do with me. I say let him warm up. He'll come around."

Before Elliott could think much more about it, Trevor grabbed his hand, and the group of them made their way out of the North Pole and to the staff room to pick up their belongings from their lockers.

Maybe they could invite the new Santa along the next time they went out after work. He knew what it was like to be the awkward outsider, and he didn't wish it on anyone.

A little friendship could go a long way, and he got the feeling that the new Santa was the kind of guy who could benefit from it.

Chapter 4

ASH

THE TOP FLOOR CONDO UNIT WAS SPOTLESS. SPARSE, MOD-ern furniture made of dark wood and white upholstery occupied the floor space, but didn't crowd it. Ash paid no mind to any of it as he let himself through the front door and locked it behind him.

He ached, and he reeked. A hot shower would fix both of those issues at once.

It was just before nine at night, but he was already exhausted. Working as Santa wasn't a physical job, but it was mentally taxing. There was nothing quite as draining as trying to understand children.

Drunk friends. Yeah. He grinned to himself. That had

made it marginally better.

Ash kicked off his shoes at the door and fanned out his toes. He shrugged the cashmere Oakford jacket he wore from his shoulders and hung it on the coat rack by the door, then stretched and tried to work some of the tension out of his shoulders.

Stress had tightened up his muscles and left them aching, like the day after a heavy workout at the gym. No wonder why so many of the floor staff were in such good shape—if being on their feet all day didn't tone them up, the tension of dealing with the public at large would do the trick.

Maybe he'd hit a club.

Ash rubbed at his irritated eyes as he padded across the reclaimed hardwood floor, destined for the master bedroom. He preferred to use the attached bathroom, because from condo to condo, his father ensured that the layout was the same. No matter which of the Ashby homes Ash visited, he could always count on the bathroom being familiar.

Sentimentality wasn't like Ash, but the sterile emptiness of the condo made it feel hollow and cold—just like every other unit he'd ever lived in.

By the time Ash made it to the bedroom, he'd unbuttoned the black Ashby's shirt he was required to wear beneath his bulky Santa costume. The buckle of his belt gaped open, and Ash undid the button of his fly and pushed his slacks down his hips. Could he even go clubbing like this?

Physically and mentally drained, and likely to suffer the same fate tomorrow when he clocked back in for work, it seemed unlikely.

What was wrong with him? Going out to party was second nature, and there had to be plenty of hot guys ready to be swept up for a night of lavish luxury with one of the world's most eligible heirs.

Except, at the moment, Ash had been cut off. *Lavish* was going to have to wait.

There was a mirror in the bedroom, and Ash used it to remove his colored contacts. The relief was instant, and tears built in the corners of his eyes as cool air met his corneas for the first time in twelve hours. Fuck, did that feel good. Ash blinked a few times, then rolled his shoulders back and stretched his neck from side to side.

If he couldn't go clubbing, he'd just go to bed. There was no shame in that, so long as no one knew he was turning in at nine. And, thanks to the disguise offered by his bleached hair and forgettably colored contacts, no one knew he was in Chicago anyway. No media outlets would be breaking the story of the geriatric Ashby's heir.

Ash's cellphone rang, stirring him from his thoughts. He fished it out of his discarded work slacks and answered.

"Hello?"

"Ash, you're on speaker phone. It's Loren."

"And Justin."

"And Ulric."

"And where the fuck are you?" The three of them

laughed, and Ash's face fell. Thank God they couldn't see him. "We're in Aspen already. The three of us have rented the same cabins as last year, and we rented yours for you in advance so that some random plebeian didn't come snatch it up to jack our flow. Where *are* you?"

"I'm stuck putting in time with Ashby's." Ash chose his words carefully. "You guys get started without me."

Hearing his friends' voices sunk his spirits, and, had he not been so gross and sweaty, he would have collapsed on the bed in total defeat. The three of them were already in Aspen for the holidays, and by the sounds of it, they were already partying. The thud of bass in the background and the dull roar of conversation didn't drown out their voices, but it created white noise that let him know exactly what he was missing.

He should have been right there alongside them, forgetting about life back at home.

"Oh my God, is your old man actually cutting you off?" Loren laughed. "My father told me that yours had to pay out a ludicrous amount of money to the NYPD to keep your name off the sex offender records or some shit like that. Said they caught you having sex in a car with some executive of the board, parked right on the street? My father said that yours was *pissed*."

Ash's mouth went dry. "Something like that."

"Tell me you've followed my advice about withdrawing funds from the family coffers to store in your offshore accounts?" Justin demanded. "It's your only insurance for situations like this. If I've told you once, Ash..."

"No. I didn't do that." There were a lot of things that Ash was, but a thief wasn't one of them. By all rights, it was his money—or it would be, once his father passed away—but he still couldn't help feeling like there was something low about siphoning it out without his father's knowledge. No matter if Justin and the rest swore by the strategy, Ash had never been able to bring himself to do it.

He may have his faults, but he was just too honest for that.

"So... what?" Ulric asked. "Are you coming to Aspen or not? Because we've got a whole empty cabin waiting for your arrival, and if you're not going to use it, we'll turn it into house party central."

"Just do your thing assuming I'm not going to be there," Ash murmured. The longer the conversation went on, the worse he felt. The four of them should have been having the time of their lives, but instead, here he was in Chicago, dealing with plummeting temperatures and inclement weather and the ridiculous triviality that was working the floor at an Ashby's department store. "I'm going to try to get down there as soon as I can, but I need my father off my back first. Which means I'm going to need some more time."

"We're going to trash your cabin," Loren said earnestly.

"I'll have a crew clean it up prior to my arrival," Ash replied. He was starting to get irritated, and he really didn't want to continue the conversation. "For now, just pretend I have the flu or something if anyone from the media comes sniffing around for me, okay? I have to lay low for a while."

"Pity." Loren didn't sound particularly upset. Ash set his lips and scowled. The three of them didn't actually give a fuck if he was there or not, did they? "Well, call us if you can afford to make it. If not, see you next year."

The call ended, and Ash tossed his phone onto the bed and stormed into the bathroom. What a mess this had become. One little mistake was all it had taken to ruin his life.

He hated it.

Ash turned the taps and let the water warm as he stripped out of his boxer briefs and threw them into the corner. While he was out at work tomorrow, the cleaning staff would deal with his laundry. At the very least, his father was still paying for his necessities. Food, menial labor, and transportation were all still covered, but for anything else, Ash had to call in and get pre-approval.

It was ridiculous. And, honestly, a little humiliating.

Three weeks, he told himself as he ran his hand under the stream of water to test its temperature. It had warmed nicely, so he pulled the lever to start the shower and stepped under the water.

Water beat hot against Ash's skin, washing away the sweat, and he let his forehead rest against the cool tile of the shower wall as it cleansed away the filth of the day. What a disaster it had been. From trying to play the role of Santa to the recent conversation with his friends in Aspen, nothing about the day had gone right.

Except for the way that nutcracker at Ashby's had stood by his side, whispering little suggestions to make his job easier.

That very attractive, definitely-not-Ash's-type nutcracker.

Ash lifted his forehead from the tile and ducked his head under the water. Hot droplets soaked into his newly blond hair and streamed down his cheeks and neck. While it was true the nutcracker wasn't his usual type, there was no denying that he was too cute to forget about. Stoic and serious about his duties as nutcracker, but then sweet and helpful when Ash needed it the most, he was a dichotomy. A mystery.

But not mysterious enough that he'd gone under Ash's gaydar.

A guy that cute couldn't be straight. Lips like those were custom-made to be wrapped around a cock—Ash's cock, if he had any say in the matter.

And what would a timid, innocent guy like that be like in bed?

Elliott, he'd heard some of the staff call him. The name fit him.

Naked on Ash's bed, hips propped up and looking back over his shoulder with his expressive blue eyes and high, rounded cheeks...

Fuck.

Ash's hand slipped down to grasp his hardening cock.

Elliott might not have been his type, but damn if that little visual didn't work Ash up in the worst way. And, after a day like the one Ash had just suffered through, he needed a little release.

Would a guy like Elliott be tight? Ash closed his eyes as he thrust into his hand, imagining it. Someone so shy would have to be. Nerves would get the best of him, and he'd have trouble relaxing, and from there...

"Oh, *shit*," Ash rasped. In his mind's eye, Elliott closed his eyes and buried his head against the pillows, bucking his hips back as Ash pushed into him. Ash imagined letting his hands explore Elliott's pale, silken skin, roaming over birthmarks, tracing along his ribs, and then gliding up to toy with his nipples.

Was it wrong, to want someone who was so innocent?

Ash loosened his hand for a moment and stopped thrusting into his fist, trying to talk himself down from what he was doing. All Elliott had done was be kind to him, and here Ash was repaying him by letting him star in his masturbatory fantasies.

But would Elliott still be so sweet if he knew who Ash was?

Ash exhaled until his lungs burned, then breathed in the humid air around him until he had his answer.

No.

If Elliott knew who Ash was, and if he realized what an advantage he could get by entertaining his favor, Elliott would have been on his knees in the staff bathroom before the end of the day, sucking Ash off. And, with lips like those, Ash wouldn't have said no.

In the end, Elliott would have been the same as his father, or any of Ash's friends. Any sensible human being would take advantage of an opportunity if presented with it, and to someone working minimum wage in retail, Ash was a huge fucking opportunity. A walking bank account. Elliott would have been crazy not to suck his cock if it had meant he'd had a shot at gleaning some benefit from Ash's fame and fortune.

But, even as Ash's hand tightened and he began to stroke himself toward orgasm—picturing Elliott laid out across his bed, taking his cock—he couldn't completely shake the twinge of guilt he felt.

It didn't stop him from coming, though.

And it was the gentle look he imagined in Elliott's rounded blue eyes and the breathy, hitched gasp of his voice that brought Ash there.

"*Ash...*"

Chapter 5

ELLIOTT

"WHAT YOU SHOULD ALWAYS LOOK FOR IN A SHIRT, to make sure you're buying the right size, is how the shoulders fit," Elliott said. He pulled at the upper sleeve of his Ashby's uniform to show off the shoulder hem. "This line right here is a great indicator of whether a shirt's going to fit you just right, and you should use it as a baseline to determine if a brand is going to work for you or not. If you end up buttoning it up and it's too tight, going up a size likely isn't going to help. Not all brands are created equal, and it's frustrating, but I guess that's fashion."

The customer in front of him nodded, and Elliott handed him the stack of shirts folded over his arm. They'd been shopping together for the last ten minutes, moving carefully through the men's wear to find the right shades and styles to complement the customer's skin and eyes. It was a balancing act, and sometimes it was a struggle, but Elliott loved helping customers find exactly what they needed.

Knowing that the gentleman who stood before him would look stylish for his first work Christmas party in five years was a big deal, and Elliott took it seriously.

"What if it winds up being too baggy?" the customer asked.

"You can get it tailored," Elliott suggested. The number of people who didn't know that services like that existed was alarming. "If you find a quality piece you know you're going to wear regularly, even if it already fits okay, it's good to get it tailored to your body. You never know how good clothes can look until you have them fitted to you. And it doesn't have to be expensive, either. There are some great, cheap services available if you look them up online. And if you're really in a pinch, my friend Trevor does tailoring work on the side. I could give you his contact information if you need someone."

Trevor had already altered all of their Christmas outfits, and despite his constant joking, he'd held back on making any of them *sexy*. Grace's baggy elf tunic fit her much better and looked far more professional, and Elliott's nutcracker outfit looked fantastic. It tapered in, following the natural lines of his body, and the sleeves fell just right. Even Jose looked amazing in his reindeer outfit.

And, one by one, Trevor was making the rounds and altering the rest of the employee costumes. None of them were to be returned at the end of the season, so personalizing them had been okayed by Ashby's headquarters, so long as no drastic changes were made. Elliott thought the terms were fair enough, and Trevor was glad to put in the work.

As Chicago's flagship store, the downtown Ashby's location prided itself on its immaculate image, and there was nothing that would make their staff look more presentable than properly tailored uniforms.

"I never realized buying clothes could be so complicated." The customer laughed. "All these years, I've just been buying whatever fits."

"Well, try tailoring at least once." Elliott winked at him. "And—"

He stopped short. Standing on the other side of the clothing rack was an Ashby's employee he didn't recognize, and that employee was staring him down. At most times, Elliott would have let it roll off his back. Sometimes, Ashby's brought in employees on transfer from other locations, and around this time of year there were tons of new temporary workers helping to relieve some of the holiday madness. But there was something about the way that employee was watching him that was different.

Like he was interested in Elliott on more than a professional level.

Elliott cleared his throat and continued, forcing himself to refocus on the customer in front of him. "If you like the results, then you'll know what to do for next time. If not, it's maybe twenty dollars wasted, but I think it's worth the chance. I'm sure that you're going to love how fitted clothes look on you."

The new employee stepped around the clothing rack to hover near their location and started to adjust a pile of men's pants that was already properly arranged and neatly stacked. Elliott couldn't help but watch him out of the corner of his eye.

His platinum blond hair was cut short and almost business-like, but it was just long enough on the top that it was still fun. He had a strong chin and a good jawline, and his cheekbones were high and dignified. Tall and fit and well groomed, he was easy on the eyes, and while he didn't exactly look like the retail type, he didn't look too out of place in his Ashby's uniform.

Elliott had never seen a guy that hot working at an Ashby's before.

"I'm going to go try these on and figure out how the shoulder's supposed to fall," the customer said. "Thanks for your help today."

"It's my pleasure." Elliott managed a timid smile. Even though the new employee had turned away, he still felt watched. Who was he? A new trainee? Martin hadn't told Elliott that he would be expected to train someone this morning.

Shirts slung over his arm, the customer made his way toward the changing rooms, and Elliott turned to look at the new guy in full. He'd stopped readjusting the stack of pants, and instead stood there, watching Elliott.

His name tag read Ben.

"Can I help you?" Elliott asked, sounding every bit as awkward as he felt. When it came to work, he was usually able to flip off his social anxiety, but it wasn't often that he found his coworkers so attractive. And the way Ben was looking back at him was definitely throwing him off his game.

Interested.

"I hope you can," Ben replied with an easy smile. Elliott's heart pounded, and he shuffled his feet to try to work out some of his nerves. There was something familiar about his voice that he couldn't place. All he knew for sure was that it was hot as hell.

Just like the rest of him.

"Are you a new trainee?" Elliott asked. Ben didn't seem too interested in volunteering his story. "Am I supposed to be training you? Who, um, who sent you here? Was it Martin?"

"It's been said I can't be trained." Ben smirked and took a step closer. Elliott's heart hammered anew in his chest and he stood frozen on the spot. "But if you want, you can still give it a shot. It could be fun."

Was that flirting? God, that was flirting, wasn't it? Elliott blinked and swallowed hard, shoulders stiff and spine board straight. The new, hot employee was *flirting* with him. That had never happened before.

"Um, well, I mean..."

"You were great with that customer," Ben continued, standing a little closer than necessary. Elliott was sure he was about to break out into a sweat. His neck and collar were on fire. "It's really great to see a guy who takes so much pride in his work. You're really devoted, aren't you?"

"I guess I am." Elliott's tongue felt too heavy for his mouth, and he knew that he was going to start stumbling over his words at any second. He simultaneously wanted to remain standing so close to Ben and longed to take a step back. "I mean, it's my job, and I take pride in it, so..."

"I bet you're just as devoted in other areas of your life." There was something darkly alluring about Ben that Elliott couldn't quite get over. He worried his bottom lip, looking up at him. "You're the kind of guy who makes his bed in the morning, right? And makes sure all the dishes are washed before... bed?"

Had he just imagined the emphasis Ben had put on the word "bed" the second time around? Was this work related? Was this even training related? Elliott glanced away, looking for Martin. If Martin, of all people, walked by while they slacked off, it wasn't going to go well for either of them, and Elliott needed to keep his job. He had rent to pay, and bills to take care of, and groceries to afford. Risking that for a gorgeous stranger wasn't worth it.

He took a step back and broke Ben's spell.

"I think maybe we should get back to work," he suggested. "Not that I'm not... um... flattered. But if Martin comes by, he's going to write us up, and I can't afford that right now."

"You definitely don't have any violations you need to worry about," Ben said with a shrug, like he'd known Elliott for years. "And if Martin comes around, let me take the blame. I'll cover for you."

"Company policy doesn't work like that," Elliott protested weakly. "It's just better if we get back to work, right? I mean... what are you doing here, anyway? Are you from another Ashby's store? I've never seen you here before. Do you need orientation?"

"No, I've already got my orientation figured out," Ben said, winking. "What I'm wondering about is yours."

Elliott felt himself go red, and he took another step back. Was this really happening?

Heart going a mile a minute, he turned his head to find Trevor on his way over. Their shift—the Christmas "A" team, as Grace had dubbed their group of elves, reindeer, and nutcrackers—was off North Pole duty today, manning the sales floor instead. Trevor was helping him cover men's apparel.

"Trevor," Elliott squeaked. "Hey."

"Hey." Trevor came to a stop beside Elliott and gave Ben the once-over. Glad for the support, Elliott faded away behind him.

Trevor was the big personality. Fun, flirty, and adventurous, he was the one who guys hit on, in the rare event that a customer was interested in making a move. Elliott was sure that with Trevor there, Ben would forget he existed, and he'd be able to get back to work.

Trevor was far better prepared to flirt back, anyway. And if he could match wits with Ben, maybe he could weave the conversation around to figure out what Ben was doing at their store.

"Now who do we have here?" Trevor asked. "I don't remember having met a Ben before—and I'm sure that I'd remember meeting a Ben who looks half as good as you do. I'm Trevor."

"Of course you have." Ben's eyes were on Trevor, but they'd lost the spark of interest they'd had while looking at Elliott. Elliott noticed. Everything about Ben drew his eye, and even the tiniest details stood out. Like his dark brows. *Ben must bleach his hair.* Blond definitely suited him, but, honestly, he probably looked hot no matter what his coloring.

"Uh, no, I'm pretty sure I haven't," Trevor replied, a little disoriented. "Remind me where we've met? If it was at a club or something, I'm so sorry. Sometimes it's all a blur, you know?"

"I'm the Ben that's helping to fill in for Santa this year. Your coworker with the purple hair seemed to know who I was."

Ben was Santa? Elliott placed his voice at once. Of course that's who Ben was. How could he have mistook a voice like his?

Eager to slink away unnoticed, Elliott took a few steps

back and made an attempt to slip behind one of the clothing racks.

"That's because Grace actually reads the weekly newsletters." Trevor laughed. "Well, Santa, I know you're off-duty right now, but what do you say I tell you what I want anyway?"

There it was. Trevor was bold in ways that Elliott could never be, and now he was going to land the hot new Santa. It was just as well. Between the overtime Elliott was putting in and the times he planned to visit Nick while he recovered, he didn't have time to date anyway.

"Maybe later." The denial was unexpected to Elliott and Trevor both, and they froze. Elliott was partially concealed behind the nearest clothing rack, but Ben's eyes were on him. "I'm wondering if Elliott might be able to take me on as his protégé. I watched him help a customer just now and I was impressed. Maybe we could do a little shopping for him as practice? I'm imagining that he'd look stunning in a Jagway shirt."

"I-I really can't afford anything in the Jagway line. Not even their socks," Elliott mumbled. He was lost in Ben's gaze. The strange hazel eyes he'd noticed the day before were trained on him, and they weren't looking away. Even though Ben spoke to Trevor, it was like Trevor wasn't even there.

"That's what employee discounts are for," Ben insisted. "From what I heard while you were serving that customer,

I'm pretty sure you're of the opinion that clothes make a man. So why not invest in some Jagway pieces?"

Trevor puffed his chest a little and stepped directly into Ben's line of sight. Happy-go-lucky and in love with life, it was seldom that he got pissed—but then again, Elliott knew that he wasn't used to being shut down and ignored, either.

"Elliott never uses his employee discount," Trevor cut in. "Not that he can't, but it's only for personal use, you know? And really, if he's buying all these clothes as an investment, isn't it more for the benefit of those looking at him, rather than for himself? And we're not supposed to use it to buy things for others."

Elliott watched the two of them, still hot and bothered and nervous all at once. How had he gotten tangled up in the middle of this? It was intoxicating to know that Ben's attention wasn't wavering, even when Trevor was doing his best to flirt, but it was a little overwhelming, too.

It wasn't often that a guy tried to crack Elliott's shell and get to know him, especially out of the blue, like Ben was doing.

"That's a shame." Ben looked over Trevor's shoulder to steal Elliott's attention again. "I'm sure he'd look fantastic."

"Hey." Trevor tried one last time to break into the conversation. Elliott heard the strain in his voice. "We were going to invite you out for drinks after work yesterday, but you disappeared."

"Yeah," Ben said with a casual shrug. "Long day."

"So you should come out with us the next time we go out, probably on Friday," Trevor insisted. "It's fun, and you don't have to stay late if you don't want to."

"Did you go?" Ben asked Elliott, still refusing to meet Trevor's eye. Trevor was clearly at his wit's end trying to keep Ben focused on him, and it looked like he wasn't going to succeed.

For some inexplicable reason, Ben seemed interested in Elliott, and Elliott alone.

Butterflies rose in Elliott's stomach and choked his reply. "Yes."

"Then maybe next time I'll go, too." Ben smiled another easy smile and took a few steps back. "I'll see you guys later. Trevor. Elliott."

"Bye," Elliott murmured.

Then Ben was gone.

"What the hell was that?" Trevor asked with a laugh once Ben was out of earshot. "I've never had someone shut me down so hard. He must be *into* you into you, Elliott. And he's a hottie to boot."

"I..." Elliott let his voice trail off, sure that Trevor was wrong, but knowing he'd never convince *him* of that. Trevor had the kind of bold self-confidence that was the polar opposite of Elliott's shy timidity.

Elliott honestly had no idea why Ben *had* kept his attention on him. It was obvious that Ben was the type who could have his pick of men, and there was no way Elliott was going to actually interest someone like that. He knew he wasn't a bad looking guy, but he definitely wasn't in the same league as Ben.

Trevor was grinning at him as he waited for Elliott's comeback, but Elliott just shrugged. He didn't have another theory to offer, other than that Ben must just be the type who flirted with everyone.

But, if that was true, why hadn't he taken the bait with Trevor?

"He *is* into you," Trevor declared, and hitched a brow playfully. "Friday can't come soon enough, right?"

Elliott's pulse raced, and he couldn't help smiling back. "Right."

Understatement of the century.

Chapter 6

ASH

THERE WERE STILL A HANDFUL OF MINUTES BEFORE ASH was supposed to report to the North Pole to play Santa for the day, and he'd discovered over the course of the week that if he hid out in the men's underwear section, he could avoid most of the kids, even while in costume. White gloves off and chucked onto one of the nearby shelves beside a package of tighty-whities, Ash scrolled through the messages on his phone.

Loren was texting him pictures of the aftermath in Aspen. As promised, the cabin designated for Ash's use was a mess. Disposable plastic cups littered the floor, there were bottles of partially consumed liquor left haphazardly on every flat surface, and Ash was pretty sure he saw a broken window or two. A bra was strung up on the chandelier, and there was some sort of slime on the stairs leading to the second floor.

Most impressively, someone had drawn a mural on one of the back walls with permanent marker. Ash knew little about art, but he knew enough to know that it was good.

It was a shame their cleaning crews would scrub it out.

And, while Ash usually would've considered any night that produced that level of damage a roaring success, the truth was, he wasn't so sure that being a part of it in Aspen would have topped the night he'd had with the crew from Ashby's.

To say it out loud was absurd—that he might be having more fun with a group of down-on-their-luck students and young adults—but it was true. Friday night, once their shifts ended, the group of them had walked down the street through the harsh Chicago cold to descend on Reggie's, a hole-in-the-wall bar that Ash never would've given a second glance to, had he not been traveling in a group. *That* group.

The floor had been grimy and sticky, and the most expensive drink on the menu had been an underwhelming twelve dollars. The bathrooms smelled of week-old urine and had been heavily covered in graffiti.

Yet, Ash had ended up having fun.

Trevor and Jose and Grace were a riot. Sean and Heidi were entertaining. Someone Ash had never met before named Jennifer had joined them as well, and she'd proven to be excellent company.

But best of all had been Elliott, who'd sat stiffly in his chair for the first half of the night, sneaking glances at Ash out of the corner of his eye. It was only once he'd made his way through his first beer that he'd started to loosen up a little, and it was then that Ash had heard him laugh.

The sound alone made the sour taste in his mouth from cheap beer worth it. When Elliott laughed, it was contagious. His eyes had lit up, and he'd buried his mouth behind his hands, and—in that moment—Ash had felt like he could see just how much Elliott had to live for, and how much love he had to share.

Once Elliott had been well into his second beer, he hadn't shied away when Ash had bumped their legs together under the table. Their affection hadn't gone any further than that, but that alone had been enough to convince Ash that he had a shot.

The cute nutcracker who'd coached him through his days on Santa's chair and who blushed the sweetest shade of pink might still be his, if he fought for him hard enough.

It wasn't like Ash to fight for any man, but then again, it wasn't like him to go after a guy like Elliott in the first place, either. There was something different about him that Ash couldn't put his finger on, and he needed to figure out what it was before it drove him crazy.

The night's only downfall had been when one of the

Ashby's crew had brought up the subject of holiday plans. Ash and Elliott had been midway through footsie, and Elliott had been drinking his beer likely a little faster than he should have, when the conversation had taken that turn. Everyone had been quick to chime in with their celebrations, and Ash had shrunk back into his chair and tried not to think about what he was missing.

Christmas had never been a happy time of year for him. Presents had meant little to a boy who'd already had everything he could want, and his father was always busier around the holiday season with company matters. Ash's mother was absent at the best of times, and she'd never been a strong presence in his life.

The best Christmases he'd had, had been spent with his nanny, but once he'd been old enough not to need one, she'd been let go with a generous severance package. Ash had jetted off to Aspen every year since, doing his best to try to forget that there were people in the world who actually *enjoyed* being around their families.

And whose families enjoyed having them around, too.

Elliott hadn't seemed to notice when Ash's foot had fallen away, wrapped up in talking about his Christmas traditions with his mother. Not even Trevor had noticed when Ash had excused himself from the table, slipping outside to compose himself and make a spontaneous call home.

Now, his phone vibrated, and the message that popped up reminded Ash just what it was he'd called and left a message about.

Waiting in his inbox was a message from his father's company email account entitled, 'Christmas Itinerary.'

Ash had called to ask what the family was doing for Christmas, and his father had sent him a canned, impersonal reply likely cobbled together by some fresh-faced intern that detailed his parents' outings and obligations, down to the hour.

Disgusted, Ash turned off his phone and shoved it back into his pocket. The Santa suit wobbled as he did.

Was that what Christmas was about? Obligations and appearances and strategic visits?

Last night he'd started to think otherwise, but obviously he'd been wrong.

Shoving down his reaction to his father's cold response, Ash left the men's wear section and made his way across the second floor toward the North Pole. On the way, some of the younger kids stared at him wide-eyed, or called out and waved. Now that it was the weekend, the crowds were bigger than ever, and there were more of them to deal with.

It was a damn good thing Elliott was there to coach him through it, because Ash didn't feel like putting on a jolly front. At its core, Christmas was nothing more than a materialistic excuse for a holiday. Commercial. Fake.

Ash didn't want to be a part of it anymore.

Struggling with the padding of the fat suit, Ash ducked under the velvet rope and headed down the red carpet toward his throne. Fake snow glimmered on either side of him, and tall Christmas trees dazzled and filled in the landscape. The reindeer employees were busy displacing the seasonal section directly across from the North Pole's arch in order to make room for the temporary fences soon to be installed—live reindeer were being brought it for the weekend.

Standing on either side of Santa's chair were two nut-crackers whom Ash hadn't worked with before.

He stopped prematurely, looking between the two of them in confusion. Over the course of the last week, he'd become so used to seeing Elliott waiting for him that it felt wrong not to have him there. If Elliott was off, who was going to carry Ash through the bad times and offer support when he needed it the most?

But the ache Ash felt ran deeper than simple disap-pointment. He'd been looking forward to seeing Elliott, and now, deprived of his presence, he missed him.

"Hey," Ash said, approaching Santa's chair to speak with the nutcrackers. "You guys know the nutcracker that usual-ly works here? Elliott?"

"Yeah," one of the nutcrackers said. "What about him?"

"Where—"

Before Ash could finish his sentence, one of the elves who monitored the lines and brought the kids down the red carpet to visit Santa ran up to them.

"The rope's coming down. Get in your positions, guys. Time to start another day."

Both of the nutcrackers assumed their rigid positions by the chair, and Ash knew his time was up. Question unanswered, he settled into his chair and adjusted his stomach as the first child was escorted down the red carpet. The professional photographer was ready. The elves looked bright and cheery and the nutcrackers were stoic and rigid.

The only one out of place was Ash.

Kids came and went. From time to time, their parents elected to have photos taken. Ash struggled to get into character and suppress his grouchiness. Without Elliott there to ground him and keep him inspired, though, the day dragged.

He zoned out.

"Ash!"

Ash's head shot up, and he was about to reply before he remembered that he was Ben here, not Ash. One of the elves was escorting the last child out of the North Pole while the other spoke to the parents and organized details about the next child's visit. At the front of the North Pole, by the main Christmas arch, two mothers were talking. Ash had only picked their conversation out from the rest because they were talking about *him*.

"I know, right? If I were a few years younger, I swear..."

"A few years younger and living in New York," the other replied, laughing. "But I agree. What a hottie. But he's totally gay. Think you could turn him?"

"Mm, yeah! But I haven't seen him in the news lately, ever since that huge incident in New York. Isn't that a shame? There was something so exciting about following his exploits. All those men... I still can't get over it."

"They're going to need to find a fix for that little scandal, aren't they?"

The next child was coming down the red carpet, but Ash wasn't interested. He'd never had the chance to hear himself spoken about so candidly.

"They will. The higher-ups at Ashby's always figure out a way to dig their golden boy out of trouble, don't they? I'm sure soon we'll be hearing all about something new that'll make us forget about November's *indecent exposure*."

"God, would I like to have seen that."

Why were they talking about him in the middle of an Ashby's? Ash sat up a little straighter in his chair and tried to still his racing heart. Paranoia had set in.

If he was discovered, what would happen? Would his father accuse him of not taking the business seriously enough? Would he be cut off for good?

Ash side-eyed the nutcrackers standing guard behind him, then searched the face of the elf bringing the next child to see him. Did any of them suspect that he wasn't who he said he was? It wasn't like he'd applied any prosthetic to change the shape of his face, and he hadn't changed his voice at all. Dyeing his hair and changing the color of his eyes felt like a weak disguise now.

He was in the middle of an Ashby's, hiding in plain sight. All it would take was a single person to do a double take to shatter the illusion, and then...

A tug at his fake beard yanked Ash's attention back into the moment. The child who'd climbed onto his lap scowled at him, fist clenched.

What the hell do you think you're doing? was what Ash wanted to say.

What he said instead was, "Ho ho ho, little boys on the nice list don't pull on Santa's beard."

"You're not Santa." Another tug at his beard. The straps holding it to his ears started to smart, and Ash winced. "Santa has *blue* eyes. Your eyes are *weird*."

"It's rude to pull on someone's beard," Ash argued. He didn't care whether the kid thought he was Santa or not. The backs of his ears were stinging.

"It's rude to pretend to be Santa!"

Ash was three seconds away from losing his temper.

"It's rude to question Santa," Ash snapped. "Don't you *believe*? I'm not going to stop by your house if you don't believe."

The kid's scowl deepened, and he tightened his hand to yank on the beard again when Ash caught movement out of the corner of his eye. The nutcrackers were changing shifts, and when one leaned over, even before he spoke, Ash instantly knew who it was.

"Isn't it exciting to be here?" Elliott asked the beard-tugger in a soft voice. His chest was pressed against Ash's shoulder, and Ash's heart skipped a beat. This close, Elliott smelled *good*. "Christmas is always such an exciting time of year. I *love* it."

He spoke with such tender enthusiasm that it was hard not to be sucked in. The kid on Ash's lap fell for it immediately, and his hand fell away from Ash's beard.

"Me, too."

"I *know*, right?" Elliott grinned. "It's such a special time of year. Pretty snow and the smell of Christmas trees and being with family are my favorite parts. What about you?"

"Getting to see my dad stay home from work during the week. It's *fun* to have him at home."

"Right?" Elliott's grin grew. "And that's what the magic of Christmas is all about, isn't it? That happiness you feel when your dad gets to stay home is the heart of that, and if you hold that joy in your heart and keep it there, then *anything* your heart desires can be yours."

Where had Elliott learned to talk so convincingly? Most of the time he was too shy to stutter his way through a full sentence, but now he'd come alive. Ash couldn't help but lean against him as he spoke, quietly extending his thanks through physical contact.

"Anything?" the boy asked, eyes wide, clearly enchanted.

"*Anything*," Elliott promised. "But you have to dip into that happiness and share it with everyone you meet—even Santa. That's why Santa has a nice list. The girls and boys who share that joy in their hearts with everyone they meet are the ones who Santa is the most generous with. Isn't that right, Santa?"

It took Ash a second to realize that Elliott was talking to him.

"Oh, uh, that's right. My trusted nutcracker is telling the truth—and he's been a very good boy this year, according to my list. You should listen to him."

With his shoulder pressed against Elliott's chest, Ash

didn't miss the sharp inhalation of breath Elliott took, even though it was silent. Flirting with him was effortless, and Elliott's reactions made it even more fun.

"Oh, okay. I, um... wow." The little boy smiled. "I'm sorry, Santa. I was wrong."

"That's okay, little boy," Ash said, summoning his best Santa. Now that Elliott had saved his ass, he didn't want to mess it up. "What's important is what's in your heart, and I can see that your heart is in the right place."

"Now that Christmas magic is alive inside of you, you should visit the Giving Tree," Elliott told him. "If you write down your wish for Christmas and leave it on the tree, it will come true."

God, was he convincing. Ash shot Elliott a look and found no stress or strain on his face. What he said, he truly believed.

There was something beautiful in that innocence, and for a moment, Ash found himself lost in it. Elliott really was something special—something he'd never experienced before.

And all of that was possible because, for the moment at least, he was *Ben*, not Ash.

There was value in the common, he was starting to understand. From nights at Reggie's with cheap beer and kind words spoken to him not out of obligation, but out of kindness...

Maybe being Ben wasn't so bad after all.

Chapter 7

ELLIOTT

THE NORTH POLE WASN'T ALL THAT FAR FROM MEN'S WEAR, and, try as he might, Elliott couldn't seem to keep himself from glancing in that direction. Repeatedly. Nick's stroke had been tragic, and, at first, Elliott had expected that his Christmas season would be tarnished for it, but as the days passed, he was coming to learn that *different* didn't necessarily equate to *bad*.

And there was certainly nothing bad about Ben.

At all.

It had been a week since the Ashby's group had gone out to Reggie's for Friday night drinks, and Elliott was still having a hard time shaking the idea of Ben from his mind.

They'd sat on the same side of the table, side by side, and at first Elliott had been too nervous to breathe, let alone look in Ben's direction. There was something about him that paralyzed Elliott. What that something was, he still wasn't sure. It wasn't just because Ben was interested in him—even, which still boggled Elliott's mind, *after* Trevor had made a play for him—and it wasn't just because Ben was hot. There was something in Ben's soul, hidden away behind his cocky demeanor, that called out to Elliott.

But that wasn't why Elliott was thinking of excuses to break away from his duties manning the floor in men's wear in order to visit the North Pole.

No. Not by a long shot. He wasn't letting Ben get under his skin. That was ridiculous. The North Pole was special to him because it was his favorite place in the world and had been ever since childhood, not because the Santa who worked there was a first-class hottie.

Not at all.

By the time he'd arrived in front of the big Christmas arch dividing the display overhang from the rest of the store, Elliott still hadn't figured out what his excuse was to be visiting the North Pole while scheduled to work men's wear, but he was certain that it would come to him. Any moment now. It definitely wasn't like he was looking for Ben. That wouldn't be like him. But whether it was like him or not didn't matter—the velvet rope was strung up over the Christmas arch, closing off the North Pole while Santa took a well-deserved break—and Elliott's heart fell.

He didn't want to admit that he was looking forward to seeing Ben, but there was no other way he could rationalize how crestfallen he felt.

Their legs had brushed under the table...

No. Elliott blinked and shook his head, turning away from the North Pole to distance himself from his thoughts. It was silly to be crushing on a guy as hot as Ben. No matter how much Ben flirted, there was no way he could actually be interested. Playing footsie wasn't a surefire indication that Ben felt anything for him. Guys that hot could afford to play around without it meaning anything.

Elliott had to be more careful with his affections. Sometimes, he knew, he was too quick to see the good in people. Too quick to trust. To see what he wanted to and let himself *believe*.

But he didn't want to get hurt.

On his way back to the men's wear department, a scene at the Giving Tree caught Elliott's eye and he came to a stop. A mother and a boy of five or six stood there, admiring the tree from afar. With a little more than two weeks to go until Christmas, the tree was only sparsely decorated with wish tags, but it was still populated enough to catch the eye.

They were struggling for money.

Someone looking from the outside wouldn't be able to tell unless they were familiar with poverty, and the two of them put on a convincing act, but Elliott had once been there himself. He could tell by the oversized shoes the boy wore, and the way his mother's coat was a little too thread-bare to be warm.

The sight reminded him poignantly of his own past.

Hand in hand, mother and son looked at the elegant tree in silence. Christmas carols played low over the speakers, and Elliott's heart melted at the sight. It felt like just yesterday that his own mother had held his hand in exactly the same way as the two of them had stood in that spot together, taking in the sight of the Giving Tree. Back then, Elliott really had thought it was magic. *Real* magic.

And now, even knowing how much went into making that kind of magic come to life, he was determined that through him, it would continue.

Without giving it a second thought, he approached the mother and son pair and fell into line beside them. The mother turned her head to look his way, but her little boy continued to stare at the tree, enchanted by it.

"Have you gone to see Santa yet?" Elliott asked, daring to stir conversation.

"Not yet," the mother replied. "Jacob wanted to come to see the tree first."

"It's a lot bigger than the one we have at home," the boy—Jacob said. Then, under his breath, he added with a heartfelt whisper, "It's so beautiful."

"It *is* beautiful," Elliott agreed, nodding and keeping his focus on the tree so he didn't come across as too overbearing. Out of the corner of his eye he could see the mother start to relax. "When I was a boy, it was always my favorite part of the Christmas display here at Ashby's. Do you know the story of the Giving Tree?"

"No," Jacob said, turning big eyes on him eagerly. "What is it?"

"The Giving Tree is a really special tree," Elliott explained, warmth spreading through his chest at the sparkle he saw in Jacob's eyes. A kindred spirit, for sure. The boy wanted to believe, and Elliott was determined to do his part to give him something to believe in... exactly the way Nick had done for him, so many years ago. "After you go see Santa, come back here and speak to one of Santa's elves," he explained. "They'll give you and your mom a tag, exactly like the ones you see on the branches. If you write the wish that you whispered to Santa on that tag and hang it here, then your wish will come true. Because the Giving Tree is magic."

Elliott didn't miss how the mother tensed at his words. It was clear that she didn't think that was true, and Elliott understood her position well. Money was tight around the holidays, and she probably knew she couldn't afford to splurge. His own mom had faced the same problem.

"Sometimes, though, not even Santa can make all of our wishes come true," Jacob's mother said, trying to deflate the dream as tenderly as she could. "Santa's very busy, and even he makes mistakes and forgets things from time to time."

"But not here," Elliott insisted. More than anything, he wanted to make the little boy's dream come true. He caught the woman's eye, willing her to understand. "As long as you whisper your wish to Santa and then put it on the tree, it's guaranteed to come true. I promise. Santa and all his helpers here at Ashby's will make sure of it."

"Mister," Jacob said, voice rising in pitch with worry, "what if I already put my tag on the tree without talking to Santa first? Will the magic still work? Santa's not there—" Jacob pointed back toward the North Pole, "—and Mom says we have to go."

"Hmm." Elliott cocked his head, pretending to think about it for a moment. "Well, Santa's taking a break to go eat lunch with Mrs. Claus right now, so I think he'll understand if you can't stick around to see him in person. Why don't you show me which tag has your Christmas wish on it? That way, I can make sure he sees it when he gets back."

Jacob's hand slipped free from his mother's and he ducked under the ropes keeping the tree separate from the aisle. The two elves on duty moved to intercept, but Elliott waved them off without a word. They backed off, grinning behind their hands as Jacob strained up on his tiptoes to point without disturbing the tree.

"It's this one!" he exclaimed.

Elliott memorized the spot and nodded. "Got it," he said. "And I'll personally make sure that Santa knows it's there. Come Christmas Eve, when Ashby's has its Children's Christmas Party, you'll find your present under the tree. So make sure you get your mom to come back, okay?"

"Okay," Jacob chimed, glowing.

He ducked back under the rope to join his mother, and Elliott made sure he gave her a reassuring look. On Christmas Eve, he was going to make sure that the present for Jacob was there, no matter what.

"I can't wait!" Jacob said, his excitement palpable as his bright eyes bounced between Elliott and his mother.

"Me neither." Elliott grinned. "The Christmas party is a lot of fun. You're going to love it—I promise."

"Let's get going, Jacob," his mother insisted. She shot Elliott a lingering glance, obviously still hesitant to believe, but—at Elliott's slight nod—looking like she was willing to take a chance. She glanced down at her son, taking his hand with a small smile. "We'll go get some lunch, too, okay?"

"Okay." Jacob was all smiles, and when the two of them left, Elliott couldn't help but smile, too. Sharing moments like that made working at Ashby's so worth it.

"Big promises," Ben murmured against the back of Elliott's ear, his warm breath tickling the delicate skin there as his voice startled Elliott.

Elliott turned too quickly and found himself chest to chest with Ben. Out of his Santa suit, he looked stunning, and Elliott took a small step back, feeling flustered. The move made him brush up against the rope that sectioned off the Giving Tree from the rest of the store, forcing him to stop. Not that being too close to Ben was a hardship.

Definitely, *definitely* not a hardship.

"How are you going to guarantee that kid gets a gift?"

Ben asked, arching a brow. "There are tons of tags on the tree, and someone has to step forward and say they'll buy whatever it is he wants. There's no guarantee it'll happen."

"Yes, there is," Elliott said. To prove his point, he ducked under the rope and plucked the tag off the tree, slipping it into his back pocket. Ben's presence had his pulse racing, and he swallowed, hoping that—despite the way it sounded in his own ears—it wasn't actually loud enough that Ben could hear it, too. "Why do you think I work so much overtime during the holiday season? I don't typically live here, you know."

"*You're* going to pay for it?" One corner of Ben's lips curved up, and he fixed Elliott with his strange hazel eyes. "But what if he asked for something expensive?"

"Well, we usually get Christmas bonuses," Elliott said. He remained standing by the tree, glad for the slight distance between himself and Ben. Ben was far too tempting otherwise. "Mine is usually is enough to cover whatever they ask for."

The upturned corner of Ben's lip fell, and he frowned. Elliott wondered if he'd said something wrong.

"'They'? Why would you spend it on kids you don't know?" Ben asked at last, sounding genuinely curious. "It's your bonus. You might even be able to spring for a Jagway shirt if you kept it for yourself."

Elliott looked back at the tree without answering right away. There were plenty of tags still hanging on it, waiting to be claimed. And he knew that as more children came to visit Santa over the next few weeks, it would fill out even further. He searched the tags already there—the written evidence of all the heartfelt wishes he'd been privileged to overhear whispered into Ben's ear from his position standing at "Santa's" side as a nutcracker. From amongst the tags, he plucked one off and dangled it by the looped ribbon on top so that Ben could see it.

"Do you remember the little girl who came in just a few days ago and asked for the toy confectioner's oven?" Elliott asked. "The one you slide the tiny little tins into and it bakes real cake?"

The rope that separated them wasn't barrier enough to keep Elliott's eyes from wandering. Even as he sought to answer Ben's question, to explain why granting children's wishes felt like a better use of his bonus money than treating himself to an expensive shirt, he couldn't help but give in to a little temptation. The way the black Ashby's uniform fit Ben's body was stunning, and seeing him in a tie instead of fat padding and a festive red suit was a treat.

"Yeah, I remember," Ben said, nodding. "What about her?"

He slid his hands into his back pockets and watched Elliott right back, and when Elliott saw *Ben's* eyes wandering, too, a delicious thrill ran down his spine.

Ben was looking at *him*.

"Do you remember why she wanted the oven?" Elliott asked, his thumb rubbing over the careful printing on the tag in his hand.

Ben's eyes tracked the movement. "No," he said.

"She said that her mother didn't get to celebrate her birthday this year because she was too busy working double shifts," Elliott reminded him. He slipped the tag into his pocket next to Jacob's. "She wanted to get the oven so she could bake her mom a birthday cake, even though her birthday had already passed."

Ben watched him, but said nothing, and Elliott continued, his self-consciousness fading away as he reached for another tag.

"Or this one? This was the nine-year-old boy who came in with his father. We don't see a lot of fathers here, so he stood out. Remember?"

"Elliott, no, not really, but—"

Elliott cut him off, wanting Ben to remember. To *understand.*

"His name was Billy, and he told us that his mother was in the hospital fighting off a 'bad sickness.' He said she wasn't going to get to come home for Christmas, so he asked for some lipstick so that he could have a present to take to her at the hospital to make sure she still had something to look forward to on Christmas morning."

Ben's expression dropped, and Elliott slipped Billy's tag into his pocket along with the others he'd just pulled from the tree.

"And, really, even if they don't have a selfless story, every kid who puts their wish on the Giving Tree deserves to see it come true," he said, believing it with every fiber of his being. He smiled. It's what Christmas was about. "There's so much unbridled joy in this time of year that you only get to experience for so long, and ruining the illusion sours that mood."

"I mean, I get all that," Ben said. "But it's not your responsibility, Elliott. Why *you*? You can't make all that much working retail at Ashby's, even if you've been here for a few years, and one day those kids are going to find out it's all fake, anyway. You're not always going to be there, you know?"

"If not me, then who?" Elliott asked. "Just because it comes from real people instead of Santa Claus, it doesn't mean it's fake, Ben. The spirit of Christmas is about all of us."

No matter what Ben said, Elliott wasn't going to change his mind. There was more value in giving like this than Ben seemed to understand, and Elliott wished he could show Ben what small gestures like buying gifts from the Giving Tree meant to the kids.

Maybe, in time, he'd see. Especially once he saw their faces at the Christmas Eve party.

Glancing around to make sure no children were around to overhear their conversation, Elliott ducked back under the ropes to rejoin Ben.

"I know that some day, those kids are going to understand that Christmas isn't what they think it is—that Santa isn't real, and that it's all just a show. But until then? Until that point, I want them to believe. Sometimes, the only thing that keeps a kid going is thinking that there's this great benevolent force out there who thinks of *them* and values *them*. That's how it was for me when I was little, living with my mom in a one-bedroom apartment in a rougher neighborhood. If I hadn't had something to look forward to, something to believe in, I don't know if I would've made it out of my childhood the way I did."

Silence lapsed between them, and normally, Elliott would have found it awkward, but his devotion to the spirit of the season eased his anxiety. Ben still hadn't said anything, but Elliott was on a roll.

"And when those kids find out that Christmas isn't really what they think it is, the ones who needed the Giving Tree the most are going to think back and they're going to realize that maybe *Santa* isn't real, but that there are kind strangers out there who bought presents for kids they'll never meet. Kids they know nothing about. And that's kind of magical in itself, isn't it? That humanity isn't all cold and sterile and cruel."

Maybe it was a trick of the light, but Elliott could have sworn he saw Ben's lips part just slightly, as though his words had finally struck a chord.

"And it's *that* belief I want to foster," Elliott said, the look in Ben's eyes making something warm blossom in his chest. "What starts as a belief in Santa and the magic of the Christmas season turns into a love of people, and of humanity, even when faced with so much injustice and inequality. It's that belief that there is *good* in people that I want to nurture. And I think that if we all did that—if we all helped kids believe just for this one day that the world is full of good and love—that there would be a whole lot less terribleness happening in the world."

The silence between them resumed, but—despite how hard his heart was beating and the fact that the underside of his jaw felt clammy—it didn't really feel awkward. With nothing more to say, Elliott relaxed his shoulders and exhaled. He'd never gone off on anyone before about his Christmas spiel, fearing he'd come across as too naive, but there was something about Ben that made him want to share.

He wanted Ben to understand where he was coming from.

And the expression on Ben's face—lips slightly parted and oddly colored eyes gentle, almost vulnerable—convinced Elliott that opening himself up had been worth it. He'd never seen Ben so stricken and soft before, and while Elliott loved how cocky and bold Ben was on a day-to-day basis, there was something intimate about this version of Ben that stirred him. Familiar butterflies rose in his stomach and crowded his lungs, and even though he breathed normally, he felt lightheaded.

Ben was gorgeous like that.

God, he had it bad, didn't he? Elliott knew he should probably look away, but he couldn't bring himself to do it. There wouldn't be too many times he'd catch Ben off-guard, he knew, and he wanted to absorb it while he could.

Once Christmas was over, they'd be going their separate ways, anyway. Maybe taking the time to commit these moments to memory was worth it.

"What are you doing after work today?" Ben asked, finally breaking the silence.

The vulnerability had leeched into his voice, and Elliott longed to hear more of it.

"It's, um, Friday, right?" Elliott no longer felt as awkward talking to Ben. Somehow, he'd cracked him and opened him up. It wasn't just Elliott who hid behind a tight shell. "On Friday nights, we all go to Reggie's for drinks. Did Trevor not invite you already?"

"He did," Ben said.

"So... do you want to go with us?" Elliott looked him over, a little confused.

"That's the problem." Ben slipped his hands from his pockets and stood a touch more formally. "I'm not really interested in the *us* part. I want to go out with *you*, Elliott."

A chill ran down Elliott's spine, but he did his best not to show it. Sometimes, Ben said things that he misconstrued. It was better that he not jump to conclusions, no matter how thrilling that statement felt.

"Well, we can definitely go together," Elliott said. "I mean... last time you came, we sat together, and that was... nice." More than nice.

"I don't think you understand what I'm getting at," Ben said lightly, the hint of a much-too-sexy smile hovering around his lips. He took a small step forward, closing some of the distance between them. "I don't want to tag along with the rest of them. I want to go out, just you and me."

The chill intensified, making Elliott shiver, and his head turned foggy as excitement clouded his senses. That was pretty hard to misconstrue, but, just to be sure...

"Like a... like a date?"

"Exactly like a date," Ben said firmly, looking at him in a way that no one ever had before.

Ben was really asking him out on a date? Elliott swallowed. His cheeks burned, and he knew he had to be blushing.

"I, um, well... okay."

"Good." Ben's charming smile dazzled him. "So I'll see you once this shift is over? I've got somewhere in mind I want to take you. For now, though, I've got to get back to work. Santa's job waits for no man."

"Right." It came out as little more than a squeak, Elliott busy turning the conversation over in his mind as he tried to pick apart its nuances. A date with Ben? It almost seemed too good to be true.

"See you later," Ben said, letting his fingers brush over the back of Elliott's hand before he headed for the escalators.

Elliott meant to say goodbye, or yes, or... something, but all he managed to do was smile like a happy fool and watch him go. He always looked forward to Friday night drinks at Reggie's, but he'd never been more excited to miss them than he was right at that moment.

Ben had asked him out on a *date*.

Chapter 8

ASH

Downtown Chicago boasted excellent restaurants of all styles, but the one Ash had been the most interested in was three blocks from Ashby's location, occupying the corner spot between East Chicago and Wabash.

L'Académie was the one restaurant he'd heard mentioned in passing by multiple friends and peers when they talked about their excursions to Chicago, but Ash had never had the chance to visit and see what all the fuss was about. Chicago had never struck him as a particularly interesting city, and, in the past, he'd spent the majority of his travel time in various Ashby homes along either coast, enjoying the ocean view and spending time on the beach. But there was no denying that there was something about Chicago on the cusp of winter that appealed to Ash in a way he never would have anticipated.

The chill of the air and the crisp way it felt in his lungs wasn't quite the same as it was in New York, and the feel of the city was different. Ash hadn't had time to explore much outside of the downtown core, but from what he'd seen so far, Chicago came alive at Christmas, and everywhere he went looked just a touch more welcoming because of it.

Or maybe it was the off-duty nutcracker at his side who should get credit for Ash's rose-colored glasses. Elliott's company—hands jammed in his coat pockets and breath fogging with each exhalation—definitely went a long way toward painting the town in such a positive light.

Elliott was glowing.

Even when he wasn't all smiles and customer service, there was a special kind of light inside him that shone forth naturally. It was just part of who he *was*. Ash saw it in his eyes and observed it in his smile, and it left him breathless. He'd never met someone who was so in tune with himself, and had never spent time with someone who was so effortlessly easy to get along with. Shy or not, caught up in his head or not, there was kindness and an openness in Elliott that nothing seemed to shake.

Ash wondered if Elliott had any idea how rare and precious that quality was.

He suspected not.

"So, where are we going again?" Elliott asked. "I don't think I've heard of the place you mentioned."

"Oh. It's probably not super well known," Ash said, shrugging. "It's just a place I've heard about from my friends a couple of times, and I thought it might be fun to try it out."

"Sounds good." There was an easy smile on Elliott's face, and even after a full shift, he still looked full of energy. "I'm... well, thanks for inviting me out."

"I've wanted to do it for a while," Ash said, realizing as he said it that it was true. "My only regret is that I didn't do it sooner."

Pink bloomed across Elliott's cheeks, and Ash knew that it wasn't from the cold. He grinned, kind of loving that he had that effect on him.

L'Académie was classically and tastefully French from the outside, having an understated elegance that—in Ash's experience—boded well for what they'd find inside. The terrace was closed for the winter, but Ash noted the small rounded tables and the heavy metal chairs set out on it that reminded him of cafes he'd enjoyed in Paris. The front door was made of glass and painted with the restaurant's name, and Ash pulled the door open to allow Elliott to enter first.

But Elliott had stopped a few paces away, looking up at the restaurant's facade with a worried expression.

Ash frowned. "What's the matter?" he asked. "Have you heard something about this place that I haven't?"

"No," Elliott said unevenly. He refocused his attention on Ash and hurried forward, stepping through the door he held open without elaborating.

As they warmed themselves by the hostess's station, Ash leaned a little closer to Elliott, lowering his voice. "If you don't think this place is up to your standards, we can go somewhere else. My heart isn't set on it."

"No, no, I'm sure it's a great restaurant," Elliott whispered back, but there was still a twinge of something in his voice that Ash couldn't place.

If Elliott hadn't heard bad things about L'Académie, why did he seem so hesitant?

The hostess approached before Ash could press him on it, and Ash took the lead, arranging to have a table prepared for them toward the back, furthest away from the kitchen doors. As Ash laid out the detail, specifying his wants as the hostess scanned her seating chart, he caught Elliott sneaking glances around the restaurant, as though he were looking for something.

What was up with that? There was clearly something wrong, but Elliott obviously didn't feel comfortable just coming out and saying it.

Once the details were finalized, the hostess led them to a suitable table and took their coats from them to be checked, a complimentary service. Ash saw Elliott seated before he sat down himself, still a little troubled by the small signs of Elliott's discomfort.

It felt strange to be out in public in an Ashby's uniform,

but at the very least they were well-made, upscale garments. The all-black ensemble looked a little out of place and a little too close to 'waiter' for Ash's taste, but having seen some of the working-class uniforms required at fast food places or less reputable chain stores, he had to be thankful that at least his father had the good sense to require at least a modicum of civility from Ashby's employees. There was value in demanding that those who worked the floors be dressed like proper gentlemen.

Or ladies, Ash supposed.

But dressed properly, regardless.

And, regardless of his and Elliott's current state of dress, they were promptly brought menus and the wine list, another sign in favor of the restaurant being a good choice. The leather backing on the menus was soft and of fine caliber, and Ash was already impressed. If L'Académie went through the trouble of perfecting the small details, he was sure that the larger ones were meticulously cared for.

Elliott's fingers tightened around the single-page menu, though, and as his eyes scanned it, his normally ever-present smile disappeared completely.

"Do you need help translating anything?" Ash asked. The menu was largely in French, but English translations were provided in small print beneath each item. In the dim light, it was likely difficult to read.

"No."

Elliott set the menu down and forced a smile back on his face. It didn't reach his eyes, lacking the light that Ash usually saw in him, and that small detail alone made Ash's soul ache.

Elliott cleared his throat. "You know, I packed a really big lunch today and I ate it all. I'm still stuffed. I think I'll maybe just get a drink and call it a night."

"Oh." There was definitely something wrong. Ash frowned. "Do you not like French cuisine? It's not all escargot and frogs legs, you know. There are some great rustic recipes on the menu that might be good if you're not feeling adventurous."

"Just not hungry," Elliott insisted, as if he actually thought Ash was going to buy that. "I think I'll get... um, do you think they serve cafe lattes here? Or something like that?"

A coffee? It had to be close to nine at night.

The garçon arrived, and Ash waved him off. He'd already made his choice, but he wasn't even remotely convinced that Elliott was telling the truth. But it was only when the sommelier arrived and Ash ordered a bottle of their exclusive Sancerre that he started to clue in to what was happening.

The second the sommelier walked away, Elliott twisted his hands together and leaned across the table.

"I um, I don't want to be... a stick in the mud." He looked like he was struggling for words. "But if you were thinking of splitting the cost of wine with me, I can't really, um, I can't pay you up front. If you still want it, that's fine, but I'll only be able to get you the money after the Christmas season is over. Maybe the second to last week of January, if I can put in some more overtime."

Ash's mouth opened, but he found he couldn't reply.

The first thing that bothered Ash was that Elliott assumed Ash wouldn't be covering the cost of dinner after Ash had been the one to invite him out. Ash may have been brash and often non-traditional, but he wasn't rude. But really, what bothered Ash most of all about the statement was that Elliott couldn't afford to split the bottle. A bottle that, honestly, Ash hadn't even looked at the price of when making his decision.

The meals at L'Académie weren't cheap, but Ash had heard they were worth the expense. Still, the truth was, he wasn't used to thinking about whether or not he could afford something. The question wasn't even on his radar, since the answer was always yes. Even with his father currently cutting him off from access to most of the luxuries he normally took for granted, it hadn't occurred to Ash to think about prices when it came to asking Elliott out. He'd just wanted to make sure they had a nice time. To take him somewhere he'd enjoy. But if Elliott couldn't afford to float seventy dollars Ash's way, then it was no wonder he was so dead set on ordering coffee and nothing else. He obviously assumed that Ash—*Ben*, as far as Elliott was concerned— was in the same boat.

"Elliott," Ash said softly, wondering if he'd ever been

out with anyone before who hadn't assumed he'd cover the bill. "I'm not asking you to pay for anything. The meal's on me, okay? So order whatever you'd like."

Found out and cornered, Elliott glanced down at the menu and then back up at Ash. Discomfort played across his face and set in his eyes, but Ash's heart tripped a little at the sight. It was discomfort at the thought of Ash over-extending himself. Elliott was worried about him.

"Can you really afford this?" Elliott asked, the flush in his cheeks deepening as he leaned forward. "It's expensive. Honestly, Ben, I'm just happy with the company. I don't need—"

"Yeah," Ash said, cutting him off. "I can, Elliott. It's okay."

He had to remember that to Elliott, he was Ben. Ashby's Santa didn't bring in a fortune, and it wasn't like he could come out and say that he was actually Ash, heir of the Ashby fortune. Regardless, though, what Elliott had said touched him.

"It sounds kind of campy," Ash said, mentally scrambling for a story that would convince Elliott. He wanted more than ever to show him some of the nicer things in life. "But every year, my dad sends me some extra money around Christmas so I can get out there and do the things I like to do. We don't really have a great relationship, so money is his way of showing me he cares."

It was the sugarcoated truth. Ash doubted that his father gave two shits about him, but he wasn't cold enough to cut Ash off from money for food. And, as long as Ash didn't get into any trouble in Chicago, he doubted his father would even notice a few hundred dollars spent on dinner in one night.

"Oh." Elliott bit down on his bottom lip like he always did when he was nervous and thinking things through, and Ash couldn't help but smile. "Well, I guess that's okay then? I mean, it's a lot to spend on just one meal, though, don't you think?"

"No." Ash remained firm, but kind. "Spending time with you is worth it. I want to treat you. If you do what you do for the kids at Ashby's, let me do this for you now."

Elliott held back a smile, but Ash knew it was there. The light had returned to his eyes, and his expression had loosened.

When the garçon returned, they placed their orders, and Ash grinned, happy, when Elliott gave in and ordered a proper dinner. Once they were alone again, Elliott shook his head and laughed.

"I've never spent so much money on a single plate of food before. It's so ridiculous."

"You'll enjoy it," Ash promised. "Once you taste the difference, you'll understand why restaurants like these charge more."

"So you come to places like this often?" Elliott grinned at him. "I can hardly afford sit-down chain restaurants. How do you manage?"

"I—" Ash blinked. Not only was he worried about

covering his tracks, but his contacts were *killing* him. "Well, I might not have been to too many, but if coming to places like this means I can convince you to join me, I might be skimping on groceries in order to eat out more often."

Deflecting with flirtation had served him well in the past, and the way Elliott blushed for him made it worth it, but Ash found himself wishing he could open up and be more candid. Elliott had been kind to him since the beginning, and Ash didn't want to lie to him. Still, he knew that if he dropped the illusion of *Ben*, things would change between them. His playboy reputation as Ash combined with his overwhelming wealth would color whatever connection they shared and change it irreversibly.

And the thought of losing Elliott knotted his stomach.

What the hell was Elliott doing to him?

Every other guy Ash had ever gone out with had used him in one way or another. Whether it was actors looking for a little screen time in the public eye, or executives who wanted to get into bed with Ashby's, or even casual guys who saw being with him as their chance at some pocket change and a taste of luxury, Ash didn't think he'd ever been on a date where there wasn't the expectation that he was the provider and his date was the leech.

Elliott was different, and Ash didn't want to lose that.

"So I guess you're the kind of guy who saves up and splurges on big items," Elliott said casually. "Is that true?"

"Go big or go home," Ash shot back. "What about you? Are you a fan of the better things in life?"

"No. I mean, I guess we all are, right?" Elliott shifted in his chair. "But I'm fine not living in luxury. I like knock-off just as well as I like brand name, so usually I go for knock-off because it's cheaper. And I'm not really the type to throw something away until it's really, really worn down."

"Like what?" Ash asked. He was surprised to find he actually wanted to know more. The men he dated were usually eye candy whom he had little interest in beyond that—he was just as guilty of using them in his own way as they were of using him—but with Elliott, it wasn't like that.

Elliott was a fantastic person inside and out, and Ash was eager to figure him out.

"Um, okay, here's an example." Elliott crossed his arms on the table and leaned forward just a little. "When I was ten or eleven, I had this pair of shoes I really liked. Growing up, my mom always bought shoes at least two sizes too big so that they'd last while I grew into them, so I grew up used to having lots of extra space around my toes."

Ash listened in silence. He couldn't imagine wearing improperly sized shoes. What about all the blisters Elliott would have gotten?

"Anyway, when I was that age, I ended up getting a really good pair that were way too big, but that I didn't seem to grow into over the years, either. I guess my feet stopped growing for a while or something. But I wore those shoes for years, until I'd worn holes through the soles and the stitching was coming undone. And even though they were falling to pieces, I couldn't bear to throw them away until the sole actually parted from the rest of the shoe and they *literally* fell apart. The day that happened, my mom and I were at free visit day at the zoo, and we had to leave early because suddenly one of my feet was barefoot."

Ash snorted and shook his head. Was that how normal people treated their possessions? There had been times he'd thrown away shoes just because of scuff damage.

"So, I guess, as long as something's going to last a while, that's the kind of thing I'm likely to buy. So a really expensive dinner? I wouldn't go out of my way to splurge on that because it only lasts for an hour, maybe, if you've got really great conversation going. But something like a high quality work shoe? Yeah. I've had the same pair of high quality non-slip shoes since I got my first paycheck from Ashby's, and I haven't regretted that purchase a single day since."

If any of Ash's friends heard the conversation he was having with Elliott, they would have doubled over laughing. The idea that a single pair of shoes would have to last until they fell apart was so unlike their reality that it sounded like a farce.

Yet Elliott spoke truthfully and sincerely, and Ash didn't doubt him.

What would Elliott have thought if Ash had talked about the cabin he was currently renting in Aspen that was going to waste? Or how having a cleaning crew scrub the house clean was more convenient than trying to curb the behavior of their house party guests?

All Ash could think about was the discomfort on Elliott's face when he'd stepped into a restaurant he knew he couldn't afford.

To Ash's friends, poverty was hilarious. To Elliott, their disregard for money would have been a travesty. The conversation just went to prove that there was no way he could ever come clean to Elliott about who he really was. Which, based on Ash's past "dating" history, shouldn't have been a problem. He didn't do long-term.

But, when it came to Elliott, the idea that the option was off the table completely didn't sit well.

Ash pushed the uncomfortable thought away, determined to enjoy the moment. The conversation continued, Ash deflecting questions with flirtation and returning fire on Elliott to keep him talking about himself. The appetizers and wine arrived together, and once Elliott started to drink, he loosened up a little more.

"Try it," Ash urged.

"No way!"

"Try it!" Grinning, he lifted one of the shells and held it across the table to Elliott, who'd sunk back into his chair and had crossed his arms. "It's actually good, and the flavor is mild. Spices and wine. What's not to like?"

"Uh, the fact that it's a *snail*." Elliott laughed. "You know, those things that crawl across the ground and leave slime everywhere?"

"You're thinking of slugs," Ash countered. Seeing Elliott in such a good mood after his initial discomfort had put Ash in a good mood. "Snails and slugs aren't the same thing. I wouldn't eat a slug."

"But you *would* eat a snail, so how can I trust your judgment?"

Ash's grin grew. "Because I'm out on a date with you, so obviously I have good taste."

Elliott looked across the table at him, concealing his smile as best he could, but it lived in his eyes and lightened his face regardless. Without a word, he uncrossed his arms and plucked the shell from Ash's fingers.

"I can't believe I'm doing this."

There was a small, long fork designed to scoop the escargot from its shell that sat on the table between them. Elliott picked it up and dug into the opening of the shell delicately.

"You can't come to a fancy French restaurant and leave without having at least said you tried the escargot," Ash insisted. "Besides, if you don't like it, you always can just spit it into your napkin." Ash winked, loving teasing Elliott. "I promise I'll look the other way if you do, but honestly, I think you're going to like it."

Meat skewered and pried from the shell, Elliott took a deep breath. "If I die, remember me as I was."

"You're not going to die." Ash rolled his eyes playfully. "Just eat the snail already."

Eyes closed, nose pushed up and wrinkled, Elliott popped the fork between his lips and ate. Seconds passed. The lack of gagging convinced Ash he hadn't been off the mark, and when Elliott swallowed and opened his eyes again, he knew he'd been right.

"Wasn't bad," Elliott admitted with a half laugh.

The rest of dinner was just as playful. Ash couldn't remember the last time he'd gone out and actually had fun.

The bill arrived, and Ash fished his father's card out of his wallet and slid it into the book to wait for processing. Elliott squinted at it.

"Is that a black card?"

Shit.

"No." Ash said it a little too quickly. "I mean, it looks like one, right? The bank I got it from offers customizations on their basic credit cards for free, so I figured that I'd mock up one of those elite cards for the laughs. I mean, who expects someone in their twenties to pull a card like that, right? I've gotten some really great reactions."

The lie held, and Elliott laughed. "God, I can only imagine. I've got to watch out for you, don't I?" The sparkle in his eyes was brighter than ever, and Ash was quickly lost in it. The atmosphere between them shifted and grew heavy, like they were caught in each other's gravities. Ash's heart beat a dull, heavy beat as anticipation built inside of him.

His gut told him to lean across the table and kiss Elliott right then and there.

His mind told him that it was a bad idea.

His mind had never spoken up like that before.

"You don't have anything to worry about," Ash told him, voice deepened from the growing attraction between them. "But I'm not going to object if you want to watch me a little more closely. I like it when your eyes are on me."

Elliott blushed and looked away, but the thick chemistry between them didn't abate.

"Let me take you home," Ash said softly.

Elliott's shoulders went rigid, and he ducked his gaze. "I um... I mean, I can just get an Uber, you know? I don't usually, um... I don't really date that much, you know? And... yeah."

Not even being shot down could spoil Ash's mood. "Then at least let me carpool with you. I don't even have to come inside; I just want to make sure you get home safe. It's late."

Elliott looked up at him then, and while hesitancy dragged at the corners of his lips, there was hope in his eyes. It lit Ash up from the inside as warmth coiled in his gut.

"Okay," Elliott said.

Ash grinned. He didn't want the night to end yet, but much to his surprise, it really *was* okay. Stealing some extra time with Elliott while seeing him home was its own reward.

Ash was smitten.

Chapter 9

ELLIOTT

THERE WAS SOMETHING MAGICAL IN THE WAY BEN OPENED the car door for him, and something even better about how he closed it after Elliott was settled. The drive out to Bronzeville would take a while, but even if it was spent in silence, so long as it was spent by Ben's side, Elliott didn't mind it so much.

Most of the time, he took the Metra in and out of work. Springing for an Uber was a little luxurious, but after Ben had paid for his entire meal, Elliott wasn't averse to the expense. He would have spent just as much at Reggie's, anyway. When he considered that, it made the Uber worth it.

Smooth jazz played at a low volume from the car stereo.

Ben settled onto the seat beside Elliott and buckled himself in. Elliott could tell that the fine wool coat he was wearing was high quality; it really did look like Ben was the type of guy who saved for luxury items. Elliott wondered if maybe he should give it a shot. Maybe a Jagway shirt wouldn't be such a bad investment after all.

Chicago streets passed. A recent snowfall made traffic a mess, but Elliott wasn't paying much attention to how long their trip was taking. His left hand rested on the middle seat, and Ben's hand lay atop it, Ben's fingers stroking over Elliott's nails tenderly.

It was instant fireworks.

Startled by how much pleasure such a simple gesture instilled in him, Elliott turned his head to look out the window and collect his racing thoughts. Not only was he out on a date for the first time in what felt like forever, but he was out on a date with the hottest guy at Ashby's. Workplace romances weren't encouraged, but company policy or not, there was no way Elliott could have brought himself to turn Ben down.

Ben made him *feel* things.

It wasn't like Elliott hadn't had boyfriends before. He'd dated a few guys, but his relationships had never lasted for long. A few weeks here, a few months there, but never anything substantial. Never anything Elliott had wanted to turn into something more.

And Elliott *never* went home with a guy on the first date. Partly just due to his own inexperience, but it also just didn't feel right to let things get that physical so soon. To Elliott, a relationship and sex weren't synonymous. A relationship was something delicate and shared—an understanding between two souls of mutual hopes and dreams. To bring sex into it too soon was to muddle the connection. Lust and love were similar, but easily enough crossed that he didn't want to confuse them. Keeping things slow and simple when getting to know someone had always been important to him.

But... no other guy had ever made him feel like Ben did.

And now, the way Ben's fingers traced along Elliott's hand, so gentle and unassuming...

Elliott closed his eyes and willed himself to calm down. The throbbing of his heart and the butterflies in his stomach weren't doing him any favors, and he knew that he had to keep a clear head so he didn't mess up what he was starting to hope might be something really, really good. Besides, Ben wasn't even coming up to his apartment. All he was going to do was sit in the Uber while it dropped Elliott off, and from there he was going home.

There was nothing for Elliott to get excited about.

Downtown Chicago faded away, replaced by the old brick apartment buildings in Bronzeville. The neighborhood was up-and-coming, but it was still a little rough around the edges. Where Elliott lived was a little shady, but not so much that he'd ever felt threatened. So long as he kept to himself, he knew he had nothing to worry about there.

The Uber came to a stop outside of his apartment building, and Elliott slid his hand out from under Ben's to undo his buckle. Ben shifted around to face him.

"Can I walk you to your door to say goodnight?"

"Um." Elliott had told himself that he'd stay in control of the situation and make sure that things ended in the Uber, but every fiber of his being urged him to say yes. He gave in. "Yeah, I guess. That's okay."

They exited the car together, but Ben shut down his attempt to pay.

"I've got it, Elliott," he said, closing his hand around Elliott's when he tried to reach for his wallet. "Please."

Elliott tried to protest, but Ben insisted with a kind of chivalry that just added to how perfect the whole night had been so far. The Uber driver waited while Ben saw him to the door.

"I had a really great time tonight," Ben said. They stood at the door together, close, but not touching. The cold bite of the air burned in Elliott's nostrils and chilled his hands. The temperature had plunged quickly over the last few days, and it had become a lot more like winter than fall.

"I did, too," Elliott said softly.

"Maybe we could do it again sometime soon," Ben continued. He reached out and took one of Elliott's hands in his own, some of his warmth seeping through Elliott's skin. "We can go do something cheaper, if you want. I hear Navy Pier is really beautiful this time of year."

"I, um, yeah." Elliott couldn't take his eyes off Ben's

lips. When he spoke, they moved in the most enchanting ways, and something shifted inside Elliott. "I'd love to do that. For sure."

"I guess this is goodnight, then," Ben whispered. When had they drawn so close? The heat of Ben's body drew Elliott closer yet, and before he knew it, the tips of their noses brushed.

The affection was delicate and sweet, and Elliott's eyelids fluttered partially closed. Ben nuzzled their noses together, gentle and tender, and then turned his head the slightest bit so that the tip of his nose nuzzled down the length of Elliott's until their lips met.

There was nothing hard or needy in the kiss they shared. A sweet affection passed between the two of them, downy in intensity. Elliott trembled and reached up, letting his fingers curl into the thick wool of Ben's jacket.

It was perfect. Soul achingly perfect.

When it broke, Elliott's resolve broke with it.

"Good ni—" Ben started to say.

Elliott didn't allow him to speak. After what they'd shared, he didn't want words. All Elliott wanted was the touch of Ben's lips again, and the heat of his body, and—mostly—the way Ben made him *feel*, like he was someone of value. Elliott pressed his lips against Ben's, eyes closed, this time bringing more passion to the kiss than they'd shared before.

Ben made a short, startled noise in the back of his throat, then relaxed and kissed him back. Elliott could feel Ben's lips curving up in a smile against his. Ben's arms tightened around him—drawing him close—and one of his hands crept up to cup the back of Elliott's head, and somehow the heated embrace made Elliott feel cherished.

Perfect.

What they shared was simple, but nothing about what Elliott felt mirrored that. Need and want and affection and lust tangled themselves in the pit of his stomach and left him aching for more, even though a part of him feared it, too.

He didn't want too much, too soon, to ruin what could be.

Heat pooled inside him as they kissed, and the possessive way Ben held him made the flame warming it burn even brighter.

When the kiss finally broke, Elliott was left struggling to catch his breath. The Uber was waiting, and it would be rude to keep the driver there when he could be picking up other fares. Ben's hand tightened around Elliott's, and Elliott looked up at him. Addled with desire, he'd looked away.

"Do you want to come inside?" he blurted, surprised by his own recklessness. "You can tell the Uber to go, and we'll call you another one later."

"You sure?" Ben asked. There was a low dip to his voice—a kind of huskiness—that Elliott had never heard in it before. It drove him wild.

"Yeah." His heart was racing, but more from excitement than nerves. Well, maybe a bit of both, but *yes*. "Come in."

He wasn't ready for the night to end.

THANK GOD THE LIVING ROOM TO HIS THIRD-FLOOR WALK-UP was clean, at least. The dishes stacked up in the attached kitchenette were neat, but what was he *doing*? Ben was the first guy he'd been on a date with that he felt something more with, and now he was threatening to ruin it by bringing him home too early.

What if Ben had second thoughts and left once he found out how inexperienced Elliott was? Nerves hit him full force as the silence of the small space surrounded them.

He turned to Ben. "I, um—"

Ben kissed him. The already-familiar taste of him made Elliott forget all about his nervousness, his apartment, everything but the anticipation that had inspired him to invite Ben up in the first place. He moaned against Ben's lips, shamelessly melting into him. Ben's lips were firm and sure of themselves, but they were sweet and giving, too. Best of all, he was a terrific kisser.

It was almost physically painful to break away, but if he didn't say something now, Ben's touch was liable to make him forget himself completely.

"Ben, I meant what I said earlier. I... I really don't bring guys home on the first date. I never have before, I mean.

I don't..." Elliott's courage failed him at getting too explicit. Feeling his cheeks heat again, he settled on, "Um, you know. I just want to get to know you first."

"That's okay." Ben stole another sweet kiss from him, and Elliott gave into it and chased it for more when Ben tried to pull away. The heat pooled inside of him worked its way down, and he felt the kind of familiar aching arousal that usually only accompanied his fantasies.

"Mm?" Elliott murmured against his lips.

"I'm not going to force you to do anything you don't want," Ben whispered back. Between words, he stole more kisses, and each and every time Elliott found himself weak to them. He *wanted* Ben, but... he wasn't ready.

"I don't... I mean..." Elliott couldn't resist the allure of Ben's lips, and he kissed him, eyes closed, as he tried to stay coherent enough to make sure Ben knew where he was coming from. "I haven't had many boyfriends, Ben. And I'm not... I don't have, um..."

The kisses were leaving him lightheaded and liable to make a stupid move. Elliott had never wanted a guy as much as he wanted Ben, and someone as attractive and potentially experienced as Ben would have to be blind not to see it.

"I'll teach you," Ben promised.

Elliott found his back pressed against the door, and they kissed again, greedier than before. Elliott was already hard, but for all Ben's obvious interest, he still wasn't pushing him.

"We'll go slow," Ben promised, not sounding at all

impatient despite what his body was quite obviously telling Elliott. "What do you feel comfortable with?"

"This," Elliott whispered back. He kissed Ben again. Each time their lips met, a new twinge of excitement twisted in his chest and urged him to act. "Just this. Forever and ever. Don't stop kissing me."

"I don't think I could if I tried."

The door supporting him from behind, Ben pinning him gently from the front, Elliott felt his knees turn to jelly. There was intensity in Ben's kiss, but it wasn't greedy. First and foremost, he put Elliott first, and Elliott could feel it in the touch of his lips and the way their bodies pressed together. Tenderness. Affection.

And, just maybe, something more.

Elliott's fingers wove through Ben's hair. He pressed against him, eager to appease the ache of his erection with friction. Ben knew exactly what he was doing, and, in seconds, he'd pulled Elliott into his arms and had backed him the short distance from the door to the couch.

They sank down together, lips only parting for a moment before Elliott kissed Ben again.

He couldn't resist.

He was horny.

God, was he horny.

The urge to push up against Ben's leg to seek relief was close to overwhelming, and based on what he could feel as Ben's body pinned him against the cushions, Ben had to feel the same way.

There was no way Elliott was ready to have sex, but he couldn't bring himself to tell Ben no when what they were doing felt so damn good. His body betrayed his mind, and when he thrust his hips up and Ben moaned in response, Elliott thought he might have gone too far. Ben wouldn't have to push hard to get him to crumble, but Elliott knew he would regret it afterward if that happened.

He didn't want to ruin what they had by taking things too fast. What he felt for Ben was insane, but Elliott wanted to move slow in order to savor and cherish the instant attraction between them. And, hopefully, to nurture it into something he'd only dreamed about finding.

"Don't," he finally managed to whisper against Ben's lips as Ben pressed against him in response to the urgent movement of Elliott's hips.

"I know," Ben whispered back.

He thrust against Elliott as he said it, and Elliott moaned and closed his eyes tightly, feeling a whole different kind of excitement.

"I promise," Ben added, his voice thick with desire. "Trust me, Elliott."

He did. Lips met lips as their coats were shed and shoes kicked off. When Ben's tongue found Elliott's, he traced it with his own as their kiss deepened, practically delirious with pleasure.

So far, Ben had been the one to remove each piece of their clothing as things had progressed, but he made no move to go for Elliott's fly. Even though Elliott had reason to believe Ben was every bit as horny and overcome with need as Elliott was, he wasn't pushing Elliott any farther than Elliott was comfortable with.

Affection diffused through Elliott's chest like a drop of dye through water, and he hummed into Ben's mouth in appreciation as they rubbed and thrust against one another, fully clothed. How was Ben so gorgeous and so understanding? It almost wasn't fair that a man so thoughtful could exist.

Or at least, it wasn't fair that he hadn't existed in Elliott's life much sooner than that moment.

Need grew between them, and Elliott trailed one of his hands down Ben's side and dipped it between their bodies, unable to resist brushing it against the bulges in their pants. Ben moaned, obviously surprised, but pleased, as Elliott's fingers explored him.

But feeling Ben up wasn't what Elliott really wanted.

Not with a barrier between them, anyway.

Deftly, his fingers undid the button of Ben's fly and worked the zipper down. He may not have been ready to have sex with Ben yet, but if he didn't let himself indulge a little before Ben left his apartment, he knew he'd regret it just as much.

Heart racing, his hand slipped along the smooth material of Ben's underwear—silk?—to feel his cock in better detail. It was *big*, and Elliott shuddered with arousal as he let his fingers play against the cotton, mouths still greedily locked together. Ben pressed into his hand eagerly, but still didn't push him for anything more.

It was almost too good to be true.

What could have been painfully awkward and potentially regretful—inviting Ben up to his apartment—was quickly turning into one of the best experiences of Elliott's life. He palmed Ben's cock, feeling bold, and savored every moan he managed to pull from Ben's lips. Loved the way Ben strained against his hand, and the rasping sound of his breath that gave evidence to just how much he was enjoying Elliott's touch.

Soon, though, it wasn't enough for either of them, and Elliott slipped his hand beneath the elastic band of Ben's underwear to grasp his length in full.

Ben gasped. The sound stirred Elliott's excitement, and he ran his hand along Ben's shaft as they kissed one last time before breaking to breathe. Never before had Elliott felt so in control of a shared intimate moment, and never before had he found himself enjoying sex so much. Being with Ben was easy, and he knew it would be easier yet to give in to him and let Ben take their relationship all the way.

"Fuck, Elliott," Ben murmured against his lips, sounding almost drunk with pleasure. "Feels good."

"Yeah?" Elliott pressed a kiss against the corner of Ben's mouth, surprising himself with how bold he had become. Ben brought out the best in him.

"Oh, fuck yeah." The breathless baritone of Ben's voice caught deep in Elliott's chest and hooked him. "W-What can I do for you?"

The question was marked by a long silence as Ben turned his head to capture Elliott's lips in full. The two of them gave in to the pleasure of each other's lips, and all the while Elliott worked his hand steadily on Ben's cock, feeling powerful. And safe. And, *God*, so, so, *so* turned on.

"S-Same," Elliott managed when their lips parted for a moment.

He wanted to know that Ben wanted him just as badly. He wanted to know what it would feel like to be at his mercy. Ben had opened up to him today, and Elliott had seen the man behind his tough facade. If that was the man Ben was, then Elliott already knew for sure that he wanted to be a fixture in his life.

What they shared now didn't cheapen their night, just because it was happening quickly. Not when Ben already meant so much to him. He trusted that Ben wasn't going to take him for granted—that wasn't the type of guy Elliott had learned that he was.

Ben's hand worked its way between their bodies, and soon Elliott's fly hung open, too. Ben's palm cupped him through his boxer briefs, just like Elliott had done to him, and, at first, Elliott contented himself with pressing up into Ben's hand as his arousal grew thicker.

And just like Elliott had done, when that touch was no longer was enough, Ben's hand slipped beneath the final cotton layer to take Elliott's cock into his hand and stroke him, skin to skin.

"Mmph," Elliott breathed, lips closed. "Ben..."

"You're so fucking hot," Ben whispered to him, claiming his lips again as both of them worked their hips and took advantage of each other's hands. Pinned beneath him, Elliott didn't have as much freedom, but, if anything, the restricted nature of his movements made what they were sharing even hotter.

Ben kissed him, harder now, bruising his lips and uniting their tongues. Elliott closed his eyes and squirmed beneath him to gain as much pleasure as he could from Ben's hand. Somewhere along the way, their pants had crept down their hips, and now Ben coaxed their underwear down, too. Finally bare, Ben lowered himself until Elliott's hand brushed against his, and without words, Elliott understood. He parted his hand from Ben's cock, and Ben opened his hand and slid his shaft up against Elliott's.

Parts of Elliott's brain fizzled and sparked, and he gasped and turned his head to the side, pressing it into the couch as his hips rose all on their own. The sleek feeling of Ben's bare skin against his was addictive. As his heart worked in overtime and his cheeks flooded with heat, Elliott let the all of the feelings he'd been holding back flood through him and wash him away.

Since they'd met, he'd had a thing for Ben, and now that they were together, those feelings were expanding into something more. It wasn't just that Ben was flirtatious, or that he made Elliott feel like he was the most import-ant person no matter where they went or who they were around. It wasn't just that Ben was drop-dead gorgeous. It was that there was a man inside of Ben that Elliott wanted to be wanted by.

There was a kindness behind Ben's cool exterior that Elliott saw in bits and slivers, and that he wanted to know in full.

Ben's cock worked against Elliott's, Ben's hand holding them together to keep them steady. The friction was in-credible, and Elliott moaned and gasped and begged Ben for more, trusting that Ben would understand what he meant.

And when the pace picked up and the heat rose be-tween them, a thrilling tightness wound through Elliott's lower stomach. Ben was going to make him come.

"Ben—"

"I know," Ben panted in response. Elliott's eyes were closed, but he knew by the sound of Ben's reply that he was just as close to the edge. "I know, baby. I want you to let it all go. Let it go for me."

"Ben," Elliott gasped in return, fighting to hold on. He never wanted the pleasure to end. He never wanted Ben to leave. "I d-don't... I wanna..."

"Come," Ben whispered against his ear. The brush of his stubble and the husky pitch of his voice, intimate and close, was too much. "Come for me, Elliott. Come."

There was no way to hold back any longer. With a shaky exhale, Elliott bucked into Ben's hand and found release.

It wasn't the first time a partner had coaxed Elliott to orgasm, but it was the first time that he'd ever felt entirely comfortable with it. With a sigh, he relaxed back onto the couch, and as he did, Ben grunted and shuddered and came as well.

They settled together on the couch, kissing lazily and catching their breath. The momentary fear that Ben would change his tune as soon as he'd used Elliott for his own gain disappeared. Ben was just as attentive as ever, his kisses soft and sweet and caring.

Elliott couldn't get enough.

Time slipped by and it was getting late.

"I've gotta go," Ben murmured against Elliott's lips between slow kisses. "I need to open tomorrow."

"I'm opening too," Elliott murmured back. "Do you have to go?"

"Yeah." Ben pulled back, and he pulled up his underwear and pants as he did. "If I stay here, I'm not going to be able to help myself, and I know you don't want that. Not right now. I respect that. That's why I've gotta go."

Elliott's heart fell at the same time that it soared. Who else but Ben would take such good care of him?

"I'll see you at work tomorrow?" Elliott asked. He sat up and watched Ben from the couch. Ben was busy at the sink in the kitchenette, cleaning off some of the mess they'd made from his shirt.

"Yeah." Ben wrung the water out of his shirt and slipped back into his shoes and his coat. When he was finished, he held Elliott's gaze, peering deep into his eyes. Elliott's heart fluttered. "Thanks for a fantastic night. I can't wait until the next time."

The next time. Three words had never meant so much. Elliott beamed.

"Until next time," he echoed back.

Ben slipped out the door and disappeared from Elliott's sight, but nothing could shake him from Elliott's mind.

He was falling for him—maybe, even, had *already* fallen—and there was no sense at all in denying it.

Chapter 10

ASH

"YOU KNOW, THAT'S A GOOD QUESTION," ASH SAID TO the customer in front of him, doing his best to stick to the training even though it was hard to stomach admitting that he was clueless. "If you can wait a second, I'll defer to my coworker and get the right answer for you."

The woman nodded, and Ash was surprised to see she didn't look angry in the least. He couldn't count the number of times his father had gone off on one of their house-cleaning staff or other professionals who provided him with service, just because of their inability to answer his questions. The idea that a paying customer would actually be okay with Ash being up front about his own ignorance was a novel idea.

And, if he were honest, a much less stressful one than having to put up a cocky front all the time.

"I'm paying these people to know the answers to my questions, Bennett," he could clearly remember his father explaining the one time he'd dared to question him on his harsh treatment of their staff. "And if they don't know, then they shouldn't be paid at all."

Douglas Ashby's voice hadn't wavered. It had obviously been a black-and-white issue to the man who had cobbled together a retail empire from the ground up, even though Ash was sure there had been plenty of times when his father hadn't had all the answers along the way.

Of course, Douglas Ashby didn't seem to see any hypocrisy in the fact that *he* was still paid, regardless.

"Thank you for your patience," Ash said, giving the customer a winning smile. "It shouldn't be long."

He bowed his head and ducked away from the line of men's shirts that the woman had been asking him about to go find Jose. The two of them were working in men's wear, and even though Ash had actually started to enjoy his stints as Santa, he didn't mind the change of pace while the part-time guy Ashby's had hired to fill in for him covered the North Pole that day.

To Ash's surprise, he'd found that he honestly didn't mind working customer service. While it was true that there were customers who considered themselves superior, for the most part, the people he met were personable and easy to get along with. The only drawback was that without the obfuscation of the Santa suit, Ash was more paranoid than ever that someone would see through his disguise. In fact, he'd been fiddling with his contacts all morning, not just because they still bothered him, but because he was nervous that they weren't doing a good job at hiding his signature blues.

"Jose," Ash said as he approached. Jose was refolding a stack of clothes that had been knocked crooked. "There's a customer asking about the origin of the textile for the Fieri Leroux line of shirts that I have no clue how to answer."

Jose snorted and set the shirt he'd been folding back down on the stack. Ash still hadn't learned how to fold clothes so they laid so flat and rectangular, and he assumed that as a temp worker he wasn't going to be taught. There were more important things to focus on during the Christmas rush—namely, getting customers in and out as fast as possible. Folding shirts wasn't going to help with that.

"You think I do, dude?" Jose asked. "Nah. But tell you what? I'll go over there and deal with her. You look pretty razzed."

"Razzed?"

"Like, uh," Jose frowned as he tried to think of the word. "Frustrated and at your wit's end, you know?"

"Oh. Razzed. Right." Ash blinked and shook his head,

even though it was probably true. He really *didn't* mind working the floor, but that didn't mean it didn't take more out of him than he was used to in his real life. "I'm okay. Really."

"You're all winky." Jose waved him off. "It's cool, dude. You look like you need to go splash some water on your face to cool down. Take a fiver and relax for a bit. I got this."

Jose abandoned the display of shirts and went to tend to the customer, and, as he left, Ash noticed another coworker pass by. Scowling, hunched, and hands in his back pockets, it looked like he was having a rough day. Ash couldn't place his face from the nights they'd all gone to Reggie's, but there was something familiar about him that nagged at the back of his mind until recognition clicked into place.

It was the guy who'd been pounding on the bathroom door, the very first day Ash had come to work at Ashby's. Kevin, if he remembered right.

Kevin turned his head to look in Ash's direction as he walked past, looking pissy. From what Ash had heard, that was pretty much the man's normal state of being. Kevin seemed to be a grump who didn't want anything to do with anyone else, least of all the customers. Martin, the shift manager, generally put him to work in the changing rooms on most days.

"He looks like he just bit into an apple to find half a worm, doesn't he?" a sweet voice asked right behind Ash's shoulder. He turned his head and recognized the lilac color at once.

"Yeah," Ash said, smiling down at Grace. "What's his deal, anyway?"

Grace moved to stand next to him and leaned across the table display that Jose had been working at. She had to be on a break. Elliott and all of his friends were hard workers, and Ash knew that none of them would slack off.

"Don't take that dirty look he shot over here personally. I just invited him out for drinks at Reggie's at the end of the week, which apparently is tantamount to spitting in his soup," Grace said. She shrugged. "I don't invite him every week because sometimes I don't have the energy to deal with his negativity, but I like to try from time to time, just in case he decides to stop being such a sourpuss. Every time it's the same, though."

"That bad, huh?" Ash let his gaze rest on the spot where Kevin had walked out of view.

"Mmhm," Grace agreed, rolling her eyes and laughing.

She seemed to be following her own advice about not taking it personally, and Ash found himself liking her all the more.

"He always looks at me as if he's disgusted that I would even talk to him," Grace said, grinning at the absurdity of such an attitude. "Then he tells me that he has *better* things to do with his Friday night than spend it with a bunch of punks sipping on bottled piss."

"Whoa." Reggie's beer was bad, but that was taking it a little too far.

Grace laughed. "Eh, it's not the end of the world. I can

only imagine the looks I'd get from everyone else if he ever did decide to come. And then, once we were at the bar? Can you imagine the group of us at our usual table, laughing and getting a little tipsy, and then, there in the middle of it all, there's *Kevin*? Sitting there with his arms crossed and scowling like he's been waiting on hold for forty-five minutes with an automated customer service menu somewhere?"

There was something really easy and fun about Grace that Ash admired. She straightened her back and rolled her shoulders to work the kinks out, then looked up at Ash and grinned even wider.

"So, speaking of Friday night and invitations to Reggie's, are you in this week? Because I know that we'd all love to have you there."

Ash couldn't help but smile back. Her good cheer was as infectious as it was genuine.

"Yeah," he readily agreed. "I'd love to come along."

"Good." Grace beamed. "Pretty sure this Friday there's a special on sweet potato fries. If you want to see Elliott go crazy, put him in front of a plate of those bad boys. Trust me, his reaction alone will make it worth the trip."

Was that so? Ash hitched an eyebrow and suppressed a smirk. Working with people who knew Elliott had certain advantages.

"Really?"

"Really." Grace winked. "So... did you two have a good time *last* Friday?"

For a minute, Ash stared at Grace and couldn't find the words to say. Last Friday, as in the night Elliott had invited Ash up to his apartment. It was Monday morning, and all three of them had worked the same shift together on Saturday, but, honestly, Ash hadn't thought that Elliott would be the kind to share details like *those* with his friends.

"You're so easy to read, Ben. I'm going to go out on a limb and guess by the expression on your face that you guys *did* have a good time," Grace said, laughing merrily. "You know, you didn't do a very good job at convincing us that you were too tired to come to Reggie's, and Elliott was almost fire-engine red when he stumbled through his explanation about why he wasn't going to be there, either. It was pretty obvious what was going on."

An unfamiliar feeling of relief flooded through Ash's chest, and he had to wonder at it. For so long he'd made a point to publicize each of his short relationships and flings—having the details of his sex life aired in the media had almost become a game—so why was he so relieved that Grace didn't know the details, this time?

"I, um." He cleared his throat. "Yeah, we had a good time out. We're going to do it again sometime soon."

His answer made Grace's smile grow even wider, but she looked genuinely happy for him, instead of predatory, the way paparazzi would have been.

"You two make a cute couple," she said, taking a few steps back from the table to look at him in full, and, as she did, Ash's phone buzzed with an incoming text message.

"Mm, yep. Picturing you and Elliott side by side, I can see it. Very nice."

Ash's fingers twitched, but he held back from checking his phone. It was Ashby's policy, and besides, it would have been rude.

"Glad we've gotten your stamp of approval," he said to Grace, winking at her.

"Nope. I wouldn't say you've earned *that* yet." Grace held up a finger to stop him in his tracks. She was still grinning, but he could tell she was serious, too. "All of us like you well enough, Ben, but you're still not through your probationary period. Just because Elliott fell for your charms doesn't mean the rest of us are going to give in so easily. And, now that you're dating one of our own, it's even more important that Trevor and Jose and I make sure that you're not going to cause trouble."

The serious look on her face faded away, and Grace laughed. He knew she meant it, but he also suspected that she assumed there was nothing all that dire to find out about him. Still, the protective mock-threat made Ash's heart pound in his chest, and he was sure that he was sweating.

If they actually managed to poke into whatever employment file had been provided on "Ben's" behalf, or tried to investigate him, then what? The whole story was going to be blown.

He'd lose Elliott.

Ash tried to calm himself down, but for some reason,

he'd felt extra paranoid all day. Maybe just because, for once, he actually had something to lose. Something that mattered.

To still his nerves and hopefully give himself something else to focus on, he slipped his phone out of his pocket and checked his messages, company policy be damned. Ulric was sending him more pictures of the destruction of the cabin in Aspen from the weekend before. The text of the message was full of glee about what a wild time they were all having. No mention of actually wishing that Ash could have made it down, though.

There was no love in the message.

None of the genuine caring between friends that was so obviously apparent in the group from Ashby's.

Ash ran his tongue along the back of his teeth and returned his phone to his pocket, leaving Ulric's message unanswered. The truth was, none of his friends in Aspen gave a shit about whether Ash was there with them or not, or any thought to what he was going through while stranded in Chicago.

They never had.

But Grace and Trevor and Jose cared. The way Grace joked at him and pushed his buttons convinced him of it.

And Elliott?

"Mm, well, my break's just about over." Grace stretched. "Gotta get back to women's wear so I can play referee as our valued customers battle it out over the last of the clearance items. Hurrah."

She'd already started to walk away, but Ash didn't want her to go just yet. "Hey."

"Yeah?" Grace turned around and continued walking backwards, albeit slowly. "What's up, loverboy?"

"Thanks for inviting me out," Ash said slowly. Finding the right words was difficult—it wasn't often that he thanked people, and when he did, it was rare that he meant it. This time was different, though. "You guys have all been really great to me. Don't think that I don't notice."

"Ohh, and so a soft side emerges." Grace's smile was as genuine as the rest of her, and even with cranky Kevin on the prowl, Ash realized that there was nowhere else he'd rather be right then. Certainly not Aspen.

"Looks like dating Elliott isn't just good for *him*," Grace added with a wink.

What? Had Grace really noticed a change in Elliott? A good one?

He took a small step forward to close some of the distance between them, eager to ask her about it, but she waved him off.

"We'll talk after. Gotta get back and bring in the big bucks. See you later." She turned on her heels and left, but Ash found himself stuck on what she'd said as if she were still there, repeating it.

Was Elliott happier? And, more importantly, why did he care so much?

Standing around thinking about it wasn't doing him any good. Jose had given him five minutes to get his head on straight, and Ash was going to make use of the few he still had left. He wove out from the aisles and cut across the floor for the bathroom when the sight of the Giving Tree caught his eye.

Working as Santa meant that he was stationary most of the day, and with the Giving Tree around the corner from the North Pole, out of sight, Ash hadn't spent much time thinking about it. But the tree had changed since he'd last seen it on Friday.

It was covered with a whole crop of new tags after the busy shopping weekend, wishes just waiting to be claimed and made true.

Hesitantly, Ash drew closer to look at it in closer detail. The tree's pine branches were thick and full, and the red and silver ornaments strung on it sparkled beneath the bright overhead lights. Tags, suspended by colorful loops of ribbon, dangled from its lowest branches. Some were high enough that Ash knew parents must have placed them, but the lower branches—the ones within a child's reach—were so heavily weighted down that it was hard to see much green between the thick paper "ornaments."

A little girl stood in front of the tree all by herself. She must have been around eight years old, and her hands were dug deeply into the pockets of her puffy pink jacket, as if she didn't trust herself to take them out. She gave the elves on duty a wide berth, taking in the whole display with wide eyes, without saying anything.

Ash wasn't sure what compelled him to do it, but

instead of taking some "me time," he approached her and fell into line beside her. She looked over at him warily.

"Are you a stranger danger, mister?"

Ash snorted. "No. I just work here. But I saw you looking at this tree, and I figured I'd come over and look at it with you." Elliott's words from the last time he'd been there rang in his head, and he smiled, adding, "Did you know that it's magic?"

The little girl turned her head back to look up at the tree, but she didn't otherwise move. "That's exactly something a stranger danger would say."

"No, I'm serious." Ash gestured at the tree, suddenly overcome with a need to make her understand, the way Elliott had done for him. "If you go visit Santa and whisper your wish in his ear, then come back here and write that wish on one of the tags Santa's elves will give you, it'll come true. And then? There's a big party right here on Christmas Eve where all of the presents get given out to the boys and girls who put their tags on the tree."

"Santa doesn't deliver the presents until nighttime on Christmas Eve," the little girl said, shaking her head skeptically. "There's no way you'd have the presents here earlier than Christmas morning. Santa doesn't work that way. He'd only deliver them when your store is all closed and everyone is at home, sleeping. That's how it *works*."

"We have a special deal with Santa," Ash replied easily, lips twitching at the absolute conviction in her voice.

The first few days that he'd worked at Ashby's as Santa,

coming up with quick responses to the huge variety of insanely imaginative and surprising things kids had said to him hadn't been easy. Elliott had swooped in to save him more than once. But, these days, the narrative came easily.

"Since we send Santa and Mrs. Claus and the reindeer all kinds of Christmas sweaters and household items they can use for the rest of the year, Santa's agreed to come early to our store so we can help him make Christmas even better than normal," Ash told the little girl, putting the ring of sincerity in his words.

"Like a trade," she said to herself, tapping her lip thoughtfully as she looked up at him. After a moment, she gave a decisive nod. "Well, okay. That makes sense. Can I put a wish of my own on the tree, then? My mom only brings me here so that I can see Santa each year. We never knew about the tree before."

"Yeah, of course you can." Ash pointed to the elves standing by at the tree, helping the few children and parents who were around on a Monday morning. "Go see Santa's helpers over there, and they'll get you to fill out the tag."

"Thanks. I guess you're not such a bad stranger after all." The girl smiled at him, then left to go greet one of the free elves. Ash puffed with pride. He was sure that Elliott would have been proud of him, if he'd seen. His delivery had been flawless.

"Hey," a woman said from right behind him. Ash turned, still beaming.

It might have been a silly thing, but he'd seen the light of belief come into the little girl's eyes. And the excitement. He couldn't remember the last time he'd felt so good.

"Has anyone ever told you that you look just like Ash?" the woman who had gotten his attention said, looking him up and down with a conspiratorial grin.

He stared at her blankly, tensing as the joy he'd just felt evaporated.

"Like, Ash *Ashby*, Ash," she said insistently, apparently taking his silence to mean he didn't know who she was talking about. "I don't even remember his real first name, but you know, the one who's always in the news for his scandalous behavior?"

"Yeah," he said slowly, trying to read her face. Had she seen through him? "I get that a lot. But Ash has different eyes and hair. And, really, I think he's a lot more handsome."

The woman paused, then laughed. "He's a hottie, that's for sure. But it's so weird that you'd look so much like him. I guess that's why they must have hired you. Maybe you should ask Ashby's to make you his public PR double or something." Her eyes softened, and she glanced over at the little girl Ash had been talking to a moment before. The woman smiled, looking back at Ash again, and added, "The real Ash would never have been as kind to my daughter as you were just now, though."

"No problem." Ash laughed awkwardly and smoothed

at the back of his head, her words making something twist in his gut.

"And seriously, you should look into the body double thing," she added, laughing. "I bet they'd snap you right up for publicity purposes!"

Story of his life. Ash swallowed, nodding as he tried to keep the smile on his face. "Yeah, thanks. I, uh, I'll get on that. Sounds like a great career opportunity."

The conversation fizzled, and the two of them watched as the woman's daughter worked with one of the elves on duty to fill out the information needed on the tag.

"Thank you for that, by the way," the mother said at last, nodding toward the little girl to let him know what she was referring to. There was a tenderness to her voice that Ash hadn't heard before. "You were really great with her. I could tell that she was convinced that what you said was true. But... I don't want her to be hurt." She cleared her throat awkwardly, lowering her voice a little. "Does the store buy the presents, or is this some kind of up-sale technique they train you on to strong-arm parents into buying more things?"

"Other customers volunteer to do it," Ash said, not offended. The little girl was on her way back, so he spoke quickly. "It's a really great tradition here at Ashby's. No child is going to be left disappointed, I promise."

She still looked worried, so Ash added, "You have my word on it. Personally."

"Hm. Well." The woman's daughter arrived, and she

smiled down at her before turning back to Ash with a soft light in her eyes. "Thank you. Coming to Ashby's has always been such a pleasant experience. It's hard to believe that a store so giving around the holiday season could be run by people like the Ashbys." She laughed ruefully, shaking her head. "I guess your similarity to Ash Ashby is only skin deep, after all."

Ash didn't reply. She was talking about *Ben*, and maybe she was right.

"Thanks again," she said, taking her leave. "Merry Christmas."

"Merry Christmas, stranger," the girl echoed.

Ash bit down on his lip, his eyes on the Giving Tree. "Merry Christmas," he wished them both.

Mother and daughter disappeared, and once he was sure they weren't coming back, he ducked under the ropes dividing the Giving Tree from the retail floor and carefully removed the newest wish from where it had been placed on one of the Giving Tree's branches.

Abigail S. was asking for a new set of colored pencils and a sketchbook.

Ash pocketed the wish and stepped back onto the floor. He would make sure she got it.

Personally.

Chapter 11

ELLIOTT

As Elliott's shift drew to a close, he could see his nutcracker replacement talking with another co-worker just beyond the North Pole's arch. More than anything, he longed to break character; to wave his arm over his head and shout out to him and switch places already. It had been a long day standing at Ben's side and helping him with the kids, made even longer by the fact that Elliott's mind was elsewhere.

He'd woken up that morning to an email from Luisa, Nick's wife, letting him know that Nick was going through a final evaluation which would determine whether or not he was ready to be released from the hospital. And, if he passed and was released to start his recovery at home, Luisa had assured him that she'd invite him over so that he could spend some time catching up with Nick.

She'd said that Nick missed working at the North Pole, and she thought it would do him good to hear about what was going on in his absence.

The truth was, it would do both of them good.

There were so many details that Elliott was eager to share. From the minor scheduling errors that had caused everything from hilarity to confusion, to the fresh new faces on the floor, to how many kids they'd already seen this season, Elliott had a lot to talk about. And, knowing Nick, Nick would also be eager to hear all about the new, full-time Santa—especially since Elliott was in such a great position to watch him while he worked.

Elliott grinned.

Talking about the new Santa wasn't going to be a hardship. At All. Elliott was pretty sure he could go on for days about Ben and still not manage to fully express what Elliott truly felt for him. Ever since their date on Friday, Elliott hadn't been able to get Ben off his mind.

Especially what had happened on Elliott's couch as the date drew to a close.

Martin circled near the red carpet, dressed in his elf outfit. Crabby Elf, Trevor had dubbed him behind his back, an appropriate nickname that made Elliott's lips twitch despite his distraction about Nick when Martin threw him a cold look that seemed custom tailored to earn him the right to the name.

Martin eyed Elliott as he passed by, and Elliott held his

amusement in, returning the crabby shift manager's gaze and standing resolute. As much as he wanted to check his phone to see if there was an update from Luisa yet, he knew that doing so would be a risk. It was against the rules when they were on the floor, and for some reason, Martin had been watching their team like a hawk today. He'd been acting like they—the most experienced employees on the floor—couldn't be trusted to handle the Christmas set-up for some reason.

Well, technically, "they" included both the most experienced and—Elliott peeked at Ben out of the corner of his eye, never a hardship—the least experienced employees of the season. He refocused his attention on Martin. Ben might have been new, but he'd caught on quickly enough, and now he was doing a fantastic job as Santa.

There was really no reason for Martin to keep hovering like he was.

It felt like hours before the replacement staff finally wandered over and nodded to the elves standing on duty at the arch to let them through. Two new nutcrackers set to stand guard over the night shift came to relieve Elliott and his counterpart, Sean, and as soon as they arrived, Elliott bolted for the break room, forgetting all about Martin as his thoughts turned to Nick and his hopes for the older man's recovery.

Switching Santas was a more delicate, more time-consuming operation than the nutcracker transition, and as Elliott left, the elves temporarily shut down the North Pole so that Ben's replacement could make the transition. The backup Santa was stuck waiting in the staff room so he didn't spoil the magical illusion for any children until Ben tagged him onto the floor, and, most of the time, Elliott waited for Ben. Walking back to the staff room with him and serving as his 'personal guard' in the eyes of any curious kids. Today, though—fueled with hope that there was good news from Luisa waiting on his phone—Elliott didn't think to wait.

He all but ran down the escalator as Ben lumbered along behind, doing his best to keep up while his fat suit jiggled and slowed him down. With Ashby's ironclad rule about employees not being permitted to look at their phones out on the floor while still in uniform, even if they were off duty, Elliott was eager to get somewhere that he could check for Luisa's update.

As soon as the staff room door swung shut behind him, he pulled his phone from his pocket to check his email. Just as he'd hoped, a new message from Luisa waited. Elliott tapped on it to open it up, eager to know what the doctors had said.

> Hi Elliott,
> Writing to let you know that Nick is home! Do you want to stop by tonight after work? He's already said he'd love to see you.
> Take care and talk soon,
> Luisa

Elliott laughed with joy and rushed to his locker to pick up his winter coat. The door to the staff room opened and Ben lumbered in, giving the Santa waiting in the wings a nod. The other man headed out to the floor to take Ben's place, leaving the two of them alone for a moment.

"Elliott?" Ben asked. There was a strained quality in his voice that Elliott hadn't heard before. Was it irritation? "What's going on?"

Elliott slipped his phone back into his pocket and rotated the dial of his lock until the mechanism released. "Hmm? What do you mean?"

"I mean," Ben pushed his palm against Elliott's locker to keep it closed, the little display of temper surprising Elliott. "You've been acting weird all day. Distracted. You haven't said more than a few words to me all day."

"Oh." Elliott supposed that was fair. His hopes and worries about Nick had been front and center in his head all day. He looked up at Ben to find Ben looking back at him, clearly pissed. "I guess you're right."

"Is it because of... Friday?" Ben asked, vulnerability and confusion creeping into his voice and leaching out the anger from a moment before. "I didn't want to do anything you didn't want. I thought, uh, that you were okay with—"

"Ben!" Elliott grinned, finding the other man's awkward uncertainty oddly endearing. And, really, how could Ben think for even a minute that Elliott *hadn't* wanted to do what they had? Elliot had been into it. Very, very into it. *Very.* "You're fine, really," he rushed to reassure him. "I had a lot of fun, and, um, well, I wouldn't mind—" Elliott could feel his face start to heat up, but he didn't let that stop him from telling the truth, "—doing it all over again."

Ben grinned, but then his features hardened again.

"Then what's going on?" The moment of good cheer slipped away, and it was clear that Ben was struggling with his emotions. "I saw how twitchy you were every time your phone vibrated today. What's happening? Do you already have a boyfriend that you forgot to tell me about or something?"

Elliott's mouth fell open in shock.

Did Ben honestly think Elliott would have been so intimate with him if he had a boyfriend? But that vulnerability was back in Ben's eyes, and Elliott realized that he didn't really know anything about Ben's past. Was this his first time dealing with jealousy? The rapid-fire swing between sounding royally pissed and almost apologetic was almost funny, and Elliott decided that the best way to deflect Ben's mood would be with humor.

Well, that, and the truth.

"You're being silly. Of course I don't have a boyfriend." The tension drained out of Ben's shoulders, and Elliott bit back a smile. Ben had nothing to worry about, but it was kind of flattering that he'd thought he might.

"I've been waiting all day for an email from Luisa... Nick's wife," Elliott explained. To illustrate that he had nothing to hide, he took his phone out and opened the message thread, turning the screen in Ben's direction.

"Nick is the man who's been playing Santa in this Ashby's ever since I was a little boy. He had a stroke right before the season was about to start—" Elliott's throat closed up for a moment, remembering how scary that moment had been. He cleared it, reminding himself that Nick was out of danger now, and went on, "—and that's why they needed to bring you in to fill the role. Nick is like a grandfather to me. He's even the one who helped me get the job here, back when I was first looking for work."

Ben's gaze flicked across the small screen of Elliott's phone, then he eased his palm from Elliott's locker and turned away, obviously distracting himself from his embarrassment by taking an extra long time to unhook his fake beard from around his ears.

"It says that you're welcome to go over there tonight," Ben finally said, sounding sheepish. He cut a look over at Elliott, then turned back to the task of removing his Santa gear. "You and I had plans though, didn't we? I was going to take you to that movie you wanted to see."

Elliott's face lit up at the reminder, and warmth bloomed in his chest. Even after what had happened in his apartment on Friday night, it still felt a little crazy that Ben had asked him out on another date, and so soon. It seemed crazy, period, to imagine that they were actually... a thing.

Not that the thing they were had a name.

Despite his little show of jealousy, Ben hadn't breathed a word about exclusivity, or being boyfriends, or anything beyond the fact that he wanted to see Elliott again. And, even if he knew what he wanted, Elliott wasn't going to let himself jump to conclusions—or get his hopes up—quite yet.

Well, maybe he couldn't totally avoid the hope part.

"Do you think maybe we could change our plans tonight?" he asked, feeling absurdly happy that Ben had been upset at the idea of missing out on their date. "We can go see that movie any time, but Nick's just been released from the hospital today. I really want to go give him my well wishes. That's something I'm only going to have the chance to do once. Maybe you can..."

Elliott let his voice trail off, wondering if inviting Ben to visit Nick with him might be getting ahead of himself for their still-undefined "thing" status. It definitely wasn't the most glamorous of dates. But Ben was smiling at him now, and the worst that could happen if Elliott suggested it was that he might shoot Elliott down.

And Elliott generally liked to hope for the best, not the worst.

He cleared his throat, continuing, "So, maybe you can come with me? You can meet Nick, and we still might be able to catch the late showing of the movie if you're really set on seeing it. But Nick matters to me, and... I'd really like it if the two of us went together."

Hopefully Ben wouldn't think that Elliott wishing Nick well meant that he hoped Ben's contract work ended soon so Nick could get back on the floor. Elliott frowned, trying to figure out how he could backtrack. After all, it was only because Nick was off sick that Ben had his job.

"I mean... you don't have to come," Elliott added, worried by Ben's silence. "Why don't we just—"

"No. I'd love to." Ben said it softly, but firmly. He took Elliott's hand, and Elliott's heart skipped a beat. "And I'm sorry that I was being a jerk to you today. I guess I'm not used to being jealous, since I don't date much. I'm still learning how to keep my emotions under control when there's someone I... care about."

Did he mean it? A smile crept onto Elliott's face, and he moved just a little closer. Being so touchy-feely at work wasn't a good idea in general, but he couldn't help himself when Ben was being so sweet and heartfelt.

"*You* don't date much? You're so hot," he blushed, but, well, it was true. "How could anyone resist you?"

"I guess I keep my heart guarded," Ben replied, moving their joined hands to cover the spot where it beat. "There are only certain people I trust with it."

The flattery didn't go unnoticed, and Elliott let himself lean a little closer, daring to brush the tip of Ben's nose with his own. Ben's lips were so close and so inviting...

"Not here," Ben murmured, even though he looked tempted, too. He took a step back and broke the spell. "Are you going to Uber over to your friend Nick's? Since I'm not paying for the movie anymore, I've got the funds to spring for one if you weren't already planning on it."

"Oh." Blinking away the sudden haze of attraction he'd all but gotten lost in—an attraction fueled as much by what Ben had just said as by his hotness factor—Elliott pulled his head back into the game. "I'd really appreciate if you'd call an Uber, but if you want to save your money, that's okay, too. I think it's warmer today than it has been for the last little while. We could always take the Metra and walk."

"Uber it is," Ben insisted, waving off the more economical suggestion. "But let me get out of this fat suit first. If I'm meeting your 'grandfather,' I want to look my best."

Even more than the earlier display of jealousy, those words stirred in Elliott's soul and left him longing for more. It wasn't *really* like Ben was meeting his family—Nick was honorary family at best—but if Elliott crossed his eyes and squinted hard enough, he could see it.

See them.

Together.

See Ben meeting Elliott's family one day, and being seen as a couple rather than just two individuals who liked to share each other's company.

He grinned, liking that vision a lot.

"Hey, don't get lost in your head again," Ben said, smiling back. He'd turned around and lifted the back of his red suit to expose the clasps on the back of his fat suit. "Unhook me before you forget I'm here and go wandering off somewhere without me. This thing is a bitch and a half to get out of on my own."

Elliott did, happier than he should probably let himself

be at the thought of spending the evening with Ben again. Date night wasn't going to go as originally planned, but with all the feelings Ben stirred up in him, Elliott was pretty sure that regardless of their change in plans, it was going to be even better than he'd originally hoped for.

Because, really, it already was.

Chapter 12

ELLIOTT

"YOU LOOK FAMILIAR," NICK SAID, SQUINTING UP AT BEN
thoughtfully.

Nick was lying in a motorized bed that was set up right
in the middle of the small living room, but even there, it
felt oddly intimate to have been invited to visit him at his
bedside. Still, Elliott couldn't be happier to see him, and he
grinned at Nick, his eyes bouncing between the two men
who he'd just introduced, and who were both important to
him in different ways.

Even dressed in everyday clothes, Nick had been known
to be mistaken for Santa around this time of year, and Elliott knew it was due to more than just his white hair and

beard, or the rosy, round cheeks that even his recent hospital stay hadn't robbed him of. Nick had always radiated a jolliness and genuine cheer that had gone a long way toward convincing young Elliott to believe in the magic of Christmas, and even stuck in bed and looking a little worse for wear, that hadn't diminished.

Luisa came out of the kitchen, carrying a silver tray. Upon it were three cups of tea, along with a small silver dish filled with sugar, a spoon, and a tiny silver pitcher filled with cream. She set the tray down by Nick's bedside and smiled cheerfully, glancing between the three of them as she caught the tail end of her husband's question.

"Do you two know each other through the store?" she asked Ben, raising an eyebrow curiously.

Elliott raised an eyebrow as he waited for Ben to answer, wondering at his apparent discomfort at the attention. Had he not wanted to come after all?

"Not unless you guys have visited Colorado without telling me," Elliott said, breaking the almost-awkward silence with the little bit that Ben had shared with him about his past. "Ben only just moved to Chicago in November, Luisa."

"Yeah," Ben said, smiling. Instead of the million-dollar smile that Elliott was used to, though, this one looked a little forlorn. "I came out this way because I was offered a position with... a company. It turns out that after I accepted it and moved out here, though, some paperwork got messed up and they'd already hired someone else. So... here I am."

Elliott looked at him, wishing he could press him for more. Now wasn't the time, but hearing the stilted information reminded Elliott how little Ben had actually shared with him about his past. He felt greedy for more. Elliott wanted to know everything about him, and he really hoped that with the way things seemed to be going between the two of them, he'd get the chance.

Nick frowned, cocking his head to the side as he searched Ben's face. After a moment, he smiled. "Well, I'm glad Ashby's got a hold of you, even if it *is* only temporary. They might not pay much, but they do take good care of their employees. You'll have a job at least until the season is over."

"That's what I'm hoping for," Ben said, his smile looking a little less strained this time.

When Nick spoke, the left side of his mouth didn't move with the rest of him. The sight made Elliott simultaneously sad and grateful. Elliott knew that there were people who became partially paralyzed after suffering a stroke, but now, seeing how much one side of Nick's face drooped, he realized just how bad the damage could be... and how lucky Nick was to have come through it as well as he had. It hurt to know that Nick had suffered, but knowing that it could have had a much scarier outcome, Elliott was beyond thankful that the doctors had considered him well enough to come home.

"Can I get you boys anything else?" Luisa offered. The long dress she wore was cinched at the hips by the strings of her apron, and she'd swept her silver hair up into a loose bun that sat low on her head.

Elliott's lips twitched at the sight. The perfect Mrs. Claus.

"Sometimes Nick likes water served alongside his tea," she went on. "Or we've got plenty of cookies. Let me bring a pack. I know how it is. After your long shift, you boys must be hungry."

"Oh, please don't worry." Elliott held up his hands. "Tea is fine. Don't put yourselves out for us."

"As far as you're concerned, Elliott, we're never putting ourselves out," Luisa said with a smile as genuine as her welcoming words. "Let me go get the cookies. Even if you don't eat any, they're so nice to have with tea."

She busied herself once more in the kitchen, leaving the three of them to talk.

Nick and Louisa owned a tiny brick house in the northern suburbs. Once, Nick had been in construction, and he'd told Elliott that he'd helped build the house himself. It showed. The place was small, but it was cozy and well-made.

It fit Nick and Luisa perfectly.

From the wood panel walls in the bedroom to the quaint little deck overlooking their tiny patch of backyard, the place was warm and welcoming. It wasn't the first time that they'd welcomed Elliott over, and each time he came back, it felt like coming home.

"Colorado, you said." Nick shuffled on the bed, his left

side motionless but his eyes bright as he looked at Ben with interest. "You a skier, then?"

Ben's face turned ashen, but his voice didn't betray whatever was causing his distress. "Yeah," he said, offering Nick another smile. "I've always loved skiing."

"You planning to move back out there if you get the chance?" Nick asked, glancing between the two of them.

"I..."

Elliott watched Ben as he struggled to reply. It was clear that trying to answer Nick's question had him torn, and Elliott liked to think that he might be the cause of some of that. It was selfish, maybe, but he *liked* Ben. And if Ben did go back to Colorado and Elliott never saw him again, Elliott wasn't sure what he would do.

It was a far way to go for someone who wasn't even officially his boyfriend yet.

But the idea of not having Ben in his life already felt... like something he didn't want to think about right now.

"I haven't made up my mind," Ben said at last, shooting Elliott a look that filled him with all the best kinds of hope. "There are a lot of great things to do and see here in Chicago. I need some time to think about it."

"Wait until the snow melts," Nick said sagely, his half-smile a vivid reminder of his condition. "If you can get through a winter in Chicago, you're meant to stay here. It's not for everyone, but—" he cut a look at Elliott, about as obvious as day, "—it's got a lot to offer."

Elliott felt himself blushing, but Ben grinned and

nodded like he agreed completely, his initial awkwardness fading away as the confident personality Elliott was more used to seeing came out again. The conversation meandered, and from time to time, with part of his face numb, Nick struggled to pronounce his words. Elliott imagined the frustration. Nick was a people person. Elliott knew he had to miss his time at Ashby's, and that not being able to get out there and talk everyone's head off must be hard on him.

He sincerely hoped that Nick would be able to get back to work soon. Ashby's was more than just a job to him, and Elliott knew he wasn't the only one who missed having Nick's perpetual cheer there.

"Nick," Elliott said, redirecting the conversation. "What have the doctors said about your stroke? What's your next step?"

Nick transitioned easily from grilling Ben to talking about his recovery. He fixed his gaze on Elliott and smiled. "Rehab."

"Rehab?" Ben asked, his eyebrows shooting up. "Was that what caused all of this? Substance abuse issues?"

Elliott and Nick laughed at the same time, and Nick shook his head. "No. I need to go to physical rehabilitation. I've lost movement on my left side, and it'll only get better if I work on it."

"Oh." Ben fell silent and busied himself with the cup of tea Luisa had brought. There was something off about his reaction, but Elliott couldn't place it. He figured that Ben was likely embarrassed, but really, he didn't need to be.

"On top of rehab, I'm on a few different medications to help stave off blood clots and lower my cholesterol," Nick explained, giving Elliott more detail. "The doctors say that I got medical attention quickly enough that it did no permanent damage to my brain, and I'm very thankful for that. Your quick reaction saved my life, Elliott. You're a good kid."

Elliott smiled and reached out to pat Nick's hand, a little amused that Nick still insisted on seeing him as a kid.

"I couldn't *not* do anything," he pointed out, touched to know that what had been instinctive had actually made a difference.

"And that's what makes you such a good person," Nick said. "You don't ignore problems or pass them off on someone else. You've got a good heart, Elliott. You always have."

Hearing it from Nick lit Elliott up from the inside. He sat a little prouder and let a comfortable silence lapse between them. Finally, Nick broke the silence.

"So, Ben," Nick said, his eyes questioning as he looked Ben over. Ben set his cup of tea back onto the tray it had been served on, fidgeting under the weight of Nick's inspection. "I take it that since you're here today with Elliott, you two must be good friends."

"Something like that," Ben said with a bow of his head. "He really is something special."

An understanding passed between the two of them, and Nick beamed at whatever it was he saw in Ben's eyes.

"Well, in that case, how would you like to hear some of my favorite Elliott stories?"

"Nick!" Elliott gasped. He knew exactly where Nick was going with that line of thought, and he wanted to shut it down before it started. "No way! We made a deal."

"And I almost died," Nick said with a laugh, waving off the protest. "Let me have a little fun, Elliott. I won't share anything *too* embarrassing."

"Embarrassing stories about Elliott?" Ben drew closer and sat in the extra chair Luisa had left by Nick's bedside, whatever awkwardness had bothered him earlier now gone completely as he warmed to the subject at hand. "Where do I sign up?"

Elliott shot Ben a look, but he couldn't keep a straight face. "Date night" wasn't turning out anything like he'd thought it would be, but Elliott was having the time of his life regardless. There was a thrill in thinking about his past laid out on the line in front of Ben, all his embarrassing moments brought to light. The truth was that Elliott had never done anything truly cringe-worthy—at least not that Nick knew of—so he knew that whatever Nick had in mind wasn't going to be too bad.

And, honestly, the idea of Ben wanting to know more about him—the same way he wished he had more details about Ben's past—made his heart feel light.

Luisa bustled into the room and placed a package of

unopened cookies on the tray, leaving again with a word about something she had brewing in the kitchen. When she was gone, Nick cleared his throat and grinned up at Ben.

"The first time I met Elliott," he said, "he was three—maybe four—years old, visiting Santa at Ashby's for the first time. Imagine a tiny, towheaded boy with the biggest, roundest owl eyes you've ever seen, looking up at you while one of the store elves urges him to say hi to Santa."

Elliott covered his eyes with his hand. *This* story. Of course.

"Elliott is a blond?" Ben grinned. "I didn't take him for the type to color his hair."

"It darkened when I got older," Elliott protested, brushing a hand over his light brown hair. "This is natural."

"So, there's Elliott, standing there and staring, and he's speechless," Nick went on, shaking his head affectionately at the memory. "The elf on duty lifted him up and settled him on my lap, and Elliott looks up at me with his big owl eyes and opens his mouth—"

"Oh, God," Ben cut in, laughing already. "He puked on you, didn't he?"

Elliott shook his head, grinning.

"No." Nick laughed. "He took a deep breath, and in a very small voice he asked if he was too big to be one of the elves back in my workshop, making toys. He assured me that he was a very hard worker who loved to help his mom sweep and do the dishes, and that he was *really* good at building with Legos, so he was sure he'd be good at making toys, too, if I'd just give him a chance."

"I can't believe I really said that," Elliott muttered, covering his eyes. He let his hand drop to find Ben looking at him, lips curved in an easy smile and eyes sparkling with something that looked a lot like adoration. The lightness in Elliott's heart turned into a warm glow, and the day Nick was referring to felt as fresh in his memory as if it were yesterday. "I remember that conversation, too. It was one of my earliest memories. And that year at the Children's Christmas Party, Santa gave me a toy tool kit and workbench and told me it was so that I could practice being a good elf for the next year."

"Little you was cute." Ben's smile grew into something that made Elliott feel all sorts of things. Ben winked at him. "Guess that's where modern day you gets it from."

Elliott's cheeks heated, but he couldn't help grinning back.

"And every year after that," Nick went on. "When Elliott came back to see me, he apologized for having grown too big to be an elf. He always promised that he'd work harder the next year to shrink back down, so he could help me out."

God. Elliott laughed and cringed at the same time. He'd been such a dorky little kid.

"Tell me more," Ben insisted, laughter lacing his words. "Watching Elliott squirm is great."

"Well..." Nick paused, thinking. "Have you ever

wondered why the Christmas trees at Ashby's are strung up with fishing wire like they are?"

"No." Elliott dropped his hands and gave Nick a hard look, trying to warn him off. "Really?"

"Yes, really," Nick grinned, obviously having no qualms about embarrassing him even more. "The boy is curious, Elliott. Aren't you, Ben?"

"Totally curious," Ben confirmed with a brisk nod. "Since the first day I walked through the doors, I've wondered why all the Christmas trees were strung up like that. Please, elaborate."

"Nick!" Elliott insisted. Still, he couldn't help but grin.

As embarrassing as it was to have Ben hear all his childhood stories, there were layers beneath the surface that made the retelling more important than it seemed. He knew Nick well enough to be confident that Nick wouldn't be so open about him with just anyone. If Nick was comfortable sharing stories like these with Ben, it meant he thought that Ben was a good guy—a guy worthy of knowing all the parts of Elliott, past and present.

It was Nick's quiet way of giving his approval.

"Well, when Elliott was six, maybe seven, he came in for his annual visit with Santa feeling a little more... energetic than usual." The twinkle in Nick's eyes showed that the trip down memory lane was good for him, too. He glanced at Elliott, a paternal warmth in his gaze, even as he continued to address Ben. "By the time he was finished filling me in about his life in the last year, and his wish for Christmas, he was full of excitement, and he took that excitement out on the Giving Tree."

"Nick, c'mon," Elliott sighed, feeling honor-bound to protest, even though the truth was that Ben's obvious interest in hearing about him made his heart swell inside his chest.

Ben looked his way and hitched a brow. "What does that mean?" he asked Nick.

"Elliott had this notion that the higher the tag was on the tree, the more likely Santa would be to notice it," Nick explained.

"Which makes *total* sense because there are so many tags at the bottom, and only a few towards the top!" Elliott cut in. "So, of *course* he would have seen it better. I still stand by my reasoning."

Ben stifled a laugh and turned his attention back to Nick. "And?"

"And so while the elves on duty were busy, Elliott decided he was going to climb up the tree to hang his tag the highest it could go—"

"I just wanted it to have the best chance possible! Santa gets busy."

"—and the tree promptly toppled over, taking Elliott with it."

"I was fine," Elliott said quickly when a look of concern flashed across Ben's face. "Just a little startled."

"And corporate was just a little startled, too," Nick laughed. "I remember the word 'lawsuit' being bandied about in fear. Ever since then, all the trees in every Ashby's location have been anchored and strung up with fishing line to make sure that if any kid got too adventurous, nothing would happen to them."

It had happened a long time ago, but Elliott still remembered the sting of pine needles pushing into his skin and the way the tree had felt heavy laying across his body. Luckily, all of the trees were artificial, and they weren't heavy enough to do any real damage. Sometimes, his mother still teased him about the incident while they were decorating the family Christmas tree together, and the mileage that the people who loved him had gotten out of teasing him over the years made up for any embarrassment it might still cause him.

"I can't believe Elliott's led such an interesting childhood," Ben remarked, grinning ear to ear. "No wonder he's so cheerful all the time—after what he went through, he must be happy just to still be alive."

Nick and Ben laughed together, and Elliott shook his head slowly. A little embarrassment was part of any new relationship, wasn't it? But more than anything, he was happy to see Nick and Ben getting along so well.

"Elliott's not the only one," Nick said. He reached for his tea and took a short sip. "Over the years, there have been plenty of troublemaker kids. Have you run into any during your days on the big chair?"

"Hm?" Ben considered the question for a moment, already smiling.

Elliott could think of a few off the top of his head, and his lips twitched as he waited to hear which stories Ben would choose to share.

"Well..." Ben started, launching into one of the funnier ones.

As Ben and Nick chatted about the kids they'd met in their role as Santa, Elliott sat back and watched. On the way to Nick's place, he'd been concerned that Ben might find visiting a man he had no connection to a boring way to spend the evening, but it didn't look like that was the case at all. From the relaxed way he sat in the chair to the contented expression on his face, Ben showed every sign of having a good time. He hit it off with Nick like the two of them had been friends for years.

Elliott couldn't have been happier.

Although Nick wasn't family by blood, he meant the world to Elliott. What Ben thought of Nick, and what Nick thought of Ben, mattered to Elliott. The evening could have been a disaster, but instead, it had turned into a fairytale. An apt analogy, since—the way Ben looked as he opened up and laughed with Nick—he was as handsome as any prince.

Elliott bit down on his bottom lip and distracted himself as his heart fluttered, reminding himself that he'd come to Nick's house to wish Nick well, not to fantasize over the man who was maybe his boyfriend.

"...and the kid with red hair who screams whenever he sees you, and who seems to come back to the store every couple of days?" Ben was asking Nick. "Is he someone you're familiar with?"

"Leonard," Nick said with a sage nod. "He's a good boy, just a little too enthusiastic. The last few years, Elliott's been using his discount to buy him the expensive Lego sets he wants. Isn't that right, Elliott?"

"Yeah," Elliott confirmed, nodding as he thought of the high-spirited boy. Hearing his name had pulled his attention back into the conversation. "He's such a sweet kid. He always cries from joy at the Children's Christmas Party. I'll be a little sad when he outgrows it, to be honest."

Ben looked between the two of them, his brow furrowing with confusion for a moment. He focused his attention on Elliott, then said, "I thought it was against the rules to use your company discount like that?"

Silence descended upon the room. Elliott's lips parted and his heart rate sped up with a sudden surge of fear, but he couldn't think of anything to say that would cover his tracks. Had he gotten too comfortable with Ben? Elliott wasn't a dishonest person, and his transgression in breaking Ashby's rules wasn't a fact that he shared with just anyone. There was only one time of year that he did it, and, in Elliott's mind, it was done for a good cause. Only a select few people were in the know—Nick amongst them—but it had seemed so natural to bring it up here that he hadn't even thought about it.

And, obviously, neither had Nick.

Elliott shifted a little on the bedside and stared at his

knees, the ease and comfort he'd felt a few moments ago evaporating as his stomach clenched.

"I mean, not that I'd tell anyone about it," Ben rushed to reassure him, breaking the silence. "It's not anyone's business at all. Mine neither. I was just... you know. Just surprised. Uh, thinking out loud. I shouldn't have said anything, Elliott."

Elliott was staring holes through the fibers of his pants, trying to still his racing heart, and didn't have it in him to respond. He wanted to trust Ben—*did* trust Ben—but the truth was, he hadn't really known him that long, and his job at Ashby's was important. Breaking the rules would put that at risk, but it wasn't like Ben would tell on him, was it?

But how could Elliott be sure?

Ben was a temp worker without any true attachment to the Ashby's brand. Sure, they'd gone out on a date—an amazing date—and they'd been work friends before that, but it didn't necessarily mean that Ben had any strong attachment to Elliott, either. No matter what Elliott had started to hope for.

The fact hit Elliott square in the face and refused to be shaken free.

No matter how well he got along with Ben, the fact was that Ben was virtually a stranger. Elliott knew next to nothing about his past, or his values, or his family.

Or how he really felt about Elliott.

While he'd pieced together the type of person he *believed* Ben to be based on his work ethic and the way he related to the rest of the floor staff, there was no telling if Ben actually *was* that person. Elliott's lack of dating experience suddenly made him feel naive and nervous. Was it possible to want something so much that he let himself be blinded to the truth?

"At Ashby's, there are rules all of us enforce for the good of the company," Nick said, filling in the uncomfortable silence that had fallen again when Ben had finished talking. "But there are also times when those rules have to be looked at as suggestions, rather than strictly enforced necessities." Nick spoke slowly and evenly. "At Christmas, with all we do, sometimes rules have to be bent a little, but in order to preserve the magic of Christmas, it's worth it. There is nothing that we're doing that's *wrong* in the spirit of the season, just... not advised in light of the Ashby's official policies."

No matter what he did, Elliott couldn't bring himself to look up at Ben. Would he be disgusted? Intrigued? Stoic? Elliott didn't want to know. Or maybe he was just scared to.

"When you see the smiling faces of the kids during the Children's Christmas Party, you'll understand," Nick promised Ben.

He reached out and patted Elliott's knee, and Elliott finally found the strength to look up. Despite the admission of Elliott's wrongdoing, Nick looked relaxed. Ben flashed Elliott a gentle smile, too, as if to tell him not to worry, and Elliott searched his eyes, finally relaxing.

It looked like things were going to be okay.

The surprise in Ben's voice earlier had just been that. Surprise at finding out Elliott had broken the rules. But not disgust. Not judgment. Ben was still *Ben*, and the tension went out of Elliott's shoulders.

Even without knowing all the details of Ben's history, Elliott's gut feeling about Ben was a good one. And he was going to go with it.

"Are you boys interested in any dinner?" Luisa asked as she swept back into the room. "You're welcome to stay for a meal if you want. It's nothing fancy, but I'm making ham."

"I think we should probably be going, actually," Elliott said. He stood, but didn't move from the bedside just yet. "Ben and I were going out to see a movie tonight, and I'm thinking we might be able to catch a later viewing if we go now."

He'd normally enjoy sharing a meal with them, but Nick was looking tired, and the truth was, Elliott wouldn't mind wrapping up their unconventional date with a little one-on-one time.

"Oh." Luisa smoothed down the front of her apron. "Well, that sounds like a good time out. You dears be safe out there, especially if you're going back downtown after dark. And call me once you get home, or I'll be worried."

There was no one sweeter than Luisa. Elliott smiled. "Of course."

"I think I'll use the bathroom before we go, if that's okay," Ben said, standing, too.

"First door down the hall to the right, dear," Luisa pointed. "You're more than welcome."

"Thanks. And it was an honor to meet you, Nick." Ben bowed his head. "I'll make sure to take care of the kids at the North Pole for you until you can make it back."

An earnestness passed between them that lit up Elliott's heart, easing the last of his earlier tension. As uncomfortable as he'd felt upon realizing how little he knew of Ben, the way Ben interacted with Nick and spoke so sincerely convinced Elliott that he didn't have any reason to worry. Ben really was a good guy, and Elliott couldn't fault him for not having shared his whole life's story over the course of the few weeks they'd known each other so far. They'd get there eventually.

At least, that was the direction Elliott was hoping their relationship was moving in.

"I won't make it back to the North Pole *this* season," Nick answered Ben, laughing easily. "But I appreciate the sentiment. And it does my heart good to know that they'll be in good hands."

Ben smiled and nodded his head in a final goodbye, then ducked out of the room to find the bathroom. Luisa took her leave, too, heading back to the kitchen, leaving Elliott and Nick alone.

"You know, Elliott," Nick said in a soft voice. "You never did get a chance to tell Santa what it was that *you* want for Christmas this year."

Memories of Nick's last day on the job flooded Elliott's head, and he remembered the true wish that had been in his heart that day. The one he'd been ready to whisper to Nick in the hopes that the true magic of Christmas might work for him once again.

Nick's recovery was a gift enough in itself, and Elliott was so glad it had been granted to him, but, yes, before that, there *had* been something else on his mind. There was no way he could tell Nick that he was hoping to find love, though. Not now.

It sounded too selfish.

Elliott glanced down at his feet, dodging the question. "I'm too old to be doing that. You know that."

"No one's too old, as long as they truly believe," Nick said, conviction making the words carry a weight that reminded Elliott vividly of the passionate trust he'd had in Christmas magic as a child. It had never let him down. Not once. "And you do still believe, don't you, Elliott?" Nick prompted in a kind voice. "Christmas lives in you as much as it lives in me."

For what felt like the thousandth time that evening, Elliott felt his cheeks heat. He stared at the polished toe of his work shoe. Nick was right, of course. Elliott was embarrassed at the thought of admitting what he really wanted to Nick, though. But at the same time, he kind of wanted to, too.

After all, every Christmas wish he had ever shared with Nick had come true, one way or another.

"I *do* believe," Elliott said, clearing his throat. "But..." Asking Santa for someone to love was different, though, than letting on that he wanted the season's latest toy. His courage failed him.

"That's okay," Nick said, putting him out of his misery when Elliott's voice trailed off. "You don't have to tell me, Elliott. Besides, I'm pretty sure Santa already knows what you want. And, I think this year, you're going to get it."

Elliott looked up to find Nick's eyes alight with joy. Heart skipping a beat, Elliott dug his hands into his pockets, grinning back.

"I hope so," he said sincerely, his eyes straying in the direction Ben had gone.

"Has Santa ever let you down?" Nick asked, winking. "Remember, Elliott. All you need to do is believe."

Chapter 13

ASH

Elliott's apartment had a miniature Christmas tree set up on the coffee table, strung up with multi-colored lights and decorated with the smallest ornaments Ash had ever seen. And, even though Christmas trees had never been that important to Ash, there was something about Elliott's that had made his heart bleed when he'd seen it.

In his youth, the Christmas trees at the various Ashby residences had always been installed by professionals, decorated with classy ornaments and white lights that complemented whichever rooms the decorator had decreed each should be put in that year.

Ash had never been allowed to touch them.

But Elliot's was different. The night before, Elliott had saved Ash five little ornaments of his own, each one mismatched from the others, to hang on his tree's minuscule branches. After catching the movie Elliott had been interested in, he'd asked Ash to come back home with him, solely so he could lend a hand in decorating the undersized little tree.

Not that decorating the tree was *all* they'd gotten up to, of course.

But—even though Elliott's lips were always tempting and his body inviting—it was the moments they'd shared decorating the tree that Ash clung to. There was something so kind and inclusive in the gesture that Ash couldn't forget it.

Or forget how it had made him feel.

Like Elliott really cared for him. For *him*, "Ben," not the Ash that so many men had been quick to fawn over or suck up to in the past.

It made Ash feel like he and Elliott could *be* something. An "us."

He'd been hung up on thinking about it all day at work. Was that what he really wanted? Ash's home was in New York, and his life was tied to the riches and prestige of the Ashby name, but being Ben and reveling in the simple pleasures of life was turning out to be far more satisfying than he'd anticipated.

With another shift over and Elliott too busy to spend time with him that day, Ash had plenty of time to think it over. Most days, he would have called an Uber to get him back to the Chicago Ashby apartment and then lounged around in bed, contemplating, but after a full day at work already spent mulling over the same questions, he knew that lounging wasn't going to get him any more clarity than he already had.

For the first time since arriving in Chicago, he skipped the Uber and decided to walk from Ashby's to—not "home"—but the residence he was staying at.

The winter chill had returned, full force. With Ashby's just a stone's throw away from Lake Michigan, the air was humid, and it made the cold into something bitter.

Ash shoved his hands into his pockets and sniffled. His nose had started to run.

Was staying in Chicago what he wanted? And, if he did stay, what did that mean for his future? Being cut off from his bank accounts and the luxuries he was used to had been tolerable for the last few weeks, but, honestly, he wasn't sure that he could keep it up forever. There were certain joys that only money could buy, no matter what the old adage said.

But, Elliott...

As he struggled to figure out the best path for himself, his phone rang. He'd left it on vibrate while he'd been at work, and he still hadn't switched the ringer back on. It was only because his hands were in his pockets that he felt it at all.

Figuring it was Elliott, Ash answered the call without bothering to look at the caller ID.

"Hey," he said, a smile already curving his lips up.

Silence crackled in the background and lasted for an uncomfortably prolonged moment, making him wonder if he'd been butt-dialed. Ash furrowed his brow and frowned, about to pull the phone away from his ear to check the number when a familiar voice answered his greeting.

"Hello, Bennett."

Ash slowed his pace and ducked behind the nearest storefront, pressing his back against the wall. "Father?"

"So paternity tests will reveal," came the humorless reply.

Ash didn't smile.

"How has Chicago been treating you?" his father asked, a false note of joviality in his voice. "It's been a while since the last time you called to complain about being stuck there."

"It's gotten better," Ash answered shortly, unwilling to go into greater detail than that. "I've been responsible. There haven't been any wild parties, and I haven't done anything scandalous. If you're looking to punish someone, it won't be me."

Douglas chuckled. "Just as testy as ever. Why would you think I'm calling to punish you?"

There were plenty of reasons. Ash's father never called because he wanted to tell him that he was proud of him.

Whenever there was communication, it was either spurred by company matters, or because Ash had gone and done something his father found deplorable.

When Douglas Ashby had first found out that his son was gay, he'd come close to disowning him on the spot. It had been a strenuous battle to try to get his father to see him for the person he was, rather than the allegedly immoral portrait of the company that Douglas clearly imagined him to be, solely due to his sexuality, and, in retrospect, it honestly wasn't one that Ash was sure had been worth fighting. Tension had been resolved once and for all after the first scandal hit the news when Ash was eighteen, but not because Douglas had come around in his personal opinions. Rather, once his father had seen how high that quarter's sales had jumped as a result of the media attention from Ash's actions, he'd ceased dragging Ash through the mud and started to treat "gay" as just one more PR asset.

But the damage to whatever tenuous father-son bond had existed prior to that had still been done.

"I just had a feeling," Ash said, responding stiffly to his father's question. "But if you're not calling to tell me what I've done to hurt the Ashby's name this time, then why are you calling? It's not like you to reach out without a motive."

"And a motive I do have," Douglas confirmed, true to form.

Ash frowned, his gaze flitting over the traffic that sped up and down the busy street. If any pedestrians overheard his half of the conversation and put two and two together... but now he was just getting paranoid. Nervous, now that there was something he didn't want to put at risk.

"I'm calling to tell you that you've served your term."

"What?" Ash asked, blinking at the unexpected statement. The irritation of his contact lenses had lessened over time, and he barely felt them now. "What do you mean by that?"

"You're no longer required to stay in Chicago," Douglas informed him briskly, the facade of friendliness from the earlier part of the conversation morphing into the more familiar, businesslike tone Ash was used to hearing from his father. "I've reactivated your cards, and you're free to go. I've already had my assistant book your itinerary for Aspen, and the details should be waiting in your inbox. I need you to be packed and ready to go by tomorrow morning."

Ash's mouth went dry. As recently as a week ago, he would have been thrilled to hear that his prison sentence had ended. But now?

"No," he said, not even having to think about it. "I can't go."

"What are you talking about, Bennett?" The surprise in Douglas's voice was impossible to miss—Ash rarely heard him caught off guard.

"I have to stay at Ashby's through Christmas Eve. I can't leave the store without a full-time Santa. It's the busiest time of the year, and we're swamped as it is."

"Are you hearing yourself right now?" Douglas asked,

sounding incredulous. "You are an *Ashby*, Bennett. Do you think that the rest of your life is to be defined by working odd jobs in department stores? You have no obligation to any of those people."

The way he spoke made it sound like the employees at Ashby's didn't matter. Like they were beneath him. Ash clenched his jaw and bit back the anger that the condescending sentiment kindled inside him.

His friends mattered.

Elliott mattered.

"It's the Christmas season," he reminded his father tightly. "I can't leave now. There's no way the store could train another Santa in the time they have. I'm obligated to stay. Is this a test to see if I'm really being responsible?"

If it was a test, Ash wasn't taking to it too kindly. Had his father not just badmouthed all of his new friends, Ash wouldn't have cared as much, but Douglas was pushing things a little too far. Ash had never had anyone to be loyal to before, but now that he was part of something bigger, he wasn't about to jump ship. Not even if that something bigger was on a scale small enough that his father would have considered it laughable, had Ash been more forthcoming.

"Bennett."

Even though it was just a voice call, Ash had no trouble picturing the expression that usually accompanied that tone in his father's voice. The cold words would be mirrored in Douglas's eyes, and he'd be rubbing at the bridge of his nose the way he always did when he started to lose patience.

"You know I don't play games," Donald said in a clipped tone. "I've already had the flight booked for you and I fully intend for you to be on it. Your time in Chicago has drawn to a close. Keeping you out of the spotlight no longer serves the good of the company. You're needed elsewhere, Bennett."

The bitter Chicago winter bit at Ash's nose and made his eyes water. It crept beneath the fine wool coat he wore and chilled him through his Ashby's shirt and tie. Powdery snow swirled around his feet, disturbed by the breeze.

But it didn't compare to the cold he felt rush through his soul at his father's uncompromising pronouncement.

"What do you mean, I'm *needed* elsewhere?" he said, determined to stay calm, even though his heart had started to race at the prospect of butting heads with the man who'd raised him. "You just said that I'm free. So if I'm done serving my time, then that means I'm free to stay here by choice."

Douglas sighed. "Have you learned nothing about responsibility since you've been away, Bennett?"

Ash didn't know where his father was going with the question, and he was hesitant when he replied. "I have. That's why I'm not leaving."

Not the only reason, but part of it.

"If you truly have, you'll go to Aspen as I've instructed.

There is more value to you being there for the company than there is in you playing at being a simple minimum wage worker, and it's your *responsibility*, as an Ashby, to put the needs of the company first."

There was something going on that Ash didn't understand. He furrowed his brow and pressed back against the wall a little more firmly, as though grounding himself against cold brick might give him answers. "Value?" he repeated, wracking his brain to make sense of it.

His only plans for Aspen had been hitting the slopes, drinking himself past the point where he gave two shits about anything, and joining his so-called "friends" in an obnoxious attempt to cause as much property damage and mayhem as they could manage.

He was embarrassed just thinking about it.

Not just embarrassed... ashamed.

Ash wanted to be a better man than that. Believed, now, that he actually could be.

"I've been monitoring sales since your last indiscretion hit the news," Douglas explained. The board member. Christopher... something. "Profits increased drastically after the incident, no doubt spurred by the brand-interest that having your exploits aired always generates. A theory supported by the fact that our numbers have started to taper back to normal levels in the subsequent weeks."

"What are you talking about?" Ash asked. He may not have kept his finger on the pulse of Ashby's business finances, but he knew the stores brought in the majority of their annual income during the Christmas shopping season. "We're not seeing Christmas money come in?"

That didn't make sense. Ashby's Chicago was packed with eager shoppers from open to close.

"Christmas sales, yes. But I want to see more of the kind of spikes we get when you're in the public eye, Bennett. I've had the analysts look over the numbers, and the consensus is that the bad press has equated to increased interest in the brand. Which means profits. The profits that fund *your* lifestyle."

"Are you serious?" The pieces finally fell into place, and Ash felt stupid for not having realized what his father was getting at right away. "You want me to go to Aspen and cause a scene? Trash the place... for the *publicity*?"

"I've had it arranged that the contact information of a few reputable male escorts be left near your bedside," Douglas said, a tacit confirmation. "Public appearances are preferable, but so long as you leave the information by the bedside for the cleaning crew to find once you leave, I'm sure it will cause enough of a commotion to see the kind of boost we're hoping for."

"No." There was no hesitation when Ash spoke.

All he could think of was Elliott, and the way his sweet face would look stricken if news like that broke. How would a revelation like that make Elliott feel? Elliott *meant* something to Ash. He meant a hell of a lot. Ash wasn't going to hire an escort, or even pretend to.

"I have friends here," he said to his father. "A *life* here. People are counting on me."

It may have still been new, the relationships all in their earliest stages, but it was still the truest thing Ash had. One he wasn't willing to throw away.

"Don't be ridiculous, Bennett," Douglas said brusquely, clearly losing patience. "I expect you to be on that plane, and I expect you to do what you were born to do—you *will* do what is best for this company, whether you like it or not."

The call ended abruptly, his father not bothering with goodbyes, and Ash pulled the phone away from his ear in disgust. Was that really what his father thought of him? Was he really so cold as to not care what Ash wanted from life?

If going back to New York meant that Ash would be expected to spend his time stirring up drama and eschewing anything more significant, it wasn't worth it. He'd rather be cut off than have to live life on a predetermined track, especially one that felt so shallow compared to what he'd just started to find in Chicago.

Disgust was soon overshadowed by anger, though, and Ash thrust his phone back into his pocket and broke for the street, enraged. The streets passed by in a blur. The importance of the Ashby family name had been drilled into him from birth, but what was the point of family if this was how family treated one another? What was the point of going back to New York if he was destined to be alone, friendless, and despised for the rest of his life?

The condo building housing the Ashby residence appeared on the horizon. Ash considered turning around and heading elsewhere. It was no true "home." The unit was owned by his father, the furniture furnished with profits from the Ashby name, the utilities paid for by Ashby money.

He had no doubt that his father would bring more pressure to bear. He'd all but promised it before hanging up on Ash, and Ash knew from experience that Douglas Ashby would expect to get his way in the end. But, for now—even though it felt hypocritical to seek refuge in the Ashby residence and depend on money he was starting to think he wanted no part of, not now that he was becoming aware of the true cost—he really didn't have anywhere else to go.

He pressed forward, his steps faltering when he caught sight of a scraggly mess of a dog hovering near the doors of the building. Ash had noticed the mutt there from time to time over the past few weeks, but had honestly never paid much attention to it before. Now, though, he felt a certain kinship. The dog was another one who seemed to keep returning to a place that didn't hold any promise for it, just because it had nowhere else to go.

No family to return to. Or, at least for one of them, none *worth* returning to.

The doorman held the door open for Ash as he

approached, giving him a deferential nod before catching sight of the mangy-looking little beast cowering near the entrance.

"Is that dog back again?" the doorman asked, scowling at it. "I've lost count of how many times I've already called animal control on the dirty mutt."

It wasn't like Ash to hover, but there was a hint of true malice in the doorman's voice, and Ash was tired of negativity. The dog hadn't done anything wrong. It wasn't the dog's fault that it was out in the cold, or that it didn't have a home.

The dog hadn't chosen the life it now found itself stuck with.

The doorman propped the door open and slipped outside, waving his hands at the dog. "Get out of here!" he shouted. "Go!"

The dog took a few startled steps back, then circled and whined. Where would it go? Ash watched it through the open door, temper boiling over once again when the doorman tried to drive it off again.

"Hey," he said, following the doorman out the door. "Leave it alone. That's my dog."

"What?" the doorman asked, startled. "No, it isn't. It's been lurking around here for months."

"It's *my* dog," Ash snapped, not caring about facts at the moment.

Sometimes, choosing to believe could make it so. If, as

Elliott has proven with the Giving Tree, someone was willing to take action, too.

Ash swept past the gaping doorman and approached the little dog. Its wiry fur was matted and dirty, but its eyes were bright. Bigger than a terrier but definitely on the small side of medium, it wasn't too tiny, but it wasn't overbearingly big, either. As Ash approached, it skittered backward as though anticipating it would be hit.

Ash calmed himself down and knelt on the cold sidewalk. Speaking soothingly, he held his hand out toward it. "Hey. Hey, come here, good dog. You're a good, nice dog, aren't you?"

"Sir?" the doorman asked. "The condo association has a strict no pet policy."

Ash turned his head to look over his shoulder. He glared. "If you have an issue with *my dog*, you can take it up with Douglas Ashby."

By the time he turned his head back, the dog had found the courage to inch closer. It sniffed Ash's hand from a short distance away, then glanced up at him and made its decision. It crept forward the rest of the way and pushed its head into Ash's hand, looking at him with big eyes that wanted to believe.

"Good dog," Ash said, its trust warming him more than it probably warranted. "That's my good dog. Now come on."

The dog was muddy, and Ash was certain it was infested with fleas. It didn't matter, though. Ugly or not, dirty or not, he was going to keep it. It deserved a shot at life, and if not from Ash, than from whom?

Carefully, aware that the dog knew as little about him as he knew about it, Ash guided it forward and scooped it up in his arms. Its legs curled up, but it didn't struggle or snap.

"Sir, you really can't bring that thing inside."

"Watch me," Ash shot back. He carried the dog through the threshold had took him directly to the elevator, leaving the doorman behind. When the doors closed behind him and the elevator started its ascent, the dog rolled his head back and licked at Ash's jaw.

What had he done?

Dread set in quickly, and Ash hefted the dog and tried to move it into a position where it wouldn't have access to his face. He'd never owned a pet before, and had no idea how to take care of it. In fact, unless the dog was a fan of leftover Pad Thai, it wasn't going to have anything to eat.

And what was he supposed to do about all the mud and potential fleas?

Ash was in over his head and he knew it.

There was no way that he was going to be able to go to Aspen. Not now. No matter what his father wanted him to do, he was going to finish the holiday season at Ashby's. After that, well...

Finally, the elevator arrived at the top floor, and Ash tucked the dog a little closer against his chest and carried it into the Ashby residence.

He didn't know what would come next, but until the day he was finished working at Ashby's, he was going to make the most of his time in Chicago.

Of his time with Elliott.

And, after that...

Ash wasn't ready to think of that.

And, thanks to the dog he'd just rescued, for the moment, he really didn't have time to.

Chapter 14

ELLIOTT

"COME OVER TO MY PLACE TONIGHT."

"Tonight?"

Elliott looked up into Ben's strange hazel eyes and shuffled his feet, pulse already speeding up. The two of them stood in the staff room at Ashby's, on break for lunch. The crew manning the North Pole all got to break at the same time, and, lately, Elliott had been using it to his advantage so he could sneak some time in with Ashby's newest Santa.

"I mean—"

"I need your help with something," Ben insisted, cutting him off with a smile that made Elliott's knees feel a little weak.

Ben took a small step closer to Elliott, closer than one employee would ever stand next to the other on purpose, and it made Elliott's already racing heart skip a beat. He leaned forward just a little to show his interest. Or maybe because he couldn't find it in him to resist temptation. Whenever Ben got close like this—so close that Elliott could smell the hint of his subtle cologne—all Elliott ever wanted to do was get closer. Trying to keep their still-undefined relationship on the down low while at work was getting harder by the day.

Ben smiled at him, and Elliott's whole world shifted on its axis to spin for him. He was toast.

"It's a time sensitive problem," Ben said, the smile never leaving his lips. "And if you're willing to help me out, Elliott, I promise you'll get a delicious free dinner out of it. Sound good?"

"You don't need to bribe me," Elliott said, biting his lip to keep his smile from breaking out. He tilted his head to the side and closed the distance between their lips so that when he spoke next, they brushed. "I want to spend time with you, Ben. I really do."

"Well then." Ben closed the kiss, smiling that same smile that always made Elliott's heart flutter. The kiss was short and sweet and perfect, the kind that made Elliott want to keep kissing him forever. "I'll meet you after work, then, and we'll go home together, okay?"

"Okay," Elliott whispered. His eyes had closed, and he didn't want to let Ben go. "Do you think maybe... maybe we could find somewhere private we could take our lunch? That was really nice."

"You're the Ashby's expert. You tell me." Ben's fingers brushed the front of Elliott's shirt and curled, locking the two of them together. It was probably against a million different company policies to do what they were doing, but Elliott didn't care. He leaned forward again and let his lips brush against Ben's, capturing them in another short, sweet kiss.

"I do know a place," he managed after a moment, relishing the taste of Ben's smile at the admission.

"Then let's go."

Lunch that day was less about eating and more about exploring each other's lips, and Elliott took it as a good sign of things to come later that night.

The rest of the day passed in a blur, and it felt like way too long before their shifts ended and their replacements showed up. Now that Christmas was drawing near, Elliott had been called to work more day shifts—something he had absolutely no problem with, especially if it meant that he could do dinner with Ben. When neither of them were too tired from work, and when their schedules lined up, Elliott found himself spending his free time in Ben's company instead of using it to relax at home. There still wasn't anything official between them, but as far as Elliott was concerned, a dinner at Ben's place was the perfect setting to define exactly what they were to each other.

Ben hadn't asked Elliott over before, and he was going

to take it as a good sign that Ben wanted to bring him home with him now.

When at last the shift was over and Ben had changed out of his fat suit, the two of them called an Uber and made their way back to Ben's place. Elliott wasn't sure what to expect. Ben had made it clear that he enjoyed luxuries, but when the Uber pulled up to a condominium off Lake Shore Drive and Ben unbuckled his seatbelt and opened his door, Elliott was floored.

"This is it?" Elliott asked in a small voice, looking up at the impressive buildings that stretched the length of the street. Modern and sleek and incredibly expensive looking, it wasn't the kind of place Elliott had been prepared for, and it definitely wasn't a location within reach for a retail clerk at Ashby's in downtown Chicago. Not by a long shot.

"Yeah," Ben answered though, like it was nothing. He stepped out of the car and walked around to open Elliott's door for him. Elliott was still looking up at the condo, spooked. "What's wrong? Have you heard there's something unsavory about these places?"

"No, that's not it." Elliott unbuckled, thanked the Uber driver, and then stepped out of the car. Following Ben's lead, he approached the front door of the closest building. Its stone gray walls and generous balconies lumbered overhead. There was a doorman waiting to let them in.

A *doorman*.

"Sir," the doorman said to Ben with a stiff nod. His voice was strained and stuffy, as if Ben had insulted him, and Elliott slanted a glance at Ben, double checking that walking into this place wasn't some kind of joke that he didn't get.

Ben looked totally relaxed, though.

"Thank you," he replied distractedly to the doorman, barely paying him any attention.

Ben let Elliott enter first, and Elliott took his time to examine the lobby. Marble floors sparkled despite the season, as if they'd never seen a slushy boot. Three elevators lined the back wall, their doors free of fingerprints and glistening. To the left and right were hallways leading to a series of doors. Signage was posted on the wall, its typography elegant and high class, stylized arrows pointing in the destination of each listed location.

Pool.

Gym.

Massage Parlor.

Spa.

"So, what were you saying outside?" Ben asked, leading him toward the elevators.

He let his hand trace down Elliott's arm until he located Elliott's hand and grasped it. Elliott spread his fingers, and Ben wove his between them, the contact reassuring.

"I mean, you *live* here?" Elliott asked, feeling like it was a little surreal that he should have to clarify his surprise. There was no way a temp's salary at Ashby's could afford something like this.

Seconds after Ben pressed the up button to hail the

elevator, one of the three doors slid open, and Ben ushered Elliott inside. The back of the elevator was made of reflective material, the floor carpeted and plush and free from winter sludge. Did they have cleaning crews in the wings waiting for someone to mess the place up? Elliott had never been in a shared living space that was so clean.

"Yeah?" Ben said, making the answer to Elliott's question sound almost like a question itself.

"But... how do you afford it?" Elliott asked, not even caring if it was rude.

If there was some secret to maintaining a luxurious lifestyle that Ben wasn't sharing with him, Elliott wanted to be let in on it. He didn't mind living in his tiny one-bedroom apartment in a rougher section of the neighborhood, but ever since he'd been little, he'd dreamed of what life would be like in the beautiful high-rises that lined Lake Shore Drive and overlooked the beaches of Lake Michigan. There was a certain magic there, winter or summer, that he'd always wanted to be a part of. He grinned. He'd never seriously considered that it might happen, but even if it was only for one night's dinner date, he was determined to enjoy being there.

"Oh." Ben was silent for a second. He pushed the button leading to the top floor, then stepped back and retook his place at Elliott's side. The doors slid closed, and they began to ascend. Ben cleared his throat. "Uh, I don't actually pay for it. My uncle is some hotshot in the advertising world, and he bought the place for his sons to use when they come back from college out of state. This year the whole family's taking a prolonged Christmas vacation in Mexico, so I was allowed to come stay here until I figure out what I'm doing with myself. You know. Since the position at that company fell through."

The threat that Ben might pack up and go back to Colorado once Christmas was over had been present in the back of Elliott's mind ever since he'd found out Ben's story, and the reminder took a little of the shine off the unexpected immersion in luxury.

Elliott didn't want Ben to leave.

He'd lived in Chicago his whole life, and, if it came to that, he wasn't sure he could move. Not even to chase Ben. Not, of course, that Ben had asked.

"That's really lucky, and nice of them," Elliott said. Then, hopeful, he asked, "Is, um, is the rest of your family in Chicago, too?"

"No."

Ben sounded upset about it, and Elliott decided not to press the matter. Tonight, they were together to have fun, not to explore emotions that were still so new to both of them. He pushed his curiosity and apprehension about the future aside just as the elevator arrived at the top floor. The doors opened, and Ben's hand tightened around Elliott's as he guided him down the hall and to the corner unit. With a twist of a key and a turn of the door handle, they were inside.

The inside was just as gorgeous as the lobby.

Ben's hand parted from Elliott's, and Elliott watched as he stepped inside and kicked off his shoes without seeming concern for the gorgeous hardwood floor that was polished, so well that it actually gleamed. Ben hung his jacket on a coat rack, then turned and smiled at Elliott. "Make yourself at home, please. We've got the matter of—"

There was a crash from another room, and Elliott jumped. Was there someone else living in Ben's apartment? Ben had never mentioned roommates, but Elliott *definitely* heard something moving.

"Goddamn it," Ben scrubbed at the bridge of his nose and shook his head. "Make yourself at home. I'll be back in a second."

"Is everything okay?" Elliott asked as Ben hurried down the short hall that opened into a spacious living room. As Ben went, Elliott lifted his heels and slid out of his shoes. "Does someone else live here with you?"

"Kind of." Ben sighed. He turned the corner and kept talking as he disappeared from sight, raising his voice so Elliott could hear. "That's why I asked you to come along tonight, Elliott. I don't really know anyone else in the city, and I know very little about these kinds of things, so—"

A door opened and Elliott heard small, skittering feet bolt across the hardwood. In a matter of seconds, a mess of wiry fur and lolling tongue skidded around the corner and rushed down the hall at him. Elliott gasped, then laughed and dropped to his knees right in time to draw the cutest, most down-on-his-luck dog he'd ever seen into his arms.

"Oh my goodness," he cooed, unable to resist the little thing. "Look at you! Aren't you just the grossest, dirtiest little scraggly puppy? Yes you are."

The dog's tail motored back and forth, and he rubbed against Elliott's chest and wheezed and whined in what Elliott assumed was joy. His gray fur—at least, Elliott assumed it was gray—was coated with mud and obviously flea ridden. In some parts, it had fallen out completely from being too matted. As Elliott rubbed the little mutt all over, he could feel ribs much too close to the surface, and, from time to time, a tick.

By the time the dog had calmed down and Elliott finally looked up, Ben was back, leaning against the wall at the end of the hallway, one arm raised and braced to hold himself up as he settled his weight against it.

He was gorgeous.

"I didn't know you had a dog," Elliott said, feeling unaccountably breathless. He worked his fingers down the dog's chest without taking his eyes off Ben, and the dog broke away from him, ran in a circle, and then fell onto his back, legs curved, tail still wagging.

"I didn't know either until yesterday," Ben replied, grinning. "I found him on the street and brought him inside."

"What's his name?" Elliott scratched at the dog's belly, loving the fact that the man he was falling for had taken in a stray.

The little mutt's tail dusted the hardwood, and its tongue hung from the corner of its mouth as it panted and squirmed. The dog had to be itchy with so much filth caked into its fur, not to mention the fleas, but despite that, it looked absolutely joyful at the attention.

"That's part of the problem I brought you here to fix," Ben said. "It doesn't have one. I, uh—" he laughed sheepishly, running a hand back through his hair, "—honestly, Elliott, I don't even know if it's a boy or a girl. But, if you're willing, I thought maybe you could name it."

Elliott stopped scratching the dog's belly. He looked up at Ben, eyes wide. "You mean that?"

"Yeah, of course I do." Ben smiled. "I'm no good with names. I'd probably just call it Dog for the rest of its life. I figure that it deserves better than that, though, and I know that you're always full of great ideas, so it seemed like a good match."

It was a simple gesture, and by all rights Elliott knew that he shouldn't be getting worked up about it, but he couldn't stop the tears that welled in his eyes. The dog picked itself up from the floor and rubbed against Elliott's chest all over again, trying to win back his attention. It had to be some kind of wire terrier mix. The face and the fur was right, but the color and the size was wrong.

Whatever its breed, though, the dog was adorable, even when dirty.

"I always wanted to have a dog," he told Ben in a low voice. "Ever since I was a little kid, it was always something I asked for, but that I was never allowed to have because of the expense."

"Me too," Ben said. "But I guess we have one now."

We.

Elliott brushed the tears from the corners of his eyes with the back of his hand and shook his head in disbelief. Tonight, he'd expected that he'd end up helping Ben make dinner, that they'd make out on the couch for a little, and then, hopefully, Ben would ask him to make things official between them.

Instead, Elliott was being treated to a whole different emotional trip.

A dog.

A dog they were going to share.

He and Ben. Together. A *we*.

Ben didn't have to make things any clearer than that. Whether he acknowledged it that night or not, Elliott knew that Ben saw them as a couple. As *partners*. He swept the dog up into his arms and buried his head against the top of its head, overcome for a moment by what that did to him. The dog's ears hung down like folded triangles, and Elliott already loved how silly they looked. He smiled against its nasty fur, happier than he could remember being in... ever.

"One year, I told Nick that I wanted a dog for Christmas. I put my tag on the Giving Tree and everything, which I knew—*knew*—meant it was going to happen. I'd read up about dogs at the library, and I knew about all of the different breeds and the care involved, and I was even ready to pick up poop if it came to that. I was determined that it was going to happen. I *believed*."

Ben remained leaned against the wall, listening as if he wanted to memorize every word. It was heady. Elliott felt the fleas hopping from the dog onto his hand, but he didn't care. A flea bath would make things right.

"In the end," Elliott continued, running a hand over the eager little mutt's head, "Nick found my mom's contact information and called her to talk about my wish. He was totally ready to make it happen for me, just like he had with my wishes every year, but my mom couldn't justify it. When you get a dog, you have to worry about all the vet bills and the food and the toys and registration at the city, and my mom was already struggling to make sure that we had power in our apartment. So, Nick..." Elliott laughed, shaking his head at the memory. Not a sad one, even if it had been the one year he hadn't gotten the gift he'd expected from the Giving Tree.

"What did he do?" Ben prompted him.

Elliott grinned. "Nick came up with this whole story so that I wouldn't be disappointed when it was time for the Children's Christmas Party and I didn't get a dog."

"What was it?" Ben asked. He picked himself up from where he leaned and walked down the hallway to close the distance between them.

The dog's tail wagged with renewed vigor, its little head bouncing back and forth between them as if it were overjoyed to have both of its people so close.

"He wrote a note. From Santa, of course." The memory was still fresh and vivid, as if Elliott had lived through it two days ago instead of two decades ago. "In it, he explained that he had my dog all ready to give to me on Christmas, but at the last minute he learned about a little boy who had no one at all to love on Christmas morning—he was an orphan, and very sad. And Santa said that he knew that I would understand if he let the other little boy have my dog so that he wouldn't have to be alone. And in return, I got a plush dog. And you know what?" Elliott scratched the dog behind his ear. "I was so happy thinking that there was a sad little boy who wasn't so sad anymore because I helped him by sharing my dog with him. When I grew older, I realized what had happened, but... it was just a really special moment to me. It's part of the reason why Nick means as much to me as he does. I don't think the man has a mean bone in his body."

Ben sat on the floor in front of him, and the dog turned and put his paws on Ben's legs so that his face was in Ben's face, and his tail whacked Elliott in the face. Elliott laughed and scooted closer.

"Did your dog back then have a name?" Ben asked.

"Yeah. I wanted to call him Donner." Elliott's lips screwed upward in a playful smile. "I always liked Donner the best of all the reindeer, because I thought he was always forgotten about. He's right in the middle of the song, and all the other reindeer have really cool names that mean things. Like Comet is fast, like the rocks in space, you know? And I always imagined Blitzen was some cool way of saying blitz, so, more speed, right? Even Cupid's name was kind of speed related, because Cupid the angel has wings, right? So he flies. But Donner? He's definitely the most under-appreciated reindeer, and I wanted him to know he was loved just as much as the rest of them."

It was embarrassing to admit it now. Elliott laughed again and shook his head. "And then, a few years after I got the toy dog instead of the real dog I wanted, I was thinking about Donner again and I did a little research on him. By then we had the internet, so I was able to play detective a little more thoroughly. And you know what? It turns out that Donner is a word that actually does have a meaning."

"Oh?" Ben's eyes were softened with something sweet, and Elliott read adoration in them. He spoke in hushed tones that made the moment more intimate. Elliott's eyelids partially descended, and he leaned closer so that their foreheads touched.

"Yeah. But not in English. In French, Donner is a verb. It means 'to give'. And when I found out, I cried, because Donner really had been a gift given to me. It felt like it was fate."

"That's beautiful." Ben's hand brushed against Elliott's knee and settled on his thigh.

"I thought so," Elliott replied with a faint smile. "It made everything in my life feel connected, you know? Like it had come around full circle."

The very first time Ben had taken him out, he'd taken him to a French restaurant. Elliott hadn't forgotten.

"Do you think we could name this dog Donner?" Ben asked. "I know it's a little late, but..."

"Yes." Elliott withdrew from Ben just enough to let their lips align. They kissed before Ben could second-guess himself anymore. "So much yes."

"Then let's get Donner cleaned up," Ben murmured back before returning Elliott's kiss with one of his own. "You'll help me, won't you?"

"Yes."

Elliott wasn't sure that Ben would ever understand what a gift like Donner meant to him.

Chapter 15

ASH

DONNER WAGGED HIS TAIL AND PADDED BACK AND FORTH along the tub as soon as Ash set him down inside it. "*His* tail"—as Elliott had just informed him—because beneath the mess of tangled hair, Donner was visibly male. Ash hadn't even thought to check.

Elliott closed the bathroom door to prevent a mid-bath escape, then set the towels Ash had gathered from the linen closet down in the sink and turned to look at the tub.

"You're going to get wet," he warned, grinning like he was looking forward to it. "From what I've read, dog baths are wild rides."

"That's fine," Ash said, meaning it. He didn't think he'd

mind anything that made Elliott glow like that, and besides, Donner needed it.

During the day, Ash had hired an assistant to go purchase the accessories they'd need to clean a dog with. The bag of goods waited beneath the sink in the guest bathroom where Elliott, Ash, and Donner now stood. Ash peeked inside the bag, asking, "We're going to start with the flea shampoo first, right?"

"Um, kind of." Elliott had moved to the medicine cabinet and was rifling through it, obviously looking for something in particular. At last, he came back holding a pair of tweezers.

"What are those for?" Ash asked, glancing between Donner and Elliott and holding in a laugh. "Are you going to detail his brows?"

"No." Elliott rolled his eyes skyward. "Donner's got some ticks on him. I'm going to take them off."

Ash blanched. Thank God Elliott was prepared to do that, because there was no way in hell that Ash was going to put his hands anywhere near a tick. If he'd known that there were some on Donner, he probably would have thought twice about carrying him into the condo.

Fleas were no big deal. But ticks? No way.

"I guess he must've been out in one of the parks recently," Elliott said, not looking like the prospect of rooting out the little bloodsuckers fazed him at all. He sank down to his knees beside Ash and started to trace his hand down

Donner's coat, totally focused. "Can you get me a glass of really hot water?"

"Sure." The water from the tub faucet heated quickly enough, so Ash turned it on and left the room briefly to fetch a glass from the kitchen. When he returned, Elliott was still going over Donner's coat, no doubt feeling for all the irregular bumps beneath his matted, wiry fur that gave the ticks' locations away.

Watching him work was incredible.

For a moment, Ash stood in the doorway, observing, heart warming to Elliott, until Elliott finally turned his head and nodded toward the running water still filling the tub. "If it runs too warm, Donner's feet will burn," he said. "Please fill the glass before that happens. I don't want him to associate the bath with bad things."

"Right." Ash closed the distance between them, filled the glass, then shut off the water.

Donner watched the water recede, tail wagging merrily. For a dog who'd been out in the cold for weeks, he certainly had made a quick recovery. Ash didn't know if he'd ever seen a dog so happy.

"If you could hold the glass for me near Donner, I'd really appreciate it." Elliott parted a section of Donner's fur and held the tips of the tweezers right up against Donner's skin. Ash did as he was told, still not sure what the glass was actually for.

"What are you—"

Elliott jerked his hand back and dropped a tick directly into the glass of water Ash held. Ash gasped, but he was steady enough not to jerk his hand away. The tick died almost instantly, but it was fat and swollen and grossed Ash out beyond belief. Its head was too tiny in proportion to its body, and its tiny little legs...

He swallowed, needing to look away for a moment.

More than ever, he was glad to have Elliott around. Dog ownership was already proving to be a lot more challenging than he'd originally anticipated. Looking down at Donner's happily wagging tail with the little guy staring back up trustingly, though, Ash had no doubt that the effort was going to be worth it.

And then, of course, there was the joy on Elliott's face.

Ash grinned. *Totally* worth it.

Tick by tick, Elliott worked his way down Donner's body. Some of the ticks were smaller than others, but some were absolutely huge. Each of them sent a chill down Ash's spine, and he marveled at how composed Elliott was as he worked. Nothing seemed to bother him. When he'd said that he was prepared to help take care of a dog, he'd meant it. Just as committed to being a part of the unpleasant parts as the more enjoyable ones.

Elliott was amazing.

Donner didn't complain at all—clearly he was the best dog, ever—and when Elliott was finally done and praised him for his good behavior, Donner put his paws up on the edge of the tub and licked at Elliott's face. Elliott laughed and sputtered, pulling away.

"We're cleared for a flea bath now," he said, grinning up at Ash. "I'm pretty sure our boy is tick free."

"Then let's get started," Ash said, totally game for it with Elliott by his side.

He ran the water, watching as Elliott lavished Donner with affection. Once the water had warmed, Ash detached the removable shower head and started to spray Donner down. Donner backed down into the tub and shook. Water went everywhere.

Elliott had been right about the whole getting wet thing.

Two rinses with the flea shampoo and two rinses with the regular shampoo later, and Donner finally looked like an actual dog again. His wiry gray fur was plastered against his skin, and he looked underfed and scraggly, but otherwise, he seemed to be in good shape.

Elliott, on the other hand, had come out of the ordeal a little worse for wear.

The black Ashby's shirt he wore was soaked through and clinging to his body. Early into the bath, both of them had ditched their ties for safety reasons after Donner had tried to hop out of the tub, forcing all his weight onto Elliott's chest. Water had soaked through the thighs of Elliott's pants, too, and, from the looks of it, even through his socks.

There was no way he could go home soaked like that when it was freezing outside.

Ash took a long moment to look him over. Elliott, oblivious, lifted Donner from the tub, grabbed a towel from the sink, and toweled Donner off before the little guy had a chance to shake water everywhere.

It was clear that Elliott had no idea how gorgeous he was, or the way he made Ash feel. Ash clamped his lips together, holding back the need to tell him. He couldn't do that. Not as Ben. Until Elliott understood who Ash really was and what he was giving up to be there with him, he'd never understand just how much he meant it. What Elliott was worth to him. One way or another, Ash was going to have to find a way to tell him the truth. But... later.

Somehow.

Until then, though, he wanted to do anything and everything in his power to show Elliott how he felt through actions alone.

As Elliott dried Donner off, cooing to him and laughing, Ash rose and stood behind him, unable to resist running a hand down his back. Elliott trembled and straightened up immediately, roused by Ash's touch. At their feet, Donner shook off his towel and shook himself from tip to tail. Beads of water went flying.

"Looks like Donner isn't the only one who needs a bath," Ash whispered against the back of Elliott's ear. The low pitch of his voice couldn't be mistaken—it alone should tell Elliott what was on his mind. "You're soaked."

"You are, too," Elliott whispered back. He didn't turn his head, but he did press back against Ash's hand.

"It's an easy fix, you know." Ash pressed his lips tenderly against the skin just below Elliott's ear, and Elliott trembled and exhaled a shaky breath. "Let me throw your clothes in the wash, then join me in the shower. What do you say?"

"Yes." The reply was instant, and Ash heard the lust start to seep into Elliott's words, fueling his own. Elliott cleared his throat, adding a hesitant, "Just, um..."

"I know." Ash wrapped his arms around Elliott and let his hands smooth down over his stomach. The tips of his fingers stopped just short of Elliott's belt. "I'm never going to do anything to you that you don't want. Never. I respect you too much."

"I, um, respect you, too," Elliott said, letting his head tip back to rest on Ash's shoulder.

The tenderness that grew between them made Ash think 'respect' was a stand-in for something much more emotional, but he didn't comment on it. Actions would have to do for now. He ducked his head and pressed another kiss against Elliott's neck, loving the needy little sigh it evoked.

"Why don't I show you to the master bath?"

"Please," Elliott whispered back.

He held himself stiffly, but Ash knew him well enough now to trust that it didn't mean he was uncomfortable with what they were doing. Apart from the one time on Elliott's couch after their dinner date, he hadn't been heavily physical with Elliott, but they'd kissed and teased each other enough that Ash was growing confident in his ability to read Elliott's body language.

He'd definitely started to learn his way around Elliott's body.

Now, the tension he could feel as Elliott pressed back against him just meant that Elliott was strung up with anticipation and excitement. Ash had nothing to worry about.

On the contrary.

He pulled himself away, and as soon as he opened the bathroom door, Donner sprinted out and tore across the attached bedroom. He ran a lap around the perimeter of the room, then hopped up on the bed and rubbed himself against the blankets. Ash didn't care. His father employed the use of a cleaning service for a reason, and the spare bedroom Ash had been keeping Donner in while he was at work was used so infrequently, dirty sheets were an afterthought at best.

As Donner made himself comfortable, Ash guided Elliott from the spare room to the master bedroom.

"I'm going to be needing... this," Ash whispered against the crook of Elliott's neck, letting his hands sweep down across Elliott's chest to toy with the first button of his shirt. It finally parted and fell open, and, one by one, Ash undid the rest as Elliott leaned back against him, obviously enraptured by the delicacy of the intimacy happening between them.

When the last button gave way to Ash's fingers, Ash slid the soaked shirt from Elliott's shoulders and pulled it free from where it was tucked into his belt. Garment collected, he let it drop to the floor so his hands could continue their exploration.

"And *this* is going to have to go," Ash murmured, brushing his fingers against the buckle of Elliott's belt.

Elliott sucked in a small, sharp breath and tilted his head back as Ash guided the belt through the buckle until it fell lax. Then, Ash pulled the belt free of its loops and ran his hand across the front of Elliott's damp pants. Elliott was already hard beneath his fly, and arousal stirred inside Ash as he rubbed Elliott's erection through the fabric.

He had done that to Elliott. Now, he was going to take care of it.

"These are wet, too," Ash remarked, fingers still tracing Elliott through the wet fabric. He kissed Elliott's neck again, and his fingers hesitated on Elliott's fly. "Looks like I'll need to take them off... to wash them."

He pressed himself against Ash's hand, and his voice was raspy with restrained excitement when he answered. "Looks like you will."

Ash grinned. It was the permission he'd been waiting for.

Deftly, he undid the button of Elliott's fly and tugged the zipper down. Elliott's pants loosened at the hips, falling to his feet, and he leaned into Ash's touch, whimpering with a need that stoked the fires of Ash's arousal. He loved the effect his touch had on Elliott... almost as much as he loved the fact that Elliott didn't try to hide it.

With one more layer to go, Ash ran his fingertips down Elliott's cock and tugged his head back, kissing the edge of his jaw before whispering playfully, "Bad news. Looks like I'm going to have to take your underwear off, too. They're soaked."

He cupped Elliott, and Elliott breathed out low and squirmed, pushing into Ash's hand in a way that clearly spoke of his desperation for *more*.

"O-okay," he uttered.

It was the last piece of permission Ash needed. His hand parted from Elliott's cock, and he hooked his fingers into the elastic band of Elliott's boxer briefs to guide them downward. They passed Elliott's slender thighs, then fell to join his pants.

Elliott toed off his socks without waiting, adding them to the pile with his back still to Ash. Knowing Elliott was finally fully naked but still unable to see him in full was torturous pleasure.

Ash loved it.

Anticipation, with Elliott, was half the pleasure.

"The shower's through that door," Ash told him, wrapping one arm around his waist and using the other to point over Elliott's shoulder. Showing him the way without letting him turn around. "Why don't you go get the water ready, baby? I'll be in to make sure you don't get lonely as soon as I take care of the laundry."

Another delectable tremble ran down Elliott's spine, and Ash let it settle before he dropped his arms and released

Elliott in full. Elliott, all gorgeous, smooth, pale skin and slender features, padded barefoot across the floor without turning. Ash's eyes devoured him from behind, following the gentle dip of his spine down to the modest curve of his ass.

He was flawless.

Ash wanted him, and not just for tonight.

Elliott's hand paused on the handle to the bathroom door, and before he entered, he spoke.

"Don't be long." The words were spoken quietly, but they carried through the silence of the room.

Ash couldn't pick up Elliott's discarded clothes fast enough.

As Elliott let himself into the bathroom and closed the door, Ash rushed back into the hall by the front door to load the wet clothes into the washer. He disrobed on the spot and added his own clothes to the pile, then set the laundry on to wash, hoping that he'd done it right. Ash had only done laundry a handful of times, but he figured that it couldn't be that easy to mess up.

And if it was, oh well. He grinned. Elliott would just have to stay overnight. What a pain.

As soon as the machine was running, Ash closed the doors to the closet it was in and hurried back to the master bathroom. He could hear the shower already running, droplets raining down onto tile with small, pattering noises. Ash eased open the bathroom door and stepped inside to find Elliott standing behind the frosted screen, already soaking underneath the warm spray. The blurred sight of him was one final layer to get past before the grand reveal, and Ash couldn't wait.

He crossed the room to the shower and slid the door open to step inside. Both of Elliott's arms were raised, and he ran his hands through his hair as the water soaked through it and slid down his body. He stood with his back to Ash, but Ash wasn't disappointed to be denied the full sight of him yet. And the way Elliott finally turned at the waist to look back at him—body on display and shame absent—made Ash suck in a sharp breath.

Slowly, Elliott's eyes made their way down Ash's body, then worked their way back up to his face. He didn't care that Ash saw him looking.

Elliott's confidence was unexpected, but sexy as hell.

Arousal spiraled low through Ash's groin, and he stepped forward to join Elliott beneath the spray, feeling blessed.

"I missed you," Elliott said with a flirtatious smile.

Ash didn't waste any time in wrapping his arms around Elliott once more, and they drew close.

"You said you'd be right in," Elliott reminded him.

"I came as fast as I could," Ash murmured back. He kissed the side of Elliott's head, and Elliott pressed back against him. His ass came into contact with Ash's abdomen, and a new wave of arousal struck Ash hard. "And I promise, that's the last time you're going to be hearing that tonight."

Since the private time they'd snuck together earlier,

over lunch—sneaking off to a back corner of receiving to kiss and fondle each other—Ash had been anticipating this moment. There was no way he'd push Elliott past his comfort zone, but Elliott was doing a fine job of being bold tonight, and it made Ash hopeful for what was to come.

How long had it been since he'd had sex? He didn't mean the fumbling, groping awkwardness in the car with Christopher whatever-his-name-was from the board, but real, full contact sex. However long it had been, it was too long. For as much airtime as Ash's sex life tended to get, the reality was that it consisted of a lot more flash than substance, and he couldn't quite remember the last time he'd had a man in his arms, skin-to-skin, with no sense of urgency other than what grew between them. Definitely too damn long. And, now that he was sharing a shower with a guy who made his heart soar and his cock throb, he wanted to fix that.

It wasn't like Ash to actually *date*.

It wasn't like him to take things slow and pursue a guy who didn't immediately want to jump into bed with him.

But it wasn't often that he met someone like Elliott, either. Someone who was loving and altruistic to a fault, who made Ash laugh instead of just cynically chuckle, who crept into his thoughts when his mind was blank, and who forced his way in, even when it wasn't.

Someone who was worth it.

Hot water rolled down Elliott's back, wetting Ash's front. Mist from the shower dampened his face as he nuzzled against the side of Elliott's head. Elliott pressed back against him, letting his ass caress Ash's hard cock as he tilted his head back to return Ash's affection.

What drew them together was more than lust. Delicate, heart-pounding, but oh-so-real, Ash felt their connection in his soul.

When he pressed his lips against Elliott's cheek and Elliott breathed out a moan, Ash wanted to hear more not because he was greedy, but because he wanted to know that Elliott felt good. That Elliott was enjoying himself.

That Elliott got as much from what they shared as Ash did.

Ash's hands slipped down the front of Elliott's body, and he traced the shape of his cock, discovering it all over again. Elliott was still hard and ready, and Ash stroked him slowly, teasing his arousal. As he worked his hand, he pressed himself against Elliott from behind, letting Elliott feel how uncomfortably hard he'd become in such a short time.

Still, Ash wanted to draw things out. Savor it.

"Why don't you get the shampoo?" he whispered against Elliott's skin. "We're here to get you cleaned up, remember?"

"Mmmmm," Elliott murmured back, the long, low sound giving evidence that he was too overcome with pleasure to manage anything more verbal. He grabbed Ash's shampoo from the mesh metal basket suspended from the shower wall and snapped the lid open.

Ash prayed that it wouldn't be the last time he heard

the stiff snap of a plastic lid that night. Tonight, if Elliott would allow it, he wanted to take him all the way.

While Elliott shampooed himself, Ash continued to work his hard length with his hand, stealing kisses every chance he got. When the thick suds began to slide down Elliott's nape, chasing Ash away, he backed off, grinning. But he didn't stop stroking. The pace was slow, but every now and then, Elliott would freeze and gasp as his body tensed while he fought off orgasm.

The fact that he held himself back from coming made Ash hotter yet.

It looked like Elliott wanted more than what they'd find together in the shower, too.

"Ben," Elliott moaned, pressing back against him and grinding his hips in a subtle way that Ash would've missed, had he not been so wired into the moment. "A-ahhh, I don't know if I can hold on if you keep doing that..."

"Then let me ask you this." Ash slowed his hand, but didn't stop it. Couldn't, when Elliott's body language was so clearly telling him how much he enjoyed it. Still, he needed to know that they both wanted the same thing. "Do you want to keep going, or do you want to let it all go right now?" Ash asked. "I'm not going to push you into doing anything, Elliott, but if you want more, I want more, too."

Elliott's posture stiffened, and he grew still. The water had washed away the suds from his hair, and now that his nape was clear of soap, Ash pressed a kiss there before drawing back. Giving him space to answer.

"I want to keep going," Elliott finally said. There was a wispy, ethereal quality to his voice that Ash couldn't get enough of. "I just... um, Ben, I haven't ever..."

"It's okay," Ash said, tenderness mingling with the heat inside him. Had he ever had sex with a virgin before? He wasn't sure. If any of the men who'd flocked to him in the past had been untouched, they hadn't let on. Still, even if Elliott had been with hundreds of men before him, Ash would have treated him the same. Elliott deserved all the affection and tenderness in the world, and no matter what, Ash would have taken things slow with him.

"I'll treat you right," he promised. "And if anything doesn't feel right or if you want to stop, all you need to do is tell me."

There was great tenderness in the way Elliott turned his head just enough to kiss him, and Ash leaned into the kiss and gave Elliott his everything. Sex this time was going to be different than what Ash was used to. It already was, because *Elliott* was different than what Ash was used to. Ash had never been the biggest fan of foreplay, but the last few weeks spent courting Elliott and teasing him had been the most fulfilling of his life—in ways that included what they did in the bedroom, but went far beyond that, too.

Not even graduating from the prestigious business program at University of Pennsylvania or jetting around the globe to some of the most exotic travel destinations the world had to offer held its weight against the time he'd spent with Elliott. A simple touch. A friendly smile. An embrace that made Ash feel like he was *worth* something as a person, independent of his accomplishments or qualifications. Or his name.

When it came down to it, Ash had never felt unconditional love before.

Now, though, he'd found that love in Elliott.

Wet and dripping, they stumbled out of the shower together. Elliott still had the good sense to turn off the water, but his efforts to reach for a towel were thwarted as Ash took him by the hand and pulled him from the bathroom. They left wet footprints in their wake, and Ash knew there'd be damage to the flooring, but he couldn't bring himself to care. Elliott was worth more than the money it would take to fix a little water damage.

He was priceless.

Wet and wrapped up in each other's arms, they tumbled onto Ash's bed. Groping, squeezing, and squirming into position, they found a comfortable place on the mattress. As soon as they did, Ash let their kissing devolve from easy and playful to heavy and needy. Elliott's tongue was in his mouth, and his hand pumping boldly at Ash's cock made the urge to pin him to the bed and fuck him senseless rise up, hot and fast, until it threatened to blot out the rest of his reasoning. He clung tight to his control and pushed the impulse aside. For the first time, Ash wanted something more than just his own release.

He wanted something sweet and meaningful. Something that would prove to Elliott what he was coming to mean to Ash. How valuable he was.

Ash pulled away and opened the bedside drawer. From inside, he pulled out a bottle of lube, opened but unused, and a condom. Elliott lay beneath him, panting as he watched, his erection flush and laying against his stomach.

"I'm ready," he insisted.

Ash grinned down at him, finding Elliott's eagerness equal parts sweet and arousing.

"No, you're not, baby." He tossed the condom onto the mattress and snapped open the lid of the lube. "You need to get warmed up a little first. I'll show you. It's okay."

No matter what Elliott did, or how sultry he tried to come across as, there was something innately cute about him that sparked a tenderness inside Ash that he'd never felt before. Elliott's enthusiasm was contagious, and it gave a new depth to the mechanics of things that Ash had done hundreds of times before.

Would Elliott always be so adorable, or would sex change him?

Ash liked to think that it wouldn't. That, no matter what, Elliott would still be the same sweet guy who'd drawn Ash's attention from day one and kept him riveted.

Without any ceremony, Ash worked the lube from the bottle onto his fingers and reached between their bodies, letting his fingertips brush against Elliott's entrance for the first time. Elliott gasped and stiffened, then relaxed, trusting. His eyes were focused on Ash's face—a blue Ash could happily get lost in—and although they were concerned, they weren't fearful.

Elliott knew that Ash wasn't going to hurt him.

When had Ash ever known someone who trusted him without reserve like that?

He leaned in to kiss Elliott as he prepared him, and Elliott returned the kiss as wholeheartedly as he did everything. The kiss went on, slow and passionate, until Ash finally felt Elliott's body start to relax. It was only then that he pressed into him—just a finger—and Elliott instantly moaned into his mouth and shifted his hips in response.

He'd meant it. He wanted this just as badly as Ash did.

For a while, there was nothing but warm lips and the silken feel of Elliott's body and the dull throb of Ash's erection begging for attention. At some point, Elliott's hand made its way back to Ash's cock, and he worked him in time with the rhythm of Ash's finger.

Then... fingers.

Delirious pleasure bonded them, and time became a lost concept. Somewhere amid stolen kisses and the intoxicating heat and tightness of Elliott's body, Elliott grabbed the condom, his enthusiasm making Ash laugh happily. The crinkling of foil broke the sound of their labored breaths and the rustling of sheets as they moved, and with a focused attention that was sexy as hell, Elliott managed to work the latex down Ash's shaft.

He didn't need much more invitation than that.

Ash had just enough sense left to lubricate the condom again before pulling Elliott into position so he could take him. He hooked Elliott's thighs over his hips, and then guided his cock to press against Elliott's entrance. A soft gust of air escaped Elliott's lips. Anticipation. And then Elliott's body gave in to him, welcoming him, and they were finally joined.

It was by no means the first time that Ash had had sex, but from the first few glorious seconds of entry, he already knew it would be the best. Elliott was tight, and warm, and, even with the condom on, it felt like they were bare. With a low groan, Ash pushed the rest of the way into him, careful not to move too fast, but also not to move too slow. And, somehow, despite his inexperience, Elliott took him in easily.

It was like they'd been made for each other.

When Ash was buried all the way, he refocused his attention on Elliott's face and found Elliott looking up at him, pupils blown wide with wonder and adoration in those gorgeous blue eyes, partially lidded with desire and lust.

Ash couldn't help himself.

He kissed Elliott, and when he pulled back and worked himself in again, he kissed him again.

Soon, the kiss didn't stop, and neither did Ash's hips. Within minutes, Elliott's body had warmed to him, and he moved eagerly into Ash's thrusts, doing his part to bring them both closer to orgasm.

How could one man be so perfect for him? Elliott's

flaws, such as they were, only added to his charm instead of detracting from it, and, even then, Ash found himself hard-pressed to remember what Elliott's flaws were. In that moment, with their bodies working together in perfect sync and Ash's heart beating in a rhythm to match, Elliott's innocence and blind trust in the good of the world didn't feel much like flaws at all.

In that moment, Ash loved each and every "flaw" just as much as he loved the rest of Elliott.

Love.

Ash laughed against Elliott's lips, a sound he didn't normally make during sex but that bubbled up within him in a spontaneous burst as the realization hit him. He *loved* him.

Elliott moaned and shifted beneath him, kissing him harder. The tight embrace of Elliott's body made Ash want to come in the worst way, but he held back on his own release. Instead, he slipped his hand between them and worked Elliott's cock as he thrust into him, wanting to make sure Elliott experienced just as much pleasure as Ash did.

Thrusting hips and rolling gyrations and the steady pump of Ash's hand were marked by the kisses they shared, and when at last Elliott broke away to pant out a warning, Ash knew that there was no more holding back. The clench low in his gut had reached a critical point, and Ash knew his strength wouldn't hold out forever.

Especially not if he watched Elliott give in to his pleasure.

"Ben, I'm... I'm gonna..."

"Come," Ash urged him.

He didn't slow his pace. The burning of his lungs begged him to stop and catch his breath, but he refused. Elliott felt too damn good to stop, and beyond that, he wanted to see Elliott lose it for him.

He wanted to see exactly what he'd done to the man who'd stolen his heart.

Elliott's breath hitched in the back of his throat, and his posture stiffened one last time. Ash surged into him, deep, and finally felt Elliott's release moments before he heard the breathy moan that accompanied it.

The new tightness of his body as Elliott clenched around him and shifted on the bed was too much. Too good. With one last thrust, Ash let himself go, filling the condom inside the perfect, perfect heat of Elliott's body.

For a while they lay together, catching their breath and stealing kisses as the mood struck. In the aftermath of orgasm, Ash regained clarity. Most times, he couldn't get out of bed to ditch his partner fast enough. This time, though, even though the sheets were wet from their shower and he knew that he should clean up the water on the wood floor, Ash didn't want to leave.

Ever.

He rolled over, pulling Elliott against his side, and Elliott immediately snuggled against him, laying his head against Ash's shoulder as if it were meant to be there.

"The sheets are dirty, now," Elliott mumbled, his

concern making Ash grin. "Maybe we should clean them, too."

"Fuck the sheets." Ash pressed a kiss to the top of Elliott's head. "Fuck everything that tries to get in the way right now. All I want is to spend time with *you*, Elliott."

Elliott smiled—Ash felt the curve of his lips against his shoulder—and it made him smile as well. Elliott alone was worth staying in Chicago for. No matter how much trouble he might find himself in for not going to Aspen, this moment alone made defying his father worth it.

"Can I stay the night?" Elliott asked.

"Yeah," Ash said, happy. "I'm thinking I'll extend the dinner deal to include breakfast, too."

Eyes closed, a smile on his face, Ash focused on the joy radiating from deep inside of him as he felt Elliott's grin grow against him. Elliott pressed a kiss into Ash's shoulder.

"How do you like your restaurant-ordered meals?" Ash asked, his arm tightening around Elliott. "Greasy or healthy?"

Elliott laughed. "You're not going to cook me dinner?"

"Are you kidding?" Ash cracked one eye open to look down at him. Flushed from sex and glowing with happiness, Elliott was stunning. "That would mean I'd have to sacrifice time cuddled up next to you. As far as I'm concerned, cooking can go fuck itself, too."

Elliott laughed, and Ash closed his eye and relaxed again.

It was the best day of his life.

But really, the best part was that Ash was sure that with Elliott by his side, there would be even better days still to come.

Chapter 16

ELLIOTT

"I GOT YOU AN UGLY CHRISTMAS SWEATER."

"You did *what*?" Elliott asked, aghast. He looked at the box Ben was holding, then looked back up at Ben himself. There was no mistaking the thin, wide box for anything else. Elliott had been gifted enough clothes over the years to know that Ben was serious.

"I got you an ugly Christmas sweater," Ben repeated, lips twitching with amusement. He shook the box a little to demonstrate. "It's in here, and I want you to wear it."

"What... why would you do that?" Elliott accepted the box, but he was still flabbergasted. At no point did he recall telling Ben that he needed to bring a gift to the tree trimming—especially a gift so unusual.

"Because—" Hands finally free of the box, Ben opened the front of his wool jacket to show off the hideous sweater he wore beneath it. He grinned. "—I thought it'd be cute if we matched."

The bright red and green and white design was gaudy enough—honestly, Elliott had never seen the normally well-dressed Ben wear anything like it—but on the front there was a depiction of what Elliott could only guess were reindeer. Elliott snickered before he could catch himself. Brown and blobby and totally artless, the only clue was that one of the brown splotches had a blob of red where he assumed the nose was supposed to go, and all of them had stick-like things poking out from the top of what Elliott guessed must be their heads.

If that was the sweater Ben had chosen for himself, Elliott dreaded to see what kind of disaster lurked in the box designated for him.

Still, disaster or not, a part of Elliott was thrilled that Ben would go through such lengths in order to coordinate Christmas outfits. Tree trimming at Elliott's mom's place wasn't all that big of a deal, but Ben was making it more special than usual.

Kind of like he did with everything.

"That's sweet, but it wasn't necessary. We don't enforce a Christmas dress code, you know."

Elliott couldn't help but smile. Not necessary at all. But... his heart warmed.

They stood in the lobby of Elliott's mom's apartment building. Ben had met him there.

"I wanted to make this special, since it's the first time I'm trimming a tree," Ben insisted, then paused and looked like he was searching for words. After a moment, he added, "I mean, with someone else. You know. Outside of the family."

Elliott's smile grew. "Really?"

"Mmhm." Ben stepped forward and let his fingers trace down Elliott's arm until they brushed against his hand. Elliott turned his palm instinctively, and Ben's hand slipped into his, feeling like it belonged there. Ben grinned, winking, and added, "Apart from the little ornaments I hung on your mini tree at the apartment, that is."

"That doesn't count," Elliott insisted. "My mom has a real Christmas tree, and we're going to decorate it from scratch."

They kissed. It was sweet and simple and short, but Elliott was hooked, and when they parted ways, his smile remained. "So... should I open this box and change into the sweater before we see my mom?"

"Absolutely," Ben said. "You can slip it on over your shirt. I'll hold your jacket."

The box was secured with a green ribbon, and Elliott tugged on the loop of the bow until it unraveled, not sure if he was excited or scared to see what sort of monstrosity awaited him inside. It was a patchwork sweater, made up of different green, white, and red Christmas swatches, and—boldly embroidered across the chest—were the words *Santa's Tallest Elf.*

Elliott stared at the sweater, instantly reminded of the story Nick had shared with Ben about Elliott's childhood. What were the odds? He looked up at Ben and narrowed his eyes suspiciously. That couldn't be a coincidence.

"*You* did this."

"I may or may not have had a hand in the creation of this sweater," Ben admitted with a grin, arching a brow playfully. "I wanted them to be about *us*. Mine has Donner on it, see?" He pointed at his chest, his finger stabbing randomly at one of the blobby reindeer.

"But, how did you do it?" Elliott asked, filled with a kind of wonder that he hadn't felt since he was a kid. He pulled the sweater out of the box and shook it out. The sleeves were striped in red and white. It was hideous, but perfect. And Ben had had it made for *him*. "It must have cost a fortune."

"Nah," Ben said, rubbing at the back of his neck as he looked away for a second. "I, um, I know some people who run an Etsy shop, and I pulled a few strings. It's all about connections."

Ben's brilliant smile distracted Elliott from pressing for more details, and between the sweater and the smile, Elliott couldn't keep his thoughts together.

"Santa's Tallest Elf," he repeated under his breath, feeling his cheeks stretch until they almost hurt. It was the sweetest thing anyone had ever done for him. "I can't even believe it."

"Believe it, and own it," Ben said firmly, holding a hand out. "Jacket off, sweater on. Let's not keep your mom waiting."

Over the last couple of weeks, since their first date, a lot had changed between them. Elliott saw it in the way Ben had opened up, and the way he interacted with others. When they'd first met, Ben had been distant and flirtatious, undeniably sexy and charismatic, but definitely not what Elliott would have considered steady boyfriend material.

But all of that was different now.

Between the times they spent simply enjoying each other's presence and the heated but sweet night they'd spent in Ben's apartment two days prior, there was something about Ben that seemed to have changed. Unfurled inside him, like a flower opening its petals to the sun, Ben's facade had slipped open to reveal the guy he was beneath, and Elliott couldn't get enough of him.

It had been a no-brainer to ask Ben to come along and decorate the family Christmas tree with him.

Elliott let go of Ben's hand and shrugged out of his jacket eagerly, laughing a little when Ben snapped his fingers imperiously to hurry him up, a teasing twinkle in his eye. Elliott set the box down and slipped the sweater over the t-shirt he wore beneath. It fit exactly right. *Exactly.* When he was done, he collected the box, took his jacket back and slung it over his arm, then led Ben up the stairs to the floor of his mom's unit, feeling warm in ways that had nothing to do with the sweater he'd donned.

Elliott hadn't told anyone yet about what was happening between himself and Ben. Grace, Trevor, and Jose seemed to have pieced it together from the way Ben and Elliott's interactions had changed while at work, but Elliott had neither confirmed nor denied their suspicions. Although he'd spent the night in Ben's bed, neither of them had actually broached the topic of what to call their budding relationship, and, while Elliott considered what they had to be real and lasting, he couldn't be totally sure that Ben felt the same way.

He could hope, though.

Virgin or not, it had been obvious to Elliott that Ben was experienced. The way Ben knew exactly how to touch him, and the way he'd worked Elliott's body in all the right ways made Elliott sure of it. There was still a chance that Ben considered his time with Elliott just something fun and temporary, despite what Elliott kept thinking he saw in his eyes.

Ben hadn't said anything, and, really, for all Elliott knew, he might end up being the kind of guy who ran at the first mention of commitment. It was an uncertainty that had held Elliott back from bringing it up on his own, but there would be plenty of time to discuss it later.

Well, he hoped there would be, at least.

He didn't know what Ben's plans were after Christmas.

Elliott pushed the thought aside firmly, reminding himself that a guy who went out of his way to meet Elliott's mom and who arranged to have a personalized sweater made definitely wasn't a guy who ran like that. Like he did in everything else, Elliott would choose to believe in Ben's good intentions, unless proven wrong.

And the truth was that even if they didn't work out, a possibility that already hurt more than Elliott would like to admit, there was still no questioning that he'd had the most fun of his life by Ben's side.

And tonight was going to be no different. It wasn't the time to worry about what might be. It was the time to enjoy what *was*.

They arrived at the front door, and Elliott knocked. His mother had obviously been waiting on them, and it didn't take her long to open the door and sweep Elliott up into her arms.

"Elliott, honey, I've *missed* you."

"I've missed you, too, Mom."

Elliott hugged her back, nostalgia for the days spent living with her hitting him hard. They'd always had a good relationship, and Elliott had only left because he was an adult, and he figured that it was the adult thing to do. She was the most important person in his life, and it was a big deal to him to bring her together with Ben.

"Is this your friend?" she asked, glancing over his shoulder with an arch of her brow.

Elliott drew out of the embrace and took a step back. He nodded. "Mom, this is Ben. Ben, this is my mom, Anna Gaffney."

"It's a pleasure to meet you, ma'am," Ben said with a nod of his head.

He held his hand out to shake hers, but of course Anna was having none of it. She stepped forward and hugged him just the same way she'd hugged Elliott.

Given how strict and practical she was, Elliott loved that his mother still found it in her heart to care for everyone. Being a single mother had been tough on her, but she'd pulled through and done an excellent job of raising him, in his opinion, and had only come out stronger for the struggle of it. Now that Elliott was grown and she was on her own, she was flourishing.

"It's a pleasure to meet you, too, Ben. I'm glad Elliott invited you along. Now come in." She released Ben and stepped back through the door, inviting them inside. "The tree has finally defrosted and its branches have spread, and it looks *way* too dark in the corner without any decorations."

Elliott entered first, and Ben followed behind him. Anna's apartment was small and sparsely decorated, but Elliott knew it well, and knew that everything she owned, she used. The Christmas tree was set up in the same corner of the living room that it had always occupied, and the boxes of Christmas ornaments and accessories were already laid out on the floor in front of it. Christmas carols and other festive tunes played at a reasonable volume from the stereo system Elliott had once bought for her on clearance at Ashby's. The CD was one he knew well, and Elliott knew what songs were coming next. It was familiar and welcoming.

As much as Elliott genuinely loved the magic and glitz of the over-the-top holiday displays at Ashby's, there was nothing that could compare with coming home for Christmas when it came to the real spirit of the season.

"Why don't I go make some hot chocolate while you boys get to work?" Anna asked, ruffling Elliott's hair like he was still a boy. He swatted at her hand, but instantly forgave her. She was his *mom*. "There are those cookies you like ready to go into the oven, Elliott. Do you want me to put them in now?"

"The kolackies?" Elliott asked, all grins as his mouth instantly started to water. "Yeah, put them in, please."

"The *what*?" Ben whispered into his ear.

"They're good," Elliott whispered back. "Promise."

There were ornaments to be unpacked. As Anna occupied herself with making hot chocolate and preheating the oven, Elliott dropped to his knees by the collection of worn, cardboard boxes and carefully opened their tops, one by one. Inside two of them were the delicate ornaments, wrapped in tissue paper to keep them safe while in storage. In a third were the durable ornaments, including all the ones Elliott had made in elementary school. His mother had even kept all the tiny bells their kindergarten teacher had had them make out of empty single serve creamer cups, glitter, and pipe cleaners.

To know that she cared that much gave him a surge of nostalgia. He didn't miss living with her—he was an adult now, after all—but he would be forever grateful that she'd made such strong, caring memories for him over the years.

In another box were the strings of Christmas lights, sockets empty, and to go with them was a smaller box filled with colored bulbs yet to be screwed in. The last thing left to uncover was the garlands, which were wrapped up around a stiff cardboard backing and stored in bags. It was a little rag-tag and chaotic, but to Elliott, the sight was the epitome of Christmas. The tiny trinkets in those boxes were tied to Elliott's heartstrings, and seeing them always filled him with joy.

Christmases in the Gaffney household had never been extravagant, but to Elliott, they'd always been magical. The special desserts his mom made, the Christmas cartoons on television, and the sleepy, cozy day that Christmas always was were cherished, no matter how simple they were.

Ben sank down to his knees beside him and was about to speak when Anna returned from the kitchen to lean against the doorway.

"Do you boys plan on staying for dinner tonight?" she asked. Before they could answer, she cocked an eyebrow up, adding, "I planned for it, if it changes your mind. I have a whole roast chicken I'm going to cook up. Call it a prelude to the turkey I'll be doing next week."

Was it really only one week until Christmas?

Elliott grinned. "I'm in," he answered her instantly. "I don't know about you, Ben? There's no pressure to stay, but I'll tell you up front that my mom makes the most amazing food."

"I'd love to have dinner with you," Ben replied. "Thanks for the invitation. It'll be good to have at least one home-cooked meal before the new year."

Anna paused, then frowned, taking in the implication of what he'd said. "Do you mean to say you don't have plans of your own for Christmas?" she asked. "Family to visit?"

"Nope," Ben said easily. The thought didn't appear to upset him like Elliott thought it should have. "My family all lives out of town, and my budget's currently, ah... tied up. It will be my first Christmas in Chicago, but I'm okay being on my own."

"Then tonight's not the only night you're staying for dinner," Anna insisted, waving off his "I'm okay" dismissively. "Come over with Elliott on Christmas and have dinner with us. There's always more than enough food, and although this place is tiny, it'll fit the three of us just fine. As long as that's alright with you, honey?"

Anna's gaze refocused on Elliott, and Elliott nodded, thrilled that his mother would offer.

"Of course it is," he said instantly, meaning it.

"Then I'd be happy to come over on Christmas." Ben flashed Anna the same charming smile that had won Elliott over in the first place, and the way it reached his eyes, Elliott knew for sure that Ben wasn't just being polite. "That's overly kind of you."

"Anything for you, dear," Anna said, giving him an answering smile. Her eyes cut to Elliott, and she added, "You're the first boyfriend Elliott's brought home, and you have no idea how glad that makes me. I worry about him being alone, you know. It's good that you have each other."

With that, she whisked back into the kitchen, leaving Elliott and Ben alone.

Elliott's mouth had gone dry. He glanced over at Ben, then looked back toward the kitchen door, momentarily too stunned for words. He hadn't told his mom that he and Ben were dating, and while he hadn't imagined she'd gloss over the fact that he'd asked permission to bring Ben along to decorate, he hadn't thought she'd assume Ben was his boyfriend when Elliott hadn't told her explicitly that such was the case. It made him worry that Ben would think he was going around telling people they were together when he might consider what they were doing only casual dating.

Unwilling to let it become a big deal, Elliott let out a breath he only just realized he'd been holding, bracing himself to face the awkwardness head on.

"I didn't tell her that we were boyfriends," he said.

"Oh," Ben said cryptically.

He sat back on his thighs and looked Elliott over, face hard to read. Elliott dreaded the fallout. He'd found something so special with Ben that he didn't want it to end, and he was worried that being pushed into talking about commitment so soon might be a nail in the coffin.

Ben's eyes softened, and his lip quirked up in a familiar, teasing grin. "Well, I'd really hate to let her down," he said. "After all, she seemed pretty happy for us."

Elliott stared, daring to hope, and Ben laughed.

"Can I please be your boyfriend, Elliott?" he asked, reaching for Elliott's hand and twining their fingers together. His voice went from teasing to sincere, and he added, "I don't want to date anyone else, and I definitely don't want to let a nice lady like your mom get the wrong idea about us."

Elliott's lips trembled, then turned up into a smile. Christmas really was a magical time.

"Yes," he said, nodding. Then he admitted, "I've wanted that for a while now, Ben."

"Then it's official." Ben tugged on his hand, pulling Elliott forward so he could kiss him where they sat. The press of his lips was short and sweet, but it filled Elliott with joy. "*We're* official."

There were few words Elliott had ever heard that sounded sweeter than that, and he bit back a smile, feeling like the gift he'd hoped for might just have come early.

Not that Elliott minded... at all.

Chapter 17

ASH

"YOU LOOK GOOD FAT," GRACE SAID WITH A GRIN. SHE poked a finger into Ash's fat suit and let it sink in past comfortable levels. He squirmed, which only made her smile grow wider. When was the last time someone had just flat-out teased him? He rolled his eyes, not really minding.

"It's very vogue," she added, winking. "Or... something."

"Is not," Trevor argued, waving a hand dismissively at the fat claim. "But at least it makes the suit look nice. You *do* make a fine Santa, Ben. And while you lack Nick's authenticity, you're a close second."

"Are you guys serious right now?" Ash asked, smiling

despite himself as he shook his head. "I asked you to help me out of the suit, not critique it."

"Sometimes the best way out is through acceptance," Trevor said with a sage nod. "Nothing like embracing who you are."

"Well, it's fortunate that I'm *not* actually Santa, then," Ash shot back with a grin. "Can you guys just unhook me, please? I really want to enjoy the rest of my lunch break without the danger of kids crawling all over me."

He stood with Grace, Trevor, Jose, and Elliott in the staff room. Sean, who worked the other nutcracker position, and the other elves and reindeer on the floor had all scattered elsewhere. Many had already escaped to take smoke breaks or otherwise had distanced themselves from the building for a few moments of much needed downtime.

Now that Christmas was less than a week away, the retail rush had reached critical levels. Customers swarmed the aisles from open to close, hunting not only for the best gifts and the best deals, but also searching for an employee—*any* employee, no matter what their assigned section was—to help them find it. Ash knew it was hard on the elves and reindeer—they were constantly being pulled aside by hurried customers urgently looking for items *right now*—but it also left Ash alone more often than not, stuck without backup as he dealt with the swarms of children off from school who had come in to visit Santa.

And it didn't end when he left the North Pole. As long as he was on the floor in "uniform," he stayed in character, but if it hadn't been for his friends guarding him on his way to the staff room, Ash was sure he wouldn't have made it that far before his lunch break ended.

And, frazzled or not, he'd take it as a compliment that he'd managed to pull off the Santa role so well that so many of the kids who came in seemed to truly believe in him.

"Here," Elliott said, eyes sparkling mischievously. "Let me set you free."

His hands slipped under Ash's shirt, and Ash was vividly reminded of more intimate moments they'd spent as he felt Elliott's fingertips brush against the costume to undo the hooks. When the first of the hooks were parted, Elliott's fingers traced along Ash's back, running over his Ashby's uniform where no one else could see. Ash grinned at his boyfriend's boldness. No one could *see*, but Ash sure as hell could feel it.

"Maybe next year you can come back and work as a sexy elf, Ben," Trevor said, grinning as he looked between the two of them as though he had his suspicions about what was going on under the fat suit. Thankfully, he didn't mention anything, though. "I'm sure Nick will be back to take his position as Lord Holly-Jolly," Trevor went on, earning a mumbled but heartfelt "I hope so" from Elliott that Ash didn't even consider taking the wrong way. Honestly, the old guy was nice, and Ash hoped Nick would be well enough to come back, too. "But Ashby's is always looking for seasonal help. With the experience you have from this season, we'd probably be able to convince Martin to let you back into the North Pole with us."

"Only if you agree to tailor my elf outfit," Ash shot back, mirroring Trevor's grin.

He pushed away the twinge of guilt he felt at playing along with the banter when he knew damn well that he wouldn't be rejoining the rest of them next Christmas. He still hadn't resolved anything with his father—hadn't even heard from him since rejecting his directive to fly to Aspen as a publicity stunt for Ashby's—but even with his future uncertain, he doubted he'd be able to take on any of the roles in the North Pole this time next year.

It felt good that they wanted him to, though. To be wanted just for *himself*. It was a new experience, and one that he wasn't willing to give up, no matter how much his father might try to force his hand.

"You know it's what I *do*," Trevor said, snorting. "In fact, if you're going to work at *this* Ashby's, there's no way I'd let you to embarrass me out on the floor in something that hadn't been properly fitted."

Ash laughed. "Well, I'm sure I could get away with a little glitz and glam and the 'I didn't know any better' defense if I showed up as a temp worker again," he said. "You think you'd be up for making that happen?"

"Me?" Trevor arched an eyebrow and quirked his lips to the side. "Do you even know who you're talking to? I'm the glitz and glam *king*."

"Then it's settled." The fat suit slumped as Elliott finally undid the last of the buckles for him, and Ash slid out of it and jammed it into his locker, grateful to be free. "Sexy elf next Christmas it is."

At least, it was fun to pretend. One way or another, though, Ash knew that his time as "Ben" was almost up.

Even if he managed to keep defying his father through Christmas, as soon as it ended, he'd have to become Ash again. Media sensation, tabloid fodder, good-only-for-what-he-could-do-for-the-Ashby-name *Ash*. He still hadn't quite figured out what to do about that, and he knew—despite Douglas Ashby's silence—that he was already working on borrowed time. If his father thought setting up some kind of scandal for him in Aspen was going to help the bottom line, there was no way he'd given up on the idea just because Ash had refused to go.

Ash just hoped he could come up with a game plan before the other shoe dropped.

"You guys are going to get in so much trouble if you bling out one of the elf outfits," Grace said, rolling her eyes and snorting back a laugh. "I thought *I* had it bad for sticking it to the man with my purple hair. I can only imagine what's going to happen when Ben shows up next year with a tunic slit up the side, covered in green rhinestones."

Ash grinned, happy to put off the unpleasant thoughts of dealing with his father in favor of the current conversation.

"Sheer stockings instead of leggings," Trevor said with a nod, closing one eye and squinting the other as he looked at Ash, obviously already seeing the sexy elf outfit take shape in his mind. "And we'll get you some cute little booties, too, Ben. Not heels, and definitely not full boots. There's a fine line between sexy and trashy, you know, and this *is* a family friendly work environment."

Grace groaned, launching another counterargument. As the two of them traded blows and laughed about his future employment options, Ash took a second to check his phone for any new messages. There were a few updates from his "friends" still stationed in Aspen, and—surprisingly, as if the man had managed to pick up on Ash's worries about not having heard from him—there was also a text message from his father.

The words were as cryptic as the fact that Douglas Ashby had sent it was ominous.

> *I hope you're still taking care of your appearance, Bennett. Even while you're pretending to be something lesser, please remember that you are still an Ashby.*

Before anyone could accidentally catch a glimpse of it over his shoulder, Ash shoved the phone back into his pocket and tried to push the confusing message out of his mind by tuning in to Trevor and Grace's back-and-forth banter. He had no idea what the real meaning behind his father's seemingly innocuous message was, but he'd deal with figuring out a response later.

"So you're fine with stockings as pants, but not *leggings* as pants?" Grace was asking Trevor, sounding incredulous.

"If something *wants* to be pants, then I accept it," Trevor replied with a Cheshire grin, clearly enjoying egging her on. "I'm not pants-ist, Grace. I'm inclusive of *all* pants groups."

"Are you dudes just about done hamming it up?" Jose asked. He was leaned against the lockers with his arms crossed over his chest, smiling as he listened, but otherwise staying uninvolved. "Do I need to remind you that we only have half an hour left to walk to the food court down the block, get our grub, and get back here? I don't know about you, but I'm not up to working the rest of the day without getting something inside me."

"*Inside* you?" Trevor parroted back, opening his mouth with a gleeful look as he visibly prepared to turn his teasing in Jose's direction.

Grace stole his thunder, smirking. "So you're saying that you *aren't* dating Barry Quartz, Jose?" she asked, all innocent. "Because I swear you said you had plans with him later today, and I'm sure he'll—"

"Shush your lips," Jose hushed her. "Shh. Shush them. Don't even go there."

Victorious, Grace winked and turned to walk toward the door to the staff room, not one to argue their need to get a move on, despite the slight diversion of trying to get a rise out of the normally unflappable Jose. Ash grabbed his coat from his locker and was about to join her and the rest when the door swung open and Martin stormed in.

The appearance of the shift manager instantly dimmed the group's lively mood, and Elliott took a small step to the side, putting distance between himself and Ash with a guilty look on his face. Right. Dating between employees was strictly discouraged. Jose stopped leaning against the locker, standing up straight and tugging at the hem of his shirt, but it was Trevor whom Martin zeroed in on.

"Consider this a verbal warning, Trevor," Martin barked, sneering at the lot of them.

"A verbal warning for what?" Trevor demanded. Faced with a conflict, he rose up to face it without any sign of fear. "You know I haven't done anything wrong, Martin."

"Oh, really?" A vicious glint flashed in Martin's eye, as though he'd anticipated Trevor's reaction and had been waiting for him to offer exactly that opening.

In the short while that Ash had been working under Martin, he'd developed an intense dislike for the man. Always one to stick by the rules to a fault, looking for the smallest mistakes to punish his staff over, Martin's militancy was a thorn in the side of every one of Ash's coworkers. Worse, from Ash's point of view, none of them deserved it. Every one of them upheld the Ashby's brand as if they genuinely cared about it, not just because Ashby's gave them a paycheck.

Martin whipped out a receipt from his back pocket, flapping it in front of Trevor's face as he demanded, "Then maybe you'd like to tell me what *this* is, hm?"

Trevor's lips hardened into a straight line. "It's a receipt. I'm not dumb, Martin. I know what a receipt is."

"I'm asking you to explain the things *on* the receipt." Martin eyeballed the list and started naming the items on it. "French chalk. Ten packs of Scheuman's sewing machine needles. A rotary cutter. Ten spools of thread. Chopsticks."

"Chopsticks?" Elliott asked. The last item had clearly surprised the word out of him despite his obvious attempts to stay under the radar.

"They're used for turning inside-out corners, or to give shape while you're pressing fabric," Trevor mumbled, "... plus, I like to eat my Chinese take-out with them, but my delivery guy keeps bringing forks."

"But what's your point, Martin?" Grace demanded, hands on her hips as she rallied to Trevor's defense. "If you're trying to stick Trevor with a charge of buying things that weren't for himself, you're off your rocker. That's all sewing stuff, and Trevor's been the one altering all of our Christmas outfits so they fit better, so he's obviously using everything himself."

"Except for the part where he's breaking a very serious rule," Martin said flatly. "No products bought with the Ashby's employee discount may be resold or otherwise used to gain profit, and I've heard it mentioned more than once that Trevor's little tailor shop is starting to take off. Ten packs of sewing machine needles? The average hobbyist won't go through that many in a year."

The tension in the air was starting to get to Ash. He glanced at Elliott out of the corner of his eye to find Elliott had subtly made his way through the group so he was standing partially behind Ash, doing his best to stay out of Martin's line of sight. Elliott was clearly uncomfortable, and thinking back to the conversation about Elliott's own use of his employee discount when they'd visited Nick, Ash understood why.

Protective instincts welled inside of him, and he puffed his chest and stepped forward.

"Then it's a damn good thing that Trevor isn't average," Ash said to Martin, ready and willing to defend the man he'd come to consider a friend in his quest to protect his boyfriend from scrutiny. "You can't prove that Trevor has done anything wrong. With all the outfits he's been tailoring, he probably *does* need those needles. And that thread, and... things."

"In corporate's eyes, I have no doubt that it will be perfectly clear what's happening," Martin sneered. "And it's going to be *my* head on the chopping block if they catch it. The rules are the rules, Trevor, and there are to be *no* exceptions. Especially not in this season. And—"

"Guys, c'mon." Ash wasn't going to listen to it anymore. "We're wasting our lunch break. Let's get out of here."

It was clear to him that Martin had no idea what kind of things corporate was actually concerned about. And if anyone actually did get on Trevor's back over some needles and some thread, Ash was going to get on *their* backs. No one would run his friends through the wringer. Working with this group over the last few weeks had convinced him that every single one of the employees who associated with Elliott was both hardworking and a true asset to Ashby's. Besides, no one deserved to be treated like a thief just for buying needles and thread. As far as Ash was concerned, Martin was way out of line, and it was almost tempting to break cover and tell him so.

Ash looked over at Elliott. But Martin had said it was just a verbal warning for Trevor, so it wasn't worth it. Not until Ash figured out how to come clean without losing Elliott.

He reached back and grabbed Elliott's arm, dragging him forward. Out of all of them, Elliott was the most timid and likely to follow his lead, and Ash knew that if he just started walking, there was a good chance Elliott wouldn't follow. He did. Trevor, chin held high, followed after Ash, too. Grace walked at his side, and Jose took up the rear.

"See you after lunch, dude," Jose told Martin in parting.

"I am *not* done!" Martin insisted. "Trevor isn't the only one—"

Ash pushed his way through the door, taking Elliott with him without waiting for the unpleasant little man to finish his sentence. The others were in hot pursuit, and the group of them walked across the floor and headed directly for the front doors, intent on salvaging a few moments of freedom. They were all wearing their winter coats to hide their uniforms, so thankfully no customers tried to stop them.

Martin was a different story.

"Hey!" he called out from behind them, storming out of the staff room after them.

But, nope. Ash didn't plan on stopping any time soon. Certainly not for Martin.

His days working on the floor at Ashby's may have been drawing to a close, but he wasn't planning on forgetting about the people who worked there. On the contrary, he was hoping they'd all stay friends, even after he eventually came out with his true identity. Regardless of that, though, if anything bad were to happen because of a ridiculous over-interpretation of the Ashby's rulebook, Ash was going to get directly involved.

Martin didn't know who he was messing with.

"Stop!" Martin's voice rang out again.

And this time, Ash did.

Not because Martin had told him to, though. He came to a halt so abruptly that Elliott ran into his back, letting out a small "oof."

"Ben?" Elliott asked from behind him, trying to peer around his shoulder to see what had caused him to come to a sudden standstill.

Ash heard him, but he couldn't bring himself to answer.

Shit.

Shit.

There were professional camera crews bearing the logos of competing gossip news stations pouring in through the front doors of the store, their equipment already running. Reporters dressed in fancy pea coats and high-heeled shoes clicked their way toward him, all but racing each other as they started shouting questions.

For a split second, Ash dared to hope their presence was a coincidence that had nothing to do with him.

"Ash! Ash! Can you confirm that you've been laying low in Chicago to pursue an illicit affair?"

"What about the executive you had sexual relations with in New York City? Is the relationship serious?"

"Is it true that you're hiding out from a jilted lover left in Aspen?"

An icy chill flooded him, freezing his feet to the floor and making his stomach clench so hard he thought he might vomit. Trevor, Grace, and Jose had all come to a stop right behind him, and Trevor peered over his shoulders at the camera crews, his eyes lighting up at the prospect of something big going down.

"What's the media doing here?" Trevor crowed.

"It sounds like Ash must be in the store. Like, *the* Ash. Ash Ashby Ash," Grace replied. She peeked over Trevor's shoulder in turn, then swiveled her neck around as she scanned the crowded floor. "Did we just miss him?"

"Ash lives in New York," Elliott said. "I don't think he's ever visited the Chicago Ashby's. They must be mistaken."

Ash knew there was no mistake. And definitely no co-incidence that the media had outed him *now*. The unstated meaning behind that morning's text message from his father suddenly clicked into place, and a helpless rage filled him as the cameras finally zeroed in on him.

He recoiled, but with all of his friends blocking the way behind him and reporters bearing down from the front, it was too late. He had nowhere to go.

"Ben?" Elliott asked, genuine concern in his voice.

Ash turned, but the rest of them had effectively created a wall behind them, and to make matters worse, he could see Martin on his way over to them, still steaming over whatever thwarted plans he'd had back in the staff room.

Elliott searched Ash's eyes. "What's wrong?" he asked. "Are you feeling okay?"

No. Ash wasn't feeling even remotely okay.

"Ash! Over here! Just a few questions, please!"

"I have to go, Elliott," Ash rasped, his voice hoarse with strain. "I can't—"

The reporters finally made it through the crowds, and one was bold enough to grab his arm and spin him around. Equally part terrified and pissed the fuck off, Ash tore his arm away from the woman, despair filling his gut as he realized there was no way to dodge the big reveal. It wasn't how he'd intended to share his identity with Elliott, and he wasn't at all certain that Elliott would understand. Not like this.

"Ash, can you tell us more about your decision to go undercover? The world's never seen you blond before. And your eyes!"

"A-Ash?" Elliott stuttered from behind him, his wide-eyed gaze bouncing between the pushy reporter and Ash. "Ben... is she talking to *you*?"

Even as the words left Elliott's mouth, Ash saw the dawning realization break in his eyes. And the sense of betrayal.

Ash's heart broke in two.

"Is this for a man?" another reporter demanded of him, shoving a microphone right in his face, obscuring his view of Elliott. There were lights and microphones dangling from overhead, cameras pointing at him from all angles, and the Ashby's customers had begun to gather round, leaving him no way out.

"Have you been having a secret affair, Ash?"

"Ash?" Elliott repeated, voice strained. Hurt and betrayal may have been in his eyes, but his voice edged on angry. "You're Ash *Ashby*, Ben?"

"There have been reports that the cabin rented under your name in Aspen has been stocked with the phone numbers for a variety of escort agencies, Ash. Were you planning on jetting off and hiring yourself some fun for Christmas?"

The crowd tittered, and Elliott's hand slipped away from his arm as the suggestive questions continued to come at him from all angles. Vaguely, he was aware that Martin had managed to breach the crowds, and the sour man hissed something in Elliott's direction that Ash had trouble understanding through the sound of the blood rushing through his ears. Martin pulled a white-faced Elliott away, and Ash's world began to dissolve into a sea of all-too-familiar media frenzy.

Ash took a step toward Elliott, but he was already gone.

The flash of a camera blinded him, and the annoying colored contacts in his eyes watered and burned. Ash squeezed his eyes closed and turned his head away, and by the time his vision recovered, the crowd had tightened around him and he'd lost sight of Grace, Trevor, and Jose, too.

Not that they had any reason to stick by him.

They would no doubt feel as betrayed as Elliott obviously did.

Ash was alone.

"Ash!" People were shouting out to him from all around, the chorus of his name deafening.

"Ash!" Each utterance of the name he hadn't been called recently was a vicious jab, reminding him that—pretend as he might—he would *never* be Ben.

"Ash!" The hurt had been heavy in Elliott's voice, and Ash knew that all of the friends he'd made likely felt the same.

He'd lied about who he was on a fundamental level, and it had come back to bite him in the ass in the worst possible way. And, even though Elliott had taught him that

Christmas wishes really could come true, after how Ash had lied to him, he couldn't find it in him to believe that Elliott would want to forgive him.

Sometimes, not even the magic of Christmas could make things right.

Chapter 18

ELLIOTT

BEN WAS ASH.

Ben—*Elliott's* Ben—was Ash Ashby.

Elliott stared blindly at the chipped edge of Martin's desk as he turned the thought over in his mind one more time. Bennett Ashby. Ben. Ash. God, how had Elliott been so blind to the truth? Ben looked *everything* like Ash. Blond hair and hazel eyes shouldn't have been enough to disguise him, but like a naive idiot, Elliott had never doubted him.

Not for a second.

He swallowed hard and tried to shake off the painful disappointment roiling in his gut. Everything he knew about Ash Ashby was negative. Ash, international playboy, morally loose man-child, and emotionally irresponsible manipulator wasn't the kind of man anyone would want to be with long-term, nor was he the kind to stick with any relationship for more than a hot second, from what the media said about him.

Ash Ashby was everything Elliott didn't believe in. And *that* was the man he'd taken home to meet his mother. The man Elliott had so willingly—*eagerly*—given up his virginity to. Not that Elliott was a prude. But it had mattered to him. And what would something so precious to Elliott be *worth* to a man like Ash?

Nothing, that's what.

Every moment with Ben—*Ash*—had been built on a lie.

All I want is you, Elliott. Elliott blinked rapidly, denying the hot prick of tears behind his eyes as Ash's tender words after they'd made love played treacherously in his mind. Elliott had believed him. Still wanted to, in fact, despite all evidence now pointing to how utterly, completely foolish such a thing would be.

"...for years now," Martin was saying, voice stiff and on the offensive. "Do you know what that means, Elliott?"

Elliott shook his head automatically, even though he wasn't really listening to the conversation. He didn't know what that meant. Hadn't even followed whatever it was Martin had so viciously pulled him into his office about.

Fingers laced and hands on his lap, Elliott squeezed his own hand to try to find some comfort. Even if Martin had actually cared, the man wouldn't understand what had just happened to him. Elliott had been invested in Ben. *Ash.* They were supposed to be serious about each other. Ash had acted excited to come over for Christmas dinner at Elliott's mom's place. A far cry from the kind of holidays he must be used to spending.

Elliott's throat tightened, and he chuffed out a breath, refusing to cry in front of Martin.

Ash had been his *boyfriend*... which sounded as impossible as it, well, was.

Ash had never been his boyfriend. Ben had been... but "Ben" was a lie.

"*Do* you, Elliott?" Martin pressed him, obviously not accepting the head shake as sufficient answer to his question.

Elliott still didn't know what they were talking about. He hadn't heard enough of what Martin had said to understand anything. His mind was elsewhere.

"No," he replied, which at least was the truth.

"Then let me lay it out for you," Martin said coldly. "This infraction goes back *years*. In cases like these, there are *no* verbal warnings. *No* written warnings to be given. We're beyond that."

"What?" Elliott pulled himself together enough to stare at Martin. "Infractions? What are you talking about?"

"Have you not been listening to me?" Martin scowled. "Since it came to management's attention that Trevor had been manipulating the system this morning, we've been combing through years of information. And do you know what we found?"

A sick feeling of dread settled into Elliott's stomach at the triumphant look Martin gave him, and Elliott shook his head, his mouth too dry to answer.

"It looks like there's just one time of year you use your employee discount, Elliott," Martin said, pinning Elliott with his gaze. "And every year, it's the same. Starting at the end of November and spanning into late December. And, go figure, the only thing you've bought with it—*ever*—are... toys. Children's toys."

Elliott swallowed. It was true. *Shit.* He had no defense because he'd actually committed the crime. He clenched his hands together tightly, trying to stop their trembling.

"Can you tell me what you're doing with dolls and fake makeup kits?" Martin asked, not bothering to wait for an answer. "Or how about the boxes upon boxes of crayons? Or the six basketballs you've bought since you started working here?"

Elliott had nothing to say. He just stared back at Martin, stunned. Only Elliott's closest friends knew what he'd done, but somehow, now, Martin did too. The shift manager was grinning like a cat who'd just caught a mouse, and Elliott felt like everything he'd believed in had just crumbled beneath him.

He wanted to cry.

"The rules are laid out in writing," Martin continued,

his enjoyment at delivering the bad news like a slap in the face. "If the infractions had been minor, perhaps I could have given you a verbal warning like I gave Trevor... but *your* infractions span years and years, and they've cost the company money, Elliott. Money you should have been paying, and so, in effect, *stole*. In fact, Ashby's might be inclined to pursue legal action to recover that money, depending on the rest of the data we dig up on you. But just from what we've found on you already, I already have no choice but to dismiss you."

"I'm fired?" Elliott whispered in disbelief, even though Martin had just so.

Martin nodded, pointing toward the door. "For your own sake, I suggest you leave now, before we find more evidence that requires me to call the authorities in to deal with your theft."

Elliott felt strangely detached, as if the conversation they were having wasn't real. He watched Martin's lips as they moved, then glanced down at Martin's desktop. It held a plain black pen cup, filled with cheap ballpoint pens. There were a few papers collected neatly in a folder pushed off to the corner, and a single paper clip shone beneath Martin's office lights.

It looked sterile and cold, just like Elliott's heart.

"But I'm one of the nutcrackers," he protested weakly. He didn't look up. "If I leave right now, there will only be one person standing up there with Santa in the North Pole." *Ben.* Ben, or Ash, was supposed to be Santa. Elliott's throat closed up. He couldn't fathom it. "It's not right, Martin. At least let me finish this shift."

"The shift disruption is better than allowing you to stay on Ashby's property," Martin said coldly. "You should be thankful that we aren't pressing charges, and leave *now*. Before we have a reason to."

"But it's *Christmas*," Elliott tried again. It was his favorite time of year. The season when all good things happened.

Tears had begun to gather in the corners of his eyes despite his best efforts to keep them at bay, but his mind still didn't fully comprehend their source. Sources, plural. It was like he was being hit from all sides, all at once.

"*Go.*" The abrupt quality of the word startled Elliott to his feet, and he dug his hands into his jacket pocket and stumbled backward for the door. He could feel the cheap, squeaky Santa head dog toy that Elliott had bought for Donner in his pocket.

Donner, their dog. His and Ben's. The one they'd named together.

Ben, who was actually Ash Ashby.

Rage and sorrow and hurt surged up inside him in a hot wave that rose so hard and fast it threatened to choke him, and Elliott tore his hand out of his pocket and spun around, heading toward the office door. As his hand brushed the handle, he came to a stop.

There was one more question he needed to ask, and he swallowed, fearing he already knew the answer.

"Who told you, Martin?"

Elliott turned back to face Martin, but the shift manager didn't bother to stand from his desk. He just watched Elliott evenly from where he sat, his face a gloating mix of smug delight and vindictive self-righteousness.

"I've got my sources." He tapped his fingers on his desktop once before continuing. "If today has shown you anything, Elliott, I'd think it would be that not all your *friends* are necessarily who they say they are, wouldn't you say? At least one of them found it more important to protect the Ashby's brand than help you cover your tracks."

Martin threw a pointed look back the direction they'd come from. He couldn't have made it clearer, and Elliott's heart officially cracked in two. He jerked the door open and fled, knowing that if he didn't keep moving, he was going to break down completely. The tears had already started to stream silently down his cheeks, and try as he might, he couldn't seem to stop them.

With less than a week to go before Christmas, Elliott had lost both the job and the man that he loved. And, even though he'd no doubt be able to find another job at some point, there was no hope of getting his boyfriend back.

Because from what Martin had just told him, it looked like the man Elliott had fallen in love with had never actually existed at all.

Chapter 19

ASH

THE CHAUFFEUR CLOSED THE CAR DOOR BEHIND HIM, granting Ash a handful of seconds of welcome privacy. Getting away from the Ashby's store had been an ordeal the likes of which he wouldn't care to go through again, and he'd never been as grateful to have a personal assistant on speed dial as when he'd flexed his Ashby's wealth and privilege and had her ensure that a car would be waiting for him on the street.

He drew his phone from his pocket and unlocked the screen, his thoughts on Elliott, but when it opened to the text from his father, Ash jammed at the back button and closed out his inbox, disgusted.

This was Douglas Ashby's doing.

His father had made it clear that he wasn't pleased about Ash skipping the flight he'd arranged for him to Aspen, but it had never occurred to Ash that his father would go to these lengths to get what he wanted. Still, there was no doubt in Ash's mind that it *was* his father who had hired someone to tip off the media as to his whereabouts. And giving the press the tidbit about the contact information for escort agencies left in "his" cabin in Aspen?

Of course.

From Douglas Ashby, Ash should have expected nothing less. The man wasn't his family—he never had been, regardless of what any paternity test might show. Ash was only valuable to him because of the influence his actions had on the Ashby empire's bottom dollar. There was no love there. No affection. Ash's father had never taken him to visit Santa, or to pick out a Christmas tree, and Ash was sure that if pressed, Douglas wouldn't even have a clue when Ash's birthday was off the top of his head.

They were simply strangers who shared blood.

Being with Elliott had taught Ash what *real* family felt like, and what he shared with his mother and father was not that. It had never been.

Before trying to win Elliott back, he was going to have to deal with that, once and for all.

Ash brought up his phone book and scrolled through the listed names until he found the one he was looking for. After so much time spent living as Ben, it was disconcerting to get back in touch with the people who knew him as Ash. He held the phone to his ear and rested his elbow flush against the base of the window. The phone rang all of three times before his most recent personal assistant picked up. He'd texted her with instructions about the car earlier, and to his shame, it took him a minute to remember her first name.

"Stacey," he said, relieved when she didn't correct him. "Charter a plane from O'Hare to New York City within the next two hours. I don't care what money you need to spend to make it happen, but it needs to leave as soon as possible."

"Mr. Ashby?" Stacey asked carefully. "Where have you been? I've been—"

"It's not important where I've been; what's important is where I'm going." A part of him silently berated himself for sounding so brusque, but his need to resolve things and try to get back to the life he'd started to build for himself overrode his new awareness of Stacey as a person deserving to be treated with a little more common courtesy. Being "Ash" was something embarrassingly easy to slip back into. "I need that chartered plane ready immediately. Concurrently, I need an assistant to take up residence in the Ashby condo unit in Chicago whose sole responsibility is to look after a small- to medium-sized gray dog with a wiry coat named Donner. The dog can be identified by his red collar and corresponding dog tags."

"A-alright," Stacey mumbled. From her end of the call,

Ash heard frantic typing. "How long should I arrange the assistant for?"

"An undetermined time. Schedule a time to check in with me every day to see if the assistant's services are still needed."

The driver entered the vehicle and sat. The car had been idling, and he wasted no time in shifting it into drive and pulling from the curb. Ash sank back into his seat, leaning against his elbow as the call went on.

"I'll need a car waiting at LaGuardia for my arrival. Make sure to coordinate that as well."

"Of course, sir," Stacey said. Her typing did not slow. "Should I have anything brought to your condo in New York? I could have a meal arranged."

"Forget it." The car merged onto Lake Shore Drive. Lake Michigan's waters were gray and choppy. "I'll arrange for that on my own when I arrive. The chartered plane, the car upon arrival, and the assistant to care for Donner at the Chicago condo are all I need."

"Of course, Mr. Ashby."

"And Stacey?" Some of the severity slipped from his tone, and he forced himself to relax his shoulders. He may have been born an Ashby, but what he did with that and how he chose to treat the people in his life were still a matter of personal choice.

And, regardless of what name he went by, Ash was going to choose to be *Ben*.

"Yes, Mr. Ashby?" Stacey prompted, crisp and professional.

"Thank you for your work," Ash said, meaning it. "I really do appreciate it."

There was a long moment of silence. Most times, Stacey—like all the Ashby family employees—was quick to respond and overly apologetic, and Ash didn't know what to make of her uncharacteristic silence. At last, he took the phone from his ear to make sure the call hadn't dropped. It hadn't.

"That's very kind of you to say, sir," Stacey said at last. She sounded flustered, but still professional. "I'll have everything prepared per your instructions. Please, don't hesitate to call me if there's anything else you need done."

"Of course." Ash paused. There were plenty of things he needed done, but none of the rest of them were within Stacey's ability to fix. If he wanted to get his life in order, he was going to have to do it himself. Delegation could only take him so far. "I'll be in touch a little later, and if not, please make sure you follow up tomorrow about the assistant. Take care."

"Sir." It was said in parting, and the call ended.

When was the last time he'd treated an assistant like a human being? Ash closed his eyes and dropped his phone into his lap. Stacey had been stunned into silence that he'd taken an extra moment to thank her sincerely. What did that say about him as a person?

What kind of a life had he been setting himself up for, before being forced to live as Ben?

When Ash had first come to Chicago, he'd arrived with a certain set of expectations and prejudices. Back then, he hadn't even been aware of them. After working as Santa and meeting Elliott and his friends, Ash understood them now.

Poverty wasn't a choice. Children weren't inherently selfish and greedy. The type of guys he'd shied away from in the past because they *weren't his type* deserved a shot.

Not that Ash was interested in giving anyone one.

If he'd actually lost Elliott—a very real possibility that made his stomach cramp just to think about—Ash wouldn't be looking to date again for a very long time.

He didn't want anyone else.

The possibility of not having Elliott in his life anymore weighed heavily on his soul and he knew that, if it happened, it would be a loss that it wouldn't be easy to shake. Ash had never allowed himself to become attached to another person before, but with Elliott—all bright eyes and sincere heart and undying enthusiasm—it had felt natural. Necessary.

And, for the first time with a man he'd dated, Ash had no doubt that Elliott's attachment to *him* hadn't been based on money or fame. Elliott had wanted "Ben" for Ben, and—before Ash had been dragged back into his old life against his will—he'd actually started to hope that he could find a way to keep on being Ben.

With Elliott.

For a long, long time.

He'd asked Elliott to be his boyfriend. Ash buried his face in his hand, a wave of despair washing through him as he remembered the look on Elliott's face when he'd realized who Ash really was. Ash had never had a boyfriend before. There were times when he was seen with the same guy over the course of a few weeks, sometimes even up to a month, but never had it been serious. Ash dated and had fun—he didn't commit. Monogamy was a fool's game.

Or so he'd believed.

Stricken, he scrambled to pick up his phone from his lap to dial Elliott, something he really should have done before getting sidetracked by his need to resolve things once and for all with his father. His elbow fell away from the window ledge, and Ash threw his head back against the seat.

On the other end of the phone, Elliott's number rang and rang, then finally went to voicemail.

Elliott's prerecorded voice, cheerful and chipper, greeted him. *"Hi! It's Elliott Gaffney, and I can't come to the phone right now. Please leave a message and I'll call you back."*

Somehow, Ash didn't think that was true.

The beep to signify the start of the recording went off, and Ash spoke. "Elliott, it's... Ben. Please call me back. I'd really like to talk to you. I'm sorry."

Spilling his emotions into a recorded message wasn't right. If Elliott called him back, he would talk then. *They* would talk then. It would have to be a give and take, because as much as Ash wanted to confess everything and make Elliott understand what had happened, he wanted to hear Elliott's side of the story, too. He wanted to understand Elliott's feelings and the depths of the betrayal he'd suffered through Ash's subterfuge.

Ash had never cared so much about what another person thought of him before.

He set the phone down and closed his eyes, silently willing Elliott to give him another chance. O'Hare was approximately forty minutes away, far out in the suburbs, and Ash had plenty of time to think through potential conversations with Elliott in his head.

When confronted with trouble, Elliott had a tendency to withdraw. Ash remembered how he'd attempted to fade away into the background when Ash had first approached him in men's wear after his first day as Santa. How Elliott had hidden behind Trevor for support.

Would Elliott be the kind of guy to hide from his problems, too? Or would he face Ash head on, teeth bared?

The possible facets of Elliott's anger and disappointment lingered with Ash all the way to O'Hare, and when he exited the car and wished the driver well, he didn't feel any better for it. If anything, with his phone remaining stubbornly silent, he felt worse.

Stacey had updated him via email with an itinerary for his chartered flight, and Ash wasted no time in striding through the airport to arrive at the appropriate check-in counter. She'd mentioned that Douglas had already chartered a plane for him. One headed for Aspen. But if his father thought he was going to jet out to Aspen now that he'd been forcefully outed, the man had another think coming. The only way Ash could ever make things right was if he weeded the problem out by its roots.

And those roots were dug deep in New York City.

"Welcome, Mr. Ashby." The TSA agent in the fast track lane smiled at him and waved him forward. Ash showed her the QR code attached to his itinerary, and she scanned it and looked it over briefly. "I'll have to call a representative over to escort you to your private gate. The section your chartered flight is in isn't accessible to the general public."

"Of course." Ash hadn't removed his shoes or his belt, and the TSA agent didn't press the issue. When asked, he stepped through the metal detector, allowed himself to be inspected with a quick sweep of the metal detecting wand, and then waited off to the side for an agent to escort him to where he needed to go.

Swarms of people waited to be passed through normal inspection. College students, families with young children, and businessmen made up the majority of the crowd. Ash watched them, acutely aware that amongst them, he was the outsider.

Until then, the division had never bothered him. The faces of the crowd had blended into one seamless blob—an obstacle Ash found inconvenient and did his best to avoid.

But that wasn't the case at all. Amongst them could have been Trevor, or Grace, or Jose. Amongst them could have been Elliott.

The people who'd come to mean so much to Ash over the course of the last few weeks weren't faceless. With as much personality as they had, Ash could see every one of them hitting it big in their own way. Trevor, with his sharp wit, charisma, and natural talent, would rise up the ranks in Hollywood given the right push. Grace, a dichotomy of sarcasm and bubbly cheer, with her edgy look and slender body, would own the modeling industry and turn it on its head. Jose, with his laid-back personality and hilarious turns of phrase, would make it as a comedian without question. And Elliott...

Ash scrubbed at his face, not wanting to think about it.

Elliott, with his kind heart and undying love of humanity, would be a shoe-in for philanthropic work.

How many more people in that once faceless crowd would Ash be able to place, just like he'd placed his friends? How many talents went unrecognized, passions went unfulfilled, and goals remained impossible because of money?

In the last hour alone, Ash had spent more money than many of them made in a whole year. Last-minute chartered flights and personal assistants of Stacey's caliber didn't come cheap. How was it that he'd never noticed the discrepancy until now? In how many ways could the money he'd spent today change one of their lives, if it had been put to a different use?

As he waited, Ash thought back to the Giving Tree. Little Abigail's tags still waited on his kitchen table. All she'd wanted was a set of colored pencils and a sketchbook.

With the money he'd spent today, how many Giving Tree tags could Ash have paid for?

"Mr. Ashby?" A man in a security uniform approached. Tall and slender, but with a defined chin edged with stubble, he was every bit Ash's type. Last month, Ash wouldn't have wasted a second flirting with him. Now, his heart ached at the thought.

Life was about more than power and money and sex. It had taken Ash years to figure it out, and now he feared that the realization may have come too late.

"One and the same," Ash replied with a brisk nod of his head and a practiced smile.

The mask was back on. Upbeat, unflappable Ash was back. Ben was gone.

"Your chartered plane is waiting. If you'd kindly follow me..."

It was always the same. Ash zoned out as he followed the airport official through a secured door and down a nondescript hallway. A set of downward winding stairs led him onto the tarmac, and not all that far from the door waited Ash's charter plane. Small and nothing much to look at from the outside, it would serve its purpose. Stacey hadn't been able to swing luxury, but the fact that the plane was waiting and cleared for departure at O'Hare in record time spoke to her abilities. Organizing an unexpected flight at LaGuardia was no less impressive.

Ash climbed the steep steps into the cabin, and a flight attendant greeted him inside and personally escorted him to his seat. As Ash settled and buckled himself in, she returned with a mixed drink.

"Something to calm your nerves, Mr. Ashby," the flight attendant said with a smile.

She had no idea how badly he needed it.

"Thank you." Ash let a beat pass, then looked up into her eyes and didn't shy away when she returned his gaze. "What's your name?"

"Oh, um..." Her professional demeanor slipped away. "It's Jolene, sir."

"And what are your plans for Christmas this year, Jolene?"

Ash had never treated his flight staff like equals before, and he knew that he had a reputation amongst flight attendants for being bitter or standoffish. Jolene's surprise was no shock, but it still shamed him.

"Well, I'm working through it and I'm scheduled to be laid over in Idaho, so my boyfriend is going to fly up so we can have Christmas at the hotel together. It's not really much, but... well, I'm just happy he gets to be there." She smiled warmly, then seemed to catch herself, a professional mask slipping back into place. She redirected the conversation to him. "Are you going back to Aspen this year? It's always a big to-do in the news."

"No." Ash took a sip of his drink and tried to soothe the dull, painful throbbing of his heart. "I'm hoping to make it back to Chicago, if you can believe it."

She grinned, becoming human again. "If you can get through the winter, Chicago's the best city in the world."

"Even if I can't get through the winter." Ash glanced out the window as the plane started to move down the runway. Chicago, despite all odds, had actually started to feel like something Ash had never truly experienced before. "The city stole my heart, and I'm going to do whatever it takes to get back to it."

Chicago had started to feel like *home*.

Chapter 20

ASH

Ashby's Corporate Tower was modern to a fault. Cold and sterile from the outside, with its broad, tinted windows and its sleek, black design, and far too modern on the inside to be welcoming. It was the face of Ashby's that the public never got to see. While the Ashby's stores were also polished and immaculately kept, there was a warmth in them that was missing here.

The corporate tower lacked heart.

Men and women in pressed business suits and polished shoes sneered after Ash as he cut his way through the lobby and toward the executive elevator. It had been ages since he'd come to the tower, but he still remembered the code to the keypad that brought the elevator to life. Following a series of numbers entered into the keypad, the elevator door slid open, and Ash stepped inside.

He was still wearing his Ashby's uniform from Chicago.

The elevator rose so smoothly and soundlessly; he almost couldn't tell it was moving at all. It was only when the top floor light flickered on and the doors parted that Ash knew he'd arrived. The lobby to his father's office was oversized and empty save for the young secretary who sat at the desk nearest the carved oak door that led into Douglas Ashby's office.

Pearl had been with Ashby's for a few years. Her glossy brown hair was twisted and pinned, and each time Ash had seen her, she'd been wearing a sheer, billowy blouse with a pencil skirt. Today was no exception.

"Hello." Pearl looked up from her typing to narrow her eyes at the unexpected visitor, then widened them with surprise. "Oh, the younger Mr. Ashby. Your blond hair threw me off for a minute. What is it that I can do for you?"

"I'm here to see my father," Ash said as he strode across the room.

Calling Douglas his father didn't feel right after what he'd done and given the seething anger that Ash harbored toward him as a result, but it was what Pearl was expecting. The last thing he needed was for her to call security and have him taken away before he reached his destination.

"Mr. Ashby isn't taking guests," Pearl twittered from

her chair, pushing away from her desk. "I'm sorry, Mr. Ashby, but you'll have to—"

"I'm not a guest. I'm his *son*."

"I realize that, but..."

Did she? Because Douglas had certainly never treated him that way.

Ash didn't stop. He stormed past Pearl's desk and toward the door leading into his father's office. Pearl scrambled up from her desk, the click of her heels against the floor sounding almost frantic. Ash heard her approaching.

"Mr. Ashby! You can't go in!"

"Mr. Ashby isn't taking orders anymore," Ash parroted back. He pulled open the door and entered his father's office. He hadn't been there for years.

Not much had changed.

The room was expansive, the back wall consisting of a floor-to-ceiling window that overlooked the city. Office buildings loomed in the distance, each of them a monolithic feat of wealth and power. Framed by them, seated in his high-backed office chair, was Douglas Ashby himself.

When Ash entered, he looked up from some paperwork. Time had turned his dark hair gray, but not even time had been able to drain the color from his turquoise eyes. Ash had inherited his looks, and one day he would inherit his fortune, but he hoped never to inherit his father's cutthroat detachment from the rest of the world.

If that was what business was, Ash didn't want any part of it.

"Mr. Ashby!" Pearl squawked from the door. "I tried to stop him, sir, but he wasn't listening to me!"

"It's fine, Pearl." Douglas collected the documents before him, tapped them into a neat pile, and then set them aside. "A visit from Bennett isn't formally penciled into the agenda, but I was expecting him regardless. You're dismissed, Pearl."

She bowed her head and ducked out of the doorway, shutting the door behind her. Ash didn't hear her go—he was too focused on what Douglas had said.

"Of course you were," Ash seethed. "After what you did, how could you think I'd stay away?"

"I was hoping you'd choose to enjoy the rest of your holiday season in Aspen, as I instructed," Douglas replied. "That you'd come to your senses about whatever hang-ups you had about leaving Chicago, and that you'd see the reason in going out of your way to bolster the company name. But I was prepared for this as well. I'm disappointed in you, Bennett. My instructions were clear."

"And so were mine!" Ash slammed his palms down onto Douglas's desk. "I told you I wasn't going to leave Chicago until Christmas was over. I told you that I had a duty to the Ashby's store, and that I couldn't leave them without a Santa."

"Someone has already been arranged to replace you," Douglas replied. "Every single person working in our stores is replaceable, Ash. Even the managers who produce the highest profit margins are disposable. Did you not think we couldn't find someone to listen to children for eight hours a day? The position was filled in seconds; money is the strongest motivator known to man."

"No, it's not," Ash replied quietly. "It's not the only thing that matters, and it's not why good people do what they do."

Elliott.

Douglas scoffed, a dismissive flick of his hand his only reaction to Ash's claim. "You're the Ashby heir, Bennett. You have a duty. Don't make me spell out what you're supposed to do again."

Ash remained steadfast where he stood, eyes narrowing. "And *you* are my father. *You're* supposed to love and respect me. I fulfilled my responsibilities in Chicago, and I made it clear that I wanted to stay there. That I had friends there."

"You have friends waiting for you in Aspen as well," Douglas replied. The stiff shoulders of his business suit grew stiffer yet as he sat back in his chair and laid his arms on its armrests. "High power, influential friends from families who will help bolster the Ashby name and our business. Friends who you *should* be spending time forging connections with."

"Those people couldn't give less of a shit about me." Ash's rage had settled down to a simmer. He stood back from the desk and did his best to bring himself back down so he could speak from a place of reason instead of emotion. "The people who actually care about me are—" He cleared his throat, knowing it might not still be true. He corrected himself, ignoring the pang it caused him. He had to get through *this* before he could start to fix things back in Chicago. "They *were* the ones you publicly outed me to in Chicago. And now they're lost."

"And easily replaced, just like anyone else." With a shake of his head, Douglas completely ignored Ash's feelings and continued with his own agenda. "I've told you already, our business is the only thing paying for your lifestyle, Bennett. Without it, you have nothing. Don't blame me for doing what serves the company in the best way possible, because in the end, doing so is ensuring that you have a future."

There was no way to get it across to him, was there?

Ash looked his father over—truly looked. It felt like ages since he'd taken the time to see the man for who he really was.

Douglas Ashby's gray hair was combed over to one side, likely masking baldness. His skin had leathered with age and was deeply wrinkled across his brow and in the corners of his mouth. Whether it was by cosmetic science or genetics, the rest of his face looked young enough, but his lips were thin and worried by stress and time, and his hands betrayed his age. Corded and thin, they weren't the hands of a healthy businessman. No matter the suit he wore or the ruthless levelheadedness he brought to the table, Douglas was losing his fight with time.

And there wasn't a soul in the world who cared.

"Ashby's is about more than just money," Ash said softly. Maybe his father would never understand, but that didn't have to stop Ash from saying it. "Ashby's means things to people. It shapes lives, it gives hope, it puts roofs over people's heads and, this time of year, it puts hope in their hearts."

"Don't be ridiculous." Douglas sat straighter in his chair. "Ashby's is designer clothes and exclusive home accessories. Ashby's is prestige and wealth. Don't be sentimental."

"I'm not being sentimental." If anything, Ash felt sorry for the small world his father had built for himself. Without love and without friendship, life was hollow. He'd learned that firsthand, and he wasn't willing to live that way anymore. "I'm still on the board, aren't I?"

"Of course you are." Douglas's eyes sharpened with sudden interest as the conversation moved into territory he was more comfortable with. "And you're welcome to come back, Bennett. Your prison sentence has been lifted. I'd be glad to have the rest of our board members go over the numbers and the results of the quarter's analysis with you. When confronted with the facts, I'm sure you'll understand how important your public persona is to maintaining elevated profit margins."

"I'm not interested in that. All I'm interested in is that I still have an executive position where my voice can be heard. And regardless of profit margins or how you spin it, I'm not going to Aspen." Ash tucked his hands into his jacket pockets and took a step back. The conversation was done. "There's somewhere else I need to be for Christmas this year, and it isn't there."

"I've already informed the press about your trip," Douglas said. "Your Aspen itinerary has been booked, and your friends are waiting. Face it. You're done in Chicago, Bennett. There is no going back to Ashby's."

Ash shook his head, his anger draining away into a kind of distant sympathy for the man who couldn't see past the walls he'd built around himself.

"Maybe not the way you see it, Father, but the way I see it, there's plenty still left for me to do back in Chicago. Money isn't everything. Money will never be everything to me again. There are bigger forces in play right now, and I need to trust in them."

Douglas scoffed. "Like what? Don't tell me you've found God, Bennett."

"No." Ash's eyes narrowed. "But I did find love, Father, and I don't care how much money it takes, or what it does to my reputation—I'm not going back to who I was before. I need to be a better man for him than that."

Without waiting for a reply, Ash turned and began to walk toward the office door. If his father wouldn't see reason, there was no point in arguing.

"When this man you're so determined to run back to turns as shallow as the rest of them and you're left with nothing, Ashby's will still be here waiting for your return," Douglas said, his parting shot. "I'll see to that."

"No matter if Elliott wants me or not," Ash's hand paused on the doorknob, "what he's shown me about love guarantees that I'll never have nothing again. I'm a changed man, Father, and I'm going to prove it to the rest of the world."

And, if things went the way he hoped, to Elliott.

Chapter 21

ELLIOTT

EVERY YEAR ON CHRISTMAS EVE, RIGHT AFTER THREE IN the afternoon, Santa bid goodbye to all the girls and boys with the promise that he'd be busy preparing for his long night of delivering presents. And then, from three until five, the North Pole was transformed. Santa's chair was hauled away, the mountains of fake snow were pushed aside and repositioned, and new ropes were set up to cordon off a circular area around where Santa's chair had once been.

The Giving Tree was moved there instead.

Absent of tags—every one claimed by generous store patrons looking to make a child's holiday wishes come true—it was placed front and center and strung up with lights, ornaments, and garlands.

Elliott had always thought it looked magical.

That it *was* magical.

A belief that hadn't diminished in the least by knowing exactly how that magic really happened.

Once the Giving Tree was installed and the scene was set, the Ashby's elves on duty brought out the gifts in huge, burlap drawstring bags and laid them out beneath it. And finally, when the final bag was placed and the scene was set, the overhead lights in the area were dimmed slightly so the glimmering lights on the tree came across more vibrantly than ever.

It was always one of Elliott's favorite moments of the year, but, this time, his enjoyment was diminished by the aftermath of what had happened.

Ben—*Ash*, he meant—wouldn't be there, and as far as management was concerned, Elliott probably shouldn't be, either. A sickening fear tightened his stomach and made him feel small, but since he hadn't formally been told not to attend, he'd refused to miss it.

At seven o'clock in the evening on Christmas Eve, the Children's Christmas Party began.

This year, the crowds were impressive. Boys and girls clustered around the roped off section of the Giving Tree while Grace and Trevor took center stage, guarding presents and keeping the kids engaged while they waited for the okay to begin gift giving. Parents stood on the other side of the ropes, watching and chatting amongst themselves. Elliott felt out of place standing with them when he'd been on the other side for so many years, but he hoped against hope that the position would make him invisible enough within the crowd that he wouldn't draw Martin's attention.

Even without an official order that he stay off Ashby's property, though, Elliott felt guilty coming back after everything Martin had said.

Elliott had never meant to steal from Ashby's. He'd never thought about it that way. But, yes, he could see now that it was technically true that he had—likely hundreds of dollars over the course of his employment—and, when it was put that way, it made Elliott feel culpable. Yes, he'd done it for a good reason, but the store policies were clear. No item was to be bought with the employee discount that wasn't for personal use. Gifts were out of the question.

He'd broken the rules, and he'd been punished for it, and he had nothing to say in his defense.

Without a job or the Christmas bonus he'd been expecting, it meant that rent would have to come out of his grocery budget for January. And, if he didn't find a new job by the first week of the new year, he might not be able to afford to eat at all come February.

But he had no one to blame but himself.

And no one to lean on to help him get through it.

Ben was gone.

Elliott had done his best not to linger on the loss, but

no matter what he told himself, it still hurt. Ben had lied to him, and Elliott had been too damn naive to see it. It hadn't been just the blond hair and hazel eyes that he'd missed, Elliott had come to realize. The illusion of "Ben" was so thin, it was almost transparent.

And Elliott *still* hadn't been able to see through it.

He'd wanted to believe that Ben was someone he could love, someone who could love Elliott back, so much that he'd ignored things that looked laughably obvious in hindsight.

Dinner at a French restaurant where the cheapest appetizers were fifty dollars a plate.

The black card.

The top floor luxury condo right off the water.

Even the custom-made Christmas sweater.

If he'd taken a second to put two and two together, he would have realized what was really going on. Instead, he'd buried his head in the sand because Ben was gorgeous and charming and interested in him. Because Elliott had been wooed. Because he thought that maybe they'd have a future together.

Because Elliott had fallen in love.

And, even now, knowing everything, it was one thing he couldn't seem to shake free of.

But Ben hadn't been who Elliott had thought he was. After finding out about Elliott's abuse of his employee discount when they'd visited Nick together, Ben must have brought it up with corporate. Maybe that's why he'd been there in the first place. Not for Elliott, of course, but to spy on how things were *really* handled out on the floor.

No wonder Martin had been so anal lately—the owner's son had quite literally been breathing down his neck.

And that hurt worse than anything. Even knowing Ben was Ash Ashby still felt a little surreal. Ash wasn't a real person. He was a media personality who Elliott had occasionally heard scandalous stories about. Having *Ben* tell corporate about Elliott's transgression was personal. Ben was real.

Or, at least, it had felt that way.

"Hello everyone! It's time to gather round."

Trevor's voice cut through the chatter, cheerful and buoyant and reminding Elliott of why he was there that night. This night, at least, wasn't about him and his troubles. It was about the children. The words Trevor spoke were directed at the kids, but they served to keep the parents informed as well, and by the time he opened his mouth again, he had everyone's attention.

Trevor grinned, always game to be the center of attention.

"We've just heard that Santa called in and that he's checked his list twice—all of the presents have arrived, and we've got the okay to start handing them out! Listen really closely for your first name and your initial, kids, and when you hear it, come on up to get your present."

Trevor was smiling almost as wide as the squealing children, if such a thing was possible, and his enthusiasm started to work on Elliott's attitude, too. Christmas really was magical, no matter what else happened.

"Remember," Trevor added, "if your mom or dad wants to have your picture taken when you come up for your present, we have photographers on site ready to do so! Now, if everyone's ready, quiet down so you can hear the first name."

The room went silent at once. It was the only time Elliott ever knew a room full of kids to go that quiet, and despite how he felt, he couldn't help but smile.

Trevor had always been a fantastic public speaker—Martin was smart to have asked him to emcee the event. Elliott had no doubt that if Trevor hadn't been such a good designer, he would have thrived in public relations. No matter what the situation, Trevor always knew what to say.

"Dude."

Elliott jumped, heart leaping into his throat. He whipped around to find Jose standing behind him, wearing his winter coat. "God, Jose, you scared me."

"Sorry, dude." Jose grinned, giving him a quick one-armed hug. "I'm glad to see you, though. The store is a mess without you here. I still can't believe what they did."

"I can."

The truth was, he'd deserved it. But it still hurt.

Elliott turned back to watch as Trevor and Grace answered questions from both parents and children. There were always a few, primarily from parents looking to buy photographs. With the carolers Ashby's hired on and the extensive decorations, it wasn't any wonder. Photographs taken at the event always turned out fantastic, and Elliott suspected that for many families—just like his own—the photographs would become treasured Christmas mementos for years to come.

"I knew what I was doing was wrong," Elliott said to Jose, not meeting his eyes. "But I did it anyway."

"Uh, dude, hello. No. You were pretty much Robin Hood," Jose said. "Total good guy, total badass. Martin's a Scrooge for letting you go. This whole North Pole thing this year? That's your baby. If he had any sort of heart at all, he would've at least kept you on until after Christmas."

"Thanks." Elliott managed a weak smile and leaned over to bump shoulders with Jose. No point telling him that it had most likely been out of Martin's hands, if Ben had taken it higher. "I miss you guys."

"We miss you, too. You should see Kevin's face since you left—smug and smirking like he's the fattest fly on Shit Mountain now that you're gone. Martin's never said, but all of us think it was him that told on you and Trevor. That dude's never been good news. He even traded his shift so he doesn't have to be here tonight and he's coming in to work on tearing down the displays on Christmas morning instead. Can you believe it?"

Kevin had never been a contender in Elliott's mind, and a sliver of hope that maybe it hadn't been Ben suddenly bloomed in his chest. Ever since the day that Ben had been outed as Ash and Elliott had been fired, Ben had been leaving short voicemails pleading with Elliott to pick up the phone and talk to him, or to call him back whenever he could.

So far, though, Elliott hadn't found the strength to do it. He'd been too hurt, and honestly wasn't sure he'd ever get to that point. The betrayal ran deep. But if Elliott was wrong... if there was a chance it hadn't been Ben who had turned him in...

Was it possible?

"I guess I can believe it of Kevin," Elliott said, ostensibly answering Jose's question.

It was something to think about. It was hope, at least, and having hope was never a bad thing, right?

Elliott cleared his throat, trying to keep his own hopes from getting the best of him. He had to remember that Ben was still *Ash*, and Elliott definitely wasn't Ash's type, no matter what Ben may or may not have done.

"Christmas just isn't special to some people," Jose said, snorting in response to Elliott's agreement about Kevin. "But that's why we've gotta make it extra special for the ones it *does* matter to. And looks like Trevor's about to do his part."

Jose pointed toward the Giving Tree, where Grace had just selected the first present from the overflowing pile and passed it to Trevor. It was starting. Trevor grinned, drawing out the moment with an appropriate level of dramatic showmanship, then opened the tag and read the name inscribed inside.

"The first present tonight is for... *Bianca F*! Bianca, are you here?"

A little girl squealed and rushed over to Trevor, looking up at him with wide eyes as she practically vibrated with excitement. Her mother came forward, too, and Trevor gave Bianca the wrapped gift and let Grace usher the two of them over to the photography station.

"Brendan L... Timothy R... Giselle N... Richard W...."

One by one, children made their way up to the front to accept their gift from Santa's favorite—and undoubtedly best-dressed—elf before either returning to the group, or joining the photographer off to the side for a photo session. It wasn't long before Elliott heard the names of some of the children he'd personally bought gifts for called up. His heart surged. No matter what the company policy said, it *had* been worth it. The children's eyes sparkled beneath the lights, and their broad grins as they accepted the gifts were exactly what made the Christmas season the magical time he'd always cherished.

For a little while at least, these children would keep believing in Christmas, and Elliott could never regret being a part of that.

He hoped that the joy of those moments would last them for a lifetime, the way it had for him.

"Here's one for... Giselle N." Trevor turned the gift over in his hand as though looking for another tag, and the surprise in his voice caught Elliott off guard.

Trevor was right to sound confused. Most of the time, there was one gift allocated per child, and Elliott's brows lowered in confusion as he watched little Giselle go up for the second time.

Another few names were called before Elliott started to hear the heavy repetition. Many of the kids in the audience were still giftless, while others were already claiming their second present.

"Oh no," Elliott whispered, leaning into Jose so Jose could hear. "You don't think they messed up and mislabeled the gifts, do you? I've never seen gifts doubled up like that before, but there are still so many kids without presents..."

"I don't know, dude." Jose pointed at the Giving Tree, cocking his head. "Look at how many presents are still left there. There are *way* more than average. You see that?"

Elliott tore his attention away from the kids to look back toward the mountain of presents. He counted them up as best as he could, then took an estimate of the number of kids gathered. It was normal for some kids not to show up—the information they gave allowed their gifts to be shipped, if they missed the party—but not even that explained the abundance of presents beneath the tree. There were more than enough there for every child to have two.

Something was off. But... maybe not in a bad way.

"Where did all those extra presents come from?" Elliott asked, breathless.

It wasn't his first time at the Children's Christmas Party, and he knew that whatever was happening was far from ordinary.

"Dunno, dude. Does it really matter?" Jose shrugged.

An almost magical prickle of awareness kissed the back of Elliott's neck a split-second before he got his answer.

"They're from me, Elliott."

Ben.

The little prickle turned into a jolt of sheer joy. It raced down Elliott's spine and buried itself in his lower back, suffusing him with a thrumming energy that suddenly made the festive decorations seem to glow all the brighter. Elliott stiffened his posture and froze as his heart raced with excitement.

There was no mistaking that voice, but Elliott's happiness died as quickly as it had appeared.

No matter what Ben made him feel, Ben wasn't real—he had to remember that it was Ash Ashby who had just answered his question, infamous playboy and spoiled socialite. The same man who'd led Elliott on for close to a month, who had promised him everything and then taken it all away.

The man who had broken his heart.

Elliott turned to face him. Ash was standing directly behind him. He looked like... Ben. Still dressed in the same wool coat he always wore, hands in his pockets, cheeks reddened as though he'd just come in from outside. He was effortlessly gorgeous, and despite knowing better, Elliott's stubborn heart insisted that even if Ben was Ash, he was still everything Elliott had always wanted.

Trying to convince himself otherwise was pointless. He was head over heels for the man, no matter what he called himself, and nothing was going to change that.

Elliott was screwed.

Chapter 22

ASH

ELLIOTT'S EYES WERE RED, LIKE HE'D BEEN CRYING, AND THE skin beneath them was puffy and darkened. He looked like he hadn't slept much since Ash had seen him last, and the sight twisted something up inside Ash. If he'd had the ability to have a single Christmas wish granted for real, it would have been that he'd never hurt Elliott.

Still, despite the strain that showed, Elliott was simply... gorgeous.

He looked exactly like everything Ash had never known he wanted.

He stood for a moment and just took him in, watching

as Elliott's lips parted, then closed again. Elliott was obviously struggling with his surprise at seeing Ash there, but Ash had no doubt that he'd find something to say any moment now. And he wouldn't blame Elliott in the least if whatever words he came up with were harsh ones.

Ash had lied to him, even after they'd shared the most intimate closeness possible. Whatever harsh words Elliott had for him would be well deserved, and Elliott had every right to say them.

Which wasn't going to make them any easier to hear.

Before Elliott could get his head on straight, Ash stepped forward to close the distance between them and sealed Elliott's lips in a gentle kiss.

It might not be fair, it might not even be welcome, but for Ash, it was as necessary as breathing.

If Elliott wanted to, he could pull away. Ash didn't hold him in place, nor was his kiss crushing or demanding. But, as simple as he kept it, it was also achingly sweet. They'd been apart for just a few days, but it felt like an eternity since Ash had felt Elliott's lips on his, or heard the already familiar, needy little inhalation Elliott always made whenever Ash touched him.

All the little things Ash had never remarked before, but that he'd missed dearly when they'd been apart. Being with Elliott felt right, and Ash wasn't going to let anything stand in the way of that.

Against all odds, Elliott returned his kiss.

He closed his eyes and hooked his fingers into the front of Ash's jacket, holding himself close. The sweet, tender moment deepened.

Then broke.

Elliott backed away and ran his arm across his eyes, clearing away unshed tears. His expressive, innocent eyes clouded with the anger and betrayal Ash had been expecting to see, and his lips—so soft a moment before—tightened into a thin line.

"Elliott, I'm sorry," Ash said before Elliott could get a word out, unable to stand it. "You have no idea how sorry I am, baby. I didn't want things to turn out this way, and it was never my intention to hurt you. You have to believe me. I came back to Chicago because I wanted to make things right, and because you inspired me. I went out of my way to make Christmas happen this year, and it's all because of you."

"You mean it's all because of Ashby's bottom line," Elliott said, the bitterness of the words not quite masking the hurt underneath.

Nothing about Elliott's expression changed, and at his side, Jose stood resolute, chest puffed and arms crossed. If things went sour, Ash knew that he would step in and come to Elliott's defenses, and a small part of him couldn't help but be glad that Elliott had people who cared about him so much.

Ash was one of them.

Now he just had to convince Elliott of that fact, and beg his forgiveness.

"No, my choices have nothing to do with Ashby's," Ash said, willing Elliott to believe him, because it was true. "They have everything to do with *you*, Elliott. And with all that you taught me while we were together. This isn't about making money or causing a media sensation or *anything* like that. The media thinks I'm heading to Aspen. No one knows I'm back here, and believe me, I don't want them to know."

The lines around Elliott's mouth loosened, but didn't completely relax. It was clear that he wasn't willing to forgive Ash just yet, but that he was also receptive to hearing what Ash had to say. From time to time, Elliott's attention flickered away as Trevor called another kid's name, or when one of the kids squealed with delight, but for the most part he remained focused on their conversation.

"I've never had the chance to appreciate Christmas until I came here and met you," Ash continued. He knew he was rambling, but he couldn't stop himself. If Elliott was giving him the chance to be heard, he wasn't going to leave anything out. "With my father busier than usual around the holidays, and with my mother as absent as she's been for my whole life, I never understood the appeal. I never got to experience trimming the tree while eating so many kolackies my stomach almost burst, or shopping for presents that have meaning rather than just an expensive price tag. But with you, treating me like I was your equal instead of a walking bank, I started to understand what the fuss was all about."

Elliott looked him over, eyes dropping down Ash's chest before rising back up to look him in the eye. Something stirred in his eyes that made Ash think he might still have a chance, and there was no way he was going to squander it.

He bared his soul.

"And beyond that..." Ash took in a deep breath. "I've never met anyone like you before. You're so special, and you don't even realize it. I'm *crazy* about you, Elliott. The time we spent together was no lie. I lov—"

"Excuse me." A new voice cut through their conversation, and Ash turned his head sharply in its direction.

A woman who looked vaguely familiar stood there, smiling. Her eyes glistened. It took Ash a second to recognize her as the mother of the little girl he'd spoken to in front of the Giving Tree. Abigail, her daughter, wasn't by her side, though.

"You're the employee who helped us by the Giving Tree, aren't you?" the woman said to Ash. "I saw you in the crowd and wanted to take a moment to thank you personally. You were right. Abigail just got called up to get her gift, and I don't think I've ever seen her so excited. Thank you for taking the time to explain the Giving Tree to her."

It was bad timing, but there was no way he could be rude to the woman. He didn't even want to be. Ash looked over at Elliott momentarily, silently apologizing, before he turned his attention to Abigail's mother.

"It was my pleasure. I'm glad to hear that she's having a good time."

The last of the presents were being passed out from the Giving Tree, and kids were starting to disperse. Abigail, the cautious little girl who Ash had spoken to, approached with two gifts—a sketchbook with a new set of colored pencils, and a miniature artist's manikin.

"Mr. Stranger," she said, smiling up at him and recognizing him instantly as the employee she'd spoken with at the Giving Tree. "I had a great time tonight. Thank you for telling me to make a wish. You were right—it really did come true."

Ash smiled. With as much hardship as he'd been through in the last few days, and for all that his future with Elliott still felt rocky and uncertain in that moment, he couldn't help but be touched by the joy on Abigail's face.

"I'm glad Santa was so good to you tonight," he said, the statement no less sincere for having played the role of Santa himself. "It pays to be good all year, doesn't it?"

"Mmhm," Abigail agreed with a decisive nod. "I think I'm going to draw Santa a picture to leave for him tonight to say thank you, along with his milk and cookies. Are you still going to be working here? I want to draw a picture for you, too."

Warmth bloomed through Ash's chest at her kindness,

and his smile grew. Was this what Elliott felt like all the time? Abigail's innocent joy was contagious.

"Nah, I was just working at Ashby's for the season," he said. "But if you want to draw me one anyway, you can send it to the employees at this store. I know they'll pass it along to me."

"Okay." She hugged the sketchbook against her chest. "I'll see you next Christmas, Mr. Stranger. Merry Christmas."

"Merry Christmas," Ash echoed back.

Abigail's mother smiled and waved, and, hand-in-hand, the two of them disappeared into the crowd. Parents had begun to lead their children away, and, relieved of their duties, Grace and Trevor were wandering in their direction. Jose intercepted them a short distance away, but Ash knew they were close enough that they would easily be able to overhear everything he and Elliott said.

He didn't care.

Clearing the air with Elliott was too important to wait, and if Ash had to do it with an audience, then so be it.

He turned back to Elliott. The lines of distress that had bracketed Elliott's normally expressive mouth a few moments before had abated, as had the anger in his eyes.

"I'm sorry about that," Ash said, gesturing in the direction that Abigail and her mother had gone.

"Don't apologize for that." Elliott glanced away as though taking a moment to compose himself. When he

298 · STELLA STARLING

turned back, his eyes were soft. "There are other things you have to apologize for, B—Ash, but *that* is not one of them."

"And I *want* to apologize for all those things." Ash breathed in deep and squared his shoulders. "But the only way I'm going to be able to do that is if you let me. I need time. Please."

The corner of Elliott's mouth trembled.

"We've got a lot to work out," Ash rushed in. "But the only way we're going to do that is if you give me a second chance. Let me prove to you that Ash is every bit of the man that Ben was, and that, regardless of what you call me, my intentions toward you have always been true."

Ash's heart beat heavily in his chest, and he fixed Elliott with a soulful stare that Elliott had begun to dodge. Something still wasn't right between them, and Ash struggled to find the right words.

"I meant what I said when I asked if you would be my boyfriend, and I'll ask it again, and *again*, if that's what it takes for you to take me back. I want to be with *you*, Elliott. The guy I was before I met you is gone. Please, let me be your boyfriend. Let me fix everything I messed up and make things right with you. Hell, I'll even come back to work the floor with you, if that will prove—"

"Martin fired me."

"*What?*"

Elliott, timid and always one to avoid conflict if he could, blinked away his tears and finally lifted his gaze to meet Ash's. "Was it you?" he asked, his voice cracking. "Did you tell him that I'd used my employee discount to buy the gifts for the Giving Tree, A-Ash?"

A part of Ash's brain noticed how Elliott had stumbled over calling him Ash, but that awareness was overridden by the pain that stabbed through his heart at the idea that Elliott would actually believe he would do something like that.

"*Hell*, no. Elliott, I would never be—"

Ash snapped his mouth closed on "betray you," frustrated that the words which burned within him might be seen as yet another lie. But it was true. The subterfuge as "Ben" had been set in motion before he'd known Elliott, but now that he did, Ash would never betray his trust again. Not intentionally. And he sure as hell hadn't in this regard.

He pinched the bridge of his nose, taking a deep breath and letting it out slowly. "Please believe me, Elliott," he said in a calmer voice. "It wasn't me, and I'm more than happy to look into where Martin got that information, but Elliott..."

Ash's shoulders drooped, and he let his argument trail off, unfinished.

Before Elliott, Ash had always been able to have whatever he wanted thanks to the Ashby name and money, but neither of those things would get him what he wanted now. Elliott had made him believe that Ash might be able to have the kind of things money couldn't buy, but with Elliott's silence stretching between them, Ash realized that he just might have to face that there were some things that would be forever beyond his reach.

That it might be too late for love.

Elliott was twisting his hands together, and Ash saw the moment that the last of his resistance stretched thin and finally snapped. Something shifted in his gaze, but he still didn't say anything. Elliott's bottom lip trembled, and he set his mouth and squared his jaw in a clear effort to hold off his emotions.

Ash knew that the secrets he'd kept and the lies he told weren't small, and that Elliott had a right to refuse to forgive him, but, deep in his heart, he'd honestly thought that he'd still had a chance. His feelings for Elliott were deep, and Elliott had always been so kind and understanding that Ash had dared to hope that the outcome of this night would be different.

Silence was the cruelest kind of rejection.

"I'm sorry," Ash whispered. He dropped his gaze and took a small step back. "You have no idea how sorry I am, Elliott. I know that I've hurt you, and I respect your decision. I won't interfere with your life anymore."

It was really over between them.

A jagged ache throbbed in Ash's ribs and left him broken. What did his life mean without Elliott in it? In three short weeks, Elliott had changed everything Ash stood for. Everything he'd known.

He didn't want to go back to the shallow person he'd been prior to his time in Chicago, but continuing on without Elliott there by his side was a new kind of pain that—now that he was actually faced with it—Ash wasn't at all sure he could deal with.

Elliott was special.

Ash swallowed, trying to find it in him to accept the loss. He'd laid his heart on the line, and Elliott's silence had been his answer. Still, no matter how long he lived, Ash knew he would never forget what Elliott had meant to him.

How he had changed--become a better man—because of him.

Ash started to turn away.

"Stop."

Elliott took a step forward to shrink the distance between them. His voice was firm and confident in a way that Ash had never heard from him before, and an almost painfully sharp spike of hope spiked through the agony of rejection in his chest.

Elliott smiled, and in a moment, everything changed. "I didn't say no, Ash."

Ash's face felt like it practically split in two, his smile stretching across it so fast and wide that he couldn't have stopped it if he'd tried.

"You didn't say yes, either," he pointed out, a fierce joy bubbling up inside him.

Somehow, they'd moved closer. There was a small distance between them still, but it felt like it stretched for miles. Ash braved it, reaching out to lay a hand on Elliott's arm.

Elliott didn't pull away.

"Can I be your boyfriend again?" Ash asked, trying his best to temper his feelings until he knew for sure that Elliott's actions meant what he desperately hoped they did. "If you can't give me a yes or a no right now, I understand, but can you at least tell me you'll think about it? That's all I ask."

Elliott shook his head, and Ash geared himself for rejection all over again, his emotions on a rollercoaster.

If Elliott was only going to tear him down, why had he made him stay? His silence had been bad enough, but this...

"I don't want you to go," Elliott said at last. The words he spoke quivered, softened still by the hint of uncertainty and fear. "I want you to stay with me, Ash, and I want you to be my boyfriend. I just don't want to be hurt again. I don't want Ash Ashby to chew me up and spit me out like you do with all the other guys you've been linked with." He swallowed nervously, but his gaze didn't waver. "When I say I want you, Ash, I don't mean for this week, or for this month... I want you unconditionally."

"You know the truth about me now." The hope swelled inside him again, and Ash grinned, letting himself believe. "There's nothing left hidden between us. I want you unconditionally, too, Elliott. I *love* you."

How long had he known it?

The words felt natural. *True.* And Ash couldn't have said whether loving Elliott had come on all at once and hit him hard—yes—or whether it had crept in slowly, rooting itself deep in his soul the more time they'd spent together—also yes.

Elliott had changed him, not because Elliott had insisted upon it, but because, with Elliott, Ash had wanted to be someone better, and Elliott had made him believe that he truly could be.

"I love you, Elliott," Ash repeated, pulling him into his arms.

Elliott's back stiffened for a moment and the breath hitched in the back of his throat delicately. But then his body began to ease, melting against Ash as he held Ash's gaze steady. His eyes had begun to water, and there was a docile affection in them that had risen up from amongst the hurt to soothe the damage done.

"I love you, too," he said, the truth of the words shining out of his eyes and making Ash catch his breath.

"Does that mean I can still come for Christmas dinner tomorrow at your mom's place?" Ash asked, his tone teasing, but the question real.

His hand slipped down Elliott's arm to take his hand, and Elliott's fingers squeezed gently to make sure Ash didn't let go. Dizzy with happiness and heart racing from the adrenaline of the moment, Ash felt like he was falling in love all over again.

Something he'd happily do every single day, if Elliott would let him.

"You really want to come over for Christmas at my mom's crummy little apartment?" Elliott asked, Ash's question startling a laugh out of him. The lights from the Giving Tree glistened in his eyes, and Ash could see that he was near tears. "We don't have anything fancy to offer you. I'm sure that you're used to luxury and riches, and you'll probably want—"

Ash silenced him with a kiss before he could say anything more. Just Elliott had been enough for him before, and he would *always* be enough going forward. No promise of luxury could change that. Ash had had luxuries. Now he wanted something more valuable.

When the kiss ended and Elliott's lidded eyes were focused on him once more, Ash whispered the words that had lived in his heart since life had brought them together. He meant them with everything he was, and everything he would be.

"Elliott, stop overthinking it. Don't you see? All I want is *you*."

Chapter 23

ELLIOTT

DONNER SKITTERED FORWARD, HIS CLAWS CLACKING against the wooden floor of Elliott's apartment. Tail wagging at about a millions miles per hour and nose to the ground, he followed the length of the wall before bolting across the room, tongue lolling, to investigate the other side. Ash set down Donner's bed by the door and his food and leash on the small table where Elliott kept his mail, his face breaking into a gorgeous smile as he watched the little dog exploring.

"Are you sure that you wouldn't rather have stayed at your place?" Elliott asked, looking at his humble apartment through fresh eyes. Or rather, eyes that tried to see it as Ash Ashby would. Elliott frowned.

The Children's Christmas Party was over, but the surprise of seeing Ash there and hearing his heartfelt confession was still fresh on Elliott's mind. Ash had said that he *loved* him, and Elliott believed him.

Part of him recognized that it might still be foolish and naive of him, but Elliott had always been someone who let his heart reign over his mind. Now that some of his hurt and sense of betrayal were allayed—he *did* believe Ash when he said he hadn't been the one to tell Martin about Elliott's transgression—he could see clearly all the little things that proved Ash was being sincere, even if he'd had to hide his identity at first. It was in the way Ash spoke to him, and the ways he acted, a thousand tiny moments that a man like Ash Ashby would have no reason to fake, that convinced Elliott that his affections were sincere.

And, based on the enthusiasm with which Grace, Trevor, and Jose had crowed and clapped and caused a scene once Ash and Elliott's declarations of love were out of the way back at the party, Elliott had reason to believe that his friends thought highly of Ash, too.

Still, Ash was used to a completely different lifestyle than he'd find at Elliott's apartment.

"Ash, are you sure—" Elliott started again, noting that Ash hadn't answered him yet.

"Nope. I'm positive," Ash said decisively, cutting him

off. The lights in the apartment were off, but the glow of the lights from Elliott's Christmas tree was bright enough that the darkness wasn't overwhelming, and Ash's eyes glowed with sincerity. "Elliott, that place isn't home to me. *You're* home. And I want to be here tonight, where everything feels like you."

Elliott glanced across his tiny apartment, moved. And... at least the place was tidy this time. The dishes were washed and drying, the living room was picked up, and he'd been able to do a load of laundry and wash the sheets before heading out to Ashby's for the party.

"You don't have to lay it on that thick, you know," he joked, hoping he wasn't overstepping any boundaries. There was still a certain rawness about their relationship that would only heal with time. "I know it's small and not what you're used to. I wouldn't mind if we—"

But before he could finish that sentence, either, Ash stepped in front of him and laid a finger over his lips. Face to face, all Elliott could do was take him in. Dark roots had started to show at the base of Ash's platinum blond hair, but he'd removed the hazel contacts that Elliott had always thought looked so odd. With them out, Ash's eyes were a shade of blue that reminded Elliott of the ocean. In the glow of the Christmas tree, they were dark and hauntingly beautiful.

A deliciously sharp flare of arousal twisted through Elliott's groin.

"You're overthinking it again," Ash insisted softly. He

let his finger slip away from Elliott's lips. "I might be an Ashby by birth, but that doesn't mean that I can't live like everybody else. Your apartment is perfect. It doesn't matter how big it is, or what caliber of furniture you furnish it with, or even if it has good water pressure."

"It doesn't," Elliott murmured, mesmerized.

"And I," Ash's eyes were lit by the light of the tiny tree, and they flashed as he leaned closer so that their lips brushed as he spoke, "don't give a shit about that. What matters to me is that we have a place where we can be *us*, and that's not going to be at my father's sterile penthouse with all the stuffy rich jerks in the homeowners' association breathing down our necks about every move we make."

The dip of Ash's voice bordered on seductive, and Elliott turned his head just a touch to the side and pressed their lips together for a soft, short kiss. Even the slightest touch from Ash got under his skin and riled him, and Elliott didn't think that was ever going to change.

"What kind of moves are we talking about?" Elliott asked in a teasing whisper. His eyelids had lowered to half-mast, and he wrapped his arms around Ash's neck loosely as they spoke, letting Ash's unwavering devotion give him confidence. "Sounds like you're thinking we're going to get into a lot of trouble."

"If I have my way," Ash whispered back, breaking his sentence to kiss Elliott a touch more firmly than Elliott had kissed him. The corkscrew of arousal that had worked itself through Elliott radiated with desire, and Elliott kissed him back while longing for more. "We'll get into every kind of trouble you can get into. All day. Every day."

"You talk big," Elliott teased, returning Ash's kiss and falling for him more with every passing second. When Ash kissed him back and wrapped his arms around Elliott's waist, pulling him close, Elliott moaned into his mouth and continued. "But can you back it up?"

The discomfort of a growing erection intensified as Ash slid his thigh between Elliott's legs, opening him up and giving him something to grind against. Bold, Elliott took him up on his offer and chased the friction his cock needed. He kissed Ash hard, and Ash held him closer and kissed him back.

It had been a tough holiday season—Elliott couldn't deny it. From the soaring highs to the crushing lows, he'd experienced fear and uncertainty and heartbreak, but he'd also found love. Safe in Ash's arms, still buzzed by the joy of hearing Ash express his love, and grateful that the relationship he'd built with Ben wasn't a sham after all, Elliott couldn't recall a time when he was happier.

There had been boyfriends in his past—guys he thought he'd loved at the time—but nothing felt as satisfying or as right as what he shared with Ash. And even should that love fizzle or prove to be another publicity stunt, Elliott knew that he would be left richer for having loved so fully and so deeply.

But his heart told him he had nothing to fear, and that Ash wasn't about to stray. That what Elliott felt, Ash felt in return. And he was going to go ahead and believe that it was true. That Ash Ashby's wild days as a celebrity playboy were really over, and that he meant every single thing he whispered so sincerely in Elliott's ears.

Ash said that he'd found his purpose, and that purpose was Elliott.

The kiss ended, and Ash withdrew his leg and tugged Elliott across the room. Donner circled their feet, overjoyed to be with them again and begging for attention. Neither Elliott nor Ash noticed.

On the way to the bedroom door, Ash pushed Elliott against the wall and kissed him once again. Elliott's cock throbbed at the display of dominance, and he wove his fingers through Ash's hair and kissed him back with everything he was worth.

When had he ever wanted somebody as badly as he wanted Ash? It wasn't just about sex, although Elliott couldn't deny that he wanted to feel Ash claim him all over again. What joined them was more substantial.

Love.

Ash *loved* him, and in his kiss, as heated as it was, Elliott felt it. The passion they shared for one another was unparalleled. "Ben" might not have been real, but the things Elliott had felt for him were.

And Ben, Elliott was accepting, *was* Ash, no matter what the media chose to believe.

The name didn't matter. It was the man he was inside that made it true.

Ash pulled Elliott back into his arms, and they stumbled together to the bedroom, shutting the door behind them. The overhead light flickered on, and Elliott broke the kiss to look toward the light switch. Ash had turned it on.

"You don't want to leave it off?" Elliott asked, a blush reddening his cheeks.

"No, baby. I want to see you," Ash replied. He pulled Elliott forward, and soon enough they'd sunk down onto the bed in a tangle of limbs, lips locked.

Neither of them had so much as shed their coats. Ash corrected that situation quickly, and Elliott obliged him by lifting his body and shifting his weight as Ash stripped him.

Love.

Would they still want one another like this in a year's time, coming home together with groceries in their arms and tired from a long walk up the stairs to their apartment? Would Ash still pin him against the wall and kiss him like he was the hottest man alive?

Elliott thought that they would.

He knew he tended to invest himself in the things he cared about. To dive in, wholeheartedly, when it mattered.

And Ash mattered.

Better, Elliott trusted that *he* mattered to Ash.

He couldn't imagine a time when they wouldn't be in love, or when he wouldn't want to touch Ash like he was touching him right now.

Elliott's shirt hit the ground, and Ash planted a heated kiss upon the center of his chest. Elliott sucked in a breath and closed his eyes. Ash's touch left Elliott speechless.

The belt around Elliott's waist loosened, then fell open. The button of his fly parted, and the zipper came undone. Elliott still hadn't opened his eyes, but he felt the bed shift, and soon he understood why. For a moment, there was a chill as Ash pulled his boxers down his thighs and exposed his rigid cock, but the next moment Elliott didn't suffer from the cold at all. Wet heat enveloped him, and he gasped and opened his eyes to watch as Ash's lips closed around his shaft. In the bright bedroom light, Ash's turquoise eyes were vivid, and they looked up at Elliott directly as Ash lowered his head and took Elliott in further.

"A-Ash," Elliott breathed. "Oh my God, Ash..."

Ash took him in even deeper, tongue darting and swirling and pressing against Elliott, and Elliott laid back and let the rampant bliss Ash shared wash over him.

It had to be some mistake. Elliott had dreamed that one day he would meet a man who treated him kindly and who loved him for who he was, naïveté and innocence included, but never had he imagined that man would be someone like Ash Ashby. And even if he'd dreamed it, Elliott knew he'd never have imagined that Ash Ashby was the kind of man that Ash really was.

Kind. Compassionate. Giving. Accepting.

It felt like he'd won the lottery.

As Ash worked him over with his mouth, sucking him

in only to back off and do it all over again, Elliott lost himself to the fantasy come to life. It wasn't the riches or the recognition that enraptured him, but the kindness of the man he'd discovered lurked in Ash's heart.

Quiet nights on the couch, wrapped in each other's arms while they watched a movie. Trips to the beach, where Ash showed off and strutted his stuff just to make Elliott laugh. Walks in the park with Donner, hand in hand, while they talked about their plans for the future.

Nothing was out of reach.

Elliott's pleasure spiked as Ash lapped over his glans and toyed with his tip, and Elliott couldn't help but lift his hips and moan loudly. "A-Ash."

"Not yet." Ash pressed a parting kiss against Elliott's cock, then drew up his body so they were chest to chest again. As he settled, Elliott felt Ash's skin against his—Ash had stripped when he wasn't watching. "Do you have condoms here, baby? I want to feel you again. I want to show you how much I love you."

Never before had Elliott been wound so tight from arousal. His body practically vibrated as he reached up, cupped the back of Ash's head, and kissed him fiercely. Ash gasped in surprise and kissed him back with just as much enthusiasm, and they kissed and ground against each other for a while, unable to tolerate the thought of splitting apart.

Drained of stamina and panting for breath, the kiss ended. Winded, Elliott gestured to the basket beneath his bedside table. "I bought them thinking that after what we did at your place, that I might need them here."

"And lube?" Ash asked, just as breathless.

"Mmhm. Same place." Embarrassment burned in Elliott's cheeks at the admission, but he was glad that he'd prepared. He wanted to feel Ash inside of him, knowing that it was a promise of more days to follow spent at his side. "Please. Hurry."

Ash didn't waste any more time. He rolled off Elliott to reach for the contents of the basket and fished around. Elliott heard the shuffle of thin cardboard as Ash slid the side of the box open, and moments later, he returned with both a condom and the bottle of lube in hand.

Elliott parted his lips to speak, but before he could, Ash kissed him into silence. Elliott forgot what he'd been about to say. Ash's lips became his focus, and he kissed them as though they were the only thing that mattered. Vaguely, he was aware of the crinkle of foil, but when Ash's tongue caressed his lips and then slipped into his mouth, Elliott didn't think any more of it.

For that moment, Ash was his, and he never wanted to lose him again.

Lost in his desire, Elliott lifted his hips easily when Ash's hand urged him to, and when Ash's fingers pressed to enter him, bearing with them slick lubricant, Elliott relaxed and prepared himself for the intrusion.

He wanted Ash more than he could put into words.

Ash's fingers prepped him, introducing lubricant and easing Elliott into sex, and Elliott closed his eyes and rode against them as his body gave in and his cock throbbed. Their kiss broke, Ash gasping for breath, and Elliott took the chance to reach down to stroke his cock as Ash played with him.

Ash's amazing turquoise eyes turned hot and needy at the sight, making Elliott feel sexy. Bold. *Loved.*

"Want you," Ash whispered, pressing a hot kiss against his neck while he continued to thrust his fingers in a maddening rhythm that was going to drive Elliott crazy. "I want you so bad, baby."

"Want you, too," Elliott managed to say through an embarrassingly loud moan as he shamelessly ground himself against Ash's hand, his own hand speeding up on his cock. "Please, Ash. *Please.* I need you."

Ash pulled his fingers out, and the sudden emptiness left Elliott feeling bereft. He groaned, reaching for Ash as Ash hefted his hips and moved him into position. Elliott needed more, and he would be out of his mind until he got it, but—for as hungry as Ash's kiss had been—he wouldn't be rushed.

Elliott could tell Ash was taking care with him, just as he had when he'd known it was Elliott's first time, and even though he was starting to feel almost desperate for Ash to do *more*, the tenderness made him feel cherished. But, finally, the weight of Ash's body pressed him into the mattress and they rocked together, shifting in a delicious slide of hot skin and slick cocks as Ash positioned himself. And then Elliott felt the thick pressure of his cock, seeking entrance.

Elliott yielded to him, gasping as Ash breached and filled him. Giving him exactly what he needed.

"Love you," Ash whispered, finally buried inside him.

Elliott arched his back, rolling his hips against the perfect weight of Ash's body. Desperate, but just as needy for the sweetness of Ash's words, the loving look he gave him, as he was for the pressure of his cock inside him.

Ash moved above him, and they struck a rhythm together that stirred Elliott in all the right ways. Tangled in each other's bodies, Elliott wrapped his arms around Ash's neck and buried his face against the crook of Ash's neck. The smell of his cologne, subtle but distinctive, flooded Elliott's nostrils and left him craving more. They hadn't been separated for long, but it was long enough that Elliott knew he never wanted to be without Ash again.

The gaping space in his heart was filled. The anguish he'd felt while they were apart was gone. Ash completed him, and no matter how Elliott had tried to persuade himself otherwise, now that he was back in Ash's arms there was no denying it.

He'd wanted someone to love for Christmas, and that was exactly what he'd gotten. He just hadn't realized how amazing it would feel to have that someone love him back so perfectly.

Elliott was blessed.

He pushed his head back against the pillows and writhed, heart pounding and mind fogging over, as primal urges took over. Ash's hands held him tight as he pinned Elliott down with the weight of his body, and Elliott didn't want to be anywhere other than right there, in the heated embrace of the man he loved.

The man who was driving him closer and closer to a release his entire body cried out for.

Time slipped away from them. The sheets rumpled, then were kicked aside. Ash's hips didn't stop, and Elliott met him every time, even when the air was stolen from his lungs and his thighs ached from strain. Ash's lips were on his, and his tongue danced across Elliott's. The hand Elliott worked across his cock kept pumping, dragging him closer and closer to the edge. Pleasure coiled inside of him, clenching low in his gut.

Their hearts beat as one and Elliott gasped as Ash crushed their mouths together, as close to the edge as Elliott was.

"I'm coming, baby," Ash groaned. "Oh fuck, Elliott. You have no idea how good you feel. Love you so much."

The blinding pleasure that had built up inside of Elliott bubbled over, and he couldn't hold himself back any longer. Ash *loved* him. Ash loved him, and he'd come back for him. They were going to have Christmas together.

They had a future.

Elliott drew in a ragged breath and tightened as release

struck. Ash was working deep inside of him, pushing against him in all the right ways to prolong his orgasm.

"Love you," Elliott gasped against Ash's lips, eyelids shut tight as he came hard. "Love you, Ash. Love you s-so much."

Ash's cock throbbed inside of him, and Elliott ground against it, taking one last huff of breath before he collapsed back onto the bed, totally spent.

In seconds, Ash joined him, pressing hot kisses to his shoulder and neck before settling down.

"Merry Christmas, baby," Ash whispered. "You up for healthy or greasy takeout tomorrow morning?"

Elliott laughed.

Despite all that had happened, somehow everything was going to be alright.

He just knew it.

Chapter 24

ASH

"I GOT YOU A LITTLE SOMETHING, TOO," ASH ADMITTED, looking up at Anna Gaffney from where he sat on the floor next to Elliott.

They were both seated in front of Elliott's mother's Christmas tree, the glow of green and yellow and red bulbs lighting them from behind. They'd donned their ugly Christmas sweaters for the occasion, and Elliott had found his old elf hat from his old Ashby's elf outfit and wore it, too.

It was the perfect level of campy for Ash's first legitimate Christmas, and he couldn't stop smiling.

Of course, he'd pretty much felt that way ever since Elliott had told him that he loved him, too.

Only a few presents were left beneath the tree now. Most had been destined for either Elliott or his mother, of course, but Ash was surprised to find that Anna had gone out of her way to make sure there were presents to open for him as well. He was now the proud owner of two pairs of fuzzy thermal socks and a thermal mug stuffed with hot chocolate packages, and regardless of what anyone in his former life might have thought about the gifts, Ash felt beyond blessed.

It looked like Elliott had inherited his kindheartedness from a very remarkable woman.

"You did not, Ash," Anna protested, crossing her arms as her cheeks went pink.

Elliott's mother had instantly adjusted to his "new" name, and hadn't made a fuss at all about who he was in any sense other than "Elliott's boyfriend." Ash appreciated that more than he could put into words, and had been genuinely eager to get her a gift.

She sat on the couch, the presents she'd already opened occupying the seat beside her. Elliott had bought her a few series box sets on DVD, some chocolate-covered cherries, and a few new plants for the spice garden she grew on the window ledge in the kitchen.

"I did," Ash admitted, grinning. "I couldn't show up to Christmas without bringing the hostess something to show my thanks."

Elliott glanced at him out of the corner of his eye, brows lightly furrowed as he visibly tried to work out what

Ash had done. Ash hadn't discussed the gift with him beforehand, because he knew Elliott would protest. It was last minute, and it was rushed, but Ash was confident that he'd put together something that Anna would truly enjoy.

And the truth was, he'd discovered that there was a joy to being the giver—especially when it was to people who mattered to him—that nothing else could compare to. His grin widened.

"I didn't see you come in with anything, Ash," Elliott said carefully.

"You're right. It's waiting outside; I just got the text." Ash picked himself up from the floor, brushed off the back of his pants, and bowed his head to Anna. "If you'll excuse me."

"What in the world is going on?" she asked, clearly startled by the whole setup.

"Give me a few more seconds and you'll see." Ash winked and jogged to the door, heart flooding with excitement.

Donner followed at his side, tail ever wagging. If everything had come together like Ash hoped it would, the gift waiting on the other side of the door was going to make an impact. When he'd brought up the idea of lavishing Elliott with a few high-end gifts the night before, Elliott had immediately shot him down, so Ash justified the gifts for Elliott's mother with the excuse that he needed to spoil *someone*.

Ash opened the front door to the apartment to find his

personal assistant, Stacey, standing on the other side. She held a thin, cheerfully wrapped box and as soon as Ash opened the door, she smiled, eyes twinkling with delight.

"Merry Christmas, Mr. Ashby," she said, sounding like she meant it. "Everything's in order. Have you been enjoying your stay?"

"Very much so," Ash replied, smiling back. Donner wandered out to circle around her legs, sniffing with curiosity, and Stacey stooped down for a moment to scratch him behind the ear. "And how has your Christmas been so far, Stacey?"

"It's going great," she said enthusiastically, sounding like she meant it. "I'm so grateful that you arranged to fly me out this way for Christmas last minute like this—you should have seen the look on my parents' faces when they opened the door this morning to find me there instead of in New York. Really, Mr. Ashby, I can't thank you enough."

Her eyes glistened, and Ash's grin widened. It really was fun to be the one who brought other people holiday cheer. He totally got why Elliott seemed addicted to it.

Stacey stood and held out the gift she'd delivered for Anna and Ash accepted the box from her.

"I'm glad you're having a good time," he told her sincerely. "Now go get back to it, okay? And let me know when, or if, you're interested in flying back to New York. Although I'm going to be staying in Chicago for the foreseeable future, and if you'd prefer to arrange living accommodations for yourself, moving expenses paid for courtesy of the Ashby's, of course, I'd be honored to keep you on as my assistant."

"I'll let you know." Stacey brushed a stray strand of hair away from her face and beamed at him. "Have a good night, Mr. Ashby."

"Goodnight."

Stacey waved and headed down the hall, and Ash whistled for Donner, then closed the door once he was back inside. With a spring in his step, he returned to the living room, gift in hand. Elliott was still seated in front of the tree, but Anna had risen from the couch and had crouched down to speak with him in private. When Ash returned, she stood and turned to face him.

"This is for you." Ash joined the pair and held the gift out to Anna. "Merry Christmas."

Anna's eyes flicked over him, both nervous and pleased. She worked one flap of the wrapping paper up and slid the box out from inside without tearing the paper. Elliott, Ash noticed, always did the same.

The box was flat but large enough in size that it wasn't small. There was little illusion about what was inside. Elliott shook his head and laughed, catching on immediately.

"*Really?*" he asked, grinning at Ash

"I couldn't leave your mom out," Ash replied, shrugging happily.

Anna lifted the top of the box to reveal a neatly folded ugly Christmas sweater inside. Hers was blue and white, covered in lopsided snowflakes and poorly constructed snowmen. Anna looked down at the sweater, looked up at Ash, and shook her head. She was smiling.

"Thank you, Ash. This was really thoughtful."

"The sweater's mandatory," Ash insisted. "We're going to have a day where we all embarrass each other by wearing them out, okay?"

"What are you talking about?" Anna hitched a brow and laughed.

"Take the sweater out of the box. You'll see."

Elliott rose to his feet and came over to watch the scene unfold. He fell into place at Ash's side and slipped his hand into Ash's, and Ash leaned against him gently and squeezed it in response.

Anna set the box down on the couch and lifted the sweater out of the box. The sweater's arms unfolded, and from inside toppled an envelope stuffed thickly with papers.

"What in the world," Anna murmured. She reached down to pick up the envelope and parted the flap. From inside, she withdrew the papers and gave them a quick glance. Her lips parted in shock, and she looked over the papers and directly at Ash.

"No," she said, even though her eyes were glowing. "Ash, I can't accept this."

"If you don't accept it, it'll go to waste. The money's already spent."

"But my job—"

"Novotex, right?" Ash asked. Her eyes rounded with

shock as he spoke, and Ash saw Elliott in them clearly. "Novotex has been partnered with Ashby's since the 1980s. I had a few phone calls made and they've agreed to let you take vacation without penalty. The money you would miss out on making is part of my gift to you, so you don't have to worry about rent or groceries."

Looking for answers, Elliott slipped his hand out of Ash's and went to peek over his mother's shoulder. "Ash!"

"What?" Ash crossed his arms stubbornly. "You told me that I wasn't allowed to spoil you, Elliott, so I'm going to ask your mom to do it on my behalf. It's only fair, if you ask me."

"An all-expenses paid trip for two to Aspen?" Anna asked, staring Ash down. The tickets were in her and Elliott's names. "Honey, this is too much. We can't accept a gift like this."

"I want to share the place I've spent so many of my Christmases at with the two of you," Ash said. "You've shared so much of your world with me, and now I want to share a little of mine with you... and hopefully make some new memories—better ones—in a place that's always felt a little hollow. If you don't like skiing, there are plenty of resort activities and shops. Of course, we could stay in and watch movies, too. The cabins are fantastic."

"I still need to worry about finding a job, Ash," Elliott admitted, embarrassed. "If I don't find something between now and the new year, I'm going to be cutting it really tight, and I might not be able to afford to keep my apartment. I'm not sure that I can go."

Donner wove around Elliott's legs, the Santa head dog toy Elliott had gifted to him clutched proudly in his mouth, and Elliott reached down to scratch his head automatically. He laughed, the sound a bit strained. Ash was still pissed that Elliott had lost his job—he'd found out that it had been Kevin, and had taken action to make sure that both the sour employee and Martin received appropriative treatment from corporate—but the worst part was seeing the strain it put on Elliott.

"About your job—"

Elliott waved him off, his shoulders relaxing. "Now's not the time. Sorry. I'll work that out a little later. Today is *Christmas*, and this is a time to be thankful and hopeful. Besides, I could always apply to places online from Aspen, right?" Elliott grinned, his natural optimism shining through. "I probably wouldn't get any interviews until the new year, anyway."

Donner had wandered off to investigate some discarded wrapping paper, and Elliott straightened his posture. Ash took the chance to step forward and kiss him, sweetly and tenderly, in an attempt to soothe his nerves.

Elliott had nothing to worry about.

It was still in the works, but Ash had already made a few phone calls early that morning while Elliott was asleep, and the charitable branch Ash wanted to set up as a subset of Ashby's looked like it would fly with the board. If the project was approved, Ash wanted Elliott on board. Given access to funds and the power to make a difference, he knew that Elliott was going to soar.

Until then, it wasn't as if Ash would ever let Elliott go without food or shelter. It was early into their relationship, but Ash felt certain it wouldn't be long until he moved in permanently, or they found their own place together.

And from there, Elliott would never have to worry again.

"We'll figure it out together, baby," he said, respecting Elliott's desire to table the subject for another time. Still, Ash couldn't help but offer a little reassurance. "Don't worry. I know there are going to be fantastic things in your future, and we're going to find them together, okay? But you deserve a vacation as much as your mom does, and I want this to happen for you."

Ash traced his fingers along Elliott's cheek, and Elliott melted into him. The tension ebbed from his shoulders, and he smiled sincerely.

"I love you," Elliott whispered, resting his head against Ash's shoulder.

"Love you, too," Ash whispered back, holding him close. "Merry Christmas."

"Hold on, boys. Christmas isn't over yet," Anna said.

There were still a few gifts left beneath the tree, and from amongst them she chose a small, square box about the size of a grapefruit wrapped in silver paper. Elliott pulled away from Ash and caught his eye, blissful with happiness.

"Elliott and I collaborated on one last present for you, Ash," Anna said, bringing the box over and handing it to him.

It barely weighed a thing, and it was packaged in such a way that Ash couldn't imagine what might be inside. He looked between the two of them as they grinned at him, and Anna drew Elliott beneath her arm and hugged him from the side as they watched Ash tear into the paper.

Inside was a nondescript box, sealed with a short piece of transparent tape. Ash worked the tape off, then opened the box from the top and drew the object out from inside. Ash turned it over in his hand, absorbing the details, before he looked back up at Elliott and Anna in awe.

They'd given him a hand-painted Christmas ornament.

Ben was written across the front of the bauble in an elegant hand, and it was painted with Christmas trees and Santa hats and nutcrackers.

"My mom and I designed it together right after you said you'd come for Christmas," Elliott explained. "She was the one who painted it, but I kind of thought it out and made sure it was something you might like. I know it's not much, but—"

"No." Ash's voice quivered when he spoke, and it surprised him. He'd never felt as pure of an emotion as he did in that moment. "It's beautiful, Elliott. Really. You have no idea how much this means to me."

"You wanna hang it up and then watch us unwrap the

rest of our socks and underwear?" Elliott asked with a laugh. "Gaffney Christmases aren't too exciting, I'm afraid."

"Gaffney Christmases are everything I always wanted, but never knew I was missing," Ash uttered. The simple truth.

He stepped forward and kissed Elliott again, letting the touch of their lips linger for longer this time around. Overcome with joy, Ash's chest was light, and he knew that if he didn't pull himself together soon, he was going to start shedding tears.

Not only had Elliott given Ash his love, but he'd given him a family. A real family. The significance of the bauble wasn't lost on him, and it had nothing to do with the kind of value Ash had grown up being told mattered. Its value was of another sort altogether.

Ash would cherish it forever.

"And so long as you'll have me, Elliott, this is the only kind of Christmas I'll ever want again."

Epilogue

ELLIOTT

Christmas, One Year Later

IT DIDN'T FEEL LIKE AN ENTIRE YEAR HAD PASSED SINCE EL-liott had last walked through the sliding front doors of Ashby's Chicago as an employee, but as he stepped in from the cold and felt his feet sink into the familiar, plush carpet—hand-in-hand with Ash—he realized that it really had been that long. Last year's Christmas debacle was history, and this year's Christmas was looking brighter than ever.

And, judging by the crowd of eager shoppers hunting for last minute deals that Elliott saw immediately upon entering, he figured that business at his former place of employment was doing just as well as his heart was.

"You think someone's going to notice me?" Ash whispered in Elliott's ear as they made their way across the floor and toward the escalator.

The cheeky humor in his words made Elliott grin, and he squeezed Ash's hand.

"If no one else notices you, I promise *I* will. You're the most attractive man in here."

"I'm afraid I'm going to have to fight you on that one," Ash whispered back. "That's your title, baby. Always has been, always will be."

Elliott shot him a playful look, but he couldn't hide his smile. After all this time, their chemistry still dazzled, and Elliott was more in love with Ash than ever.

"But to answer your question honestly, you might get a few people coming up to you, but I don't anticipate you're going to be swamped like you were last year. Your father has no reason to call any camera crews on you." Elliott grinned, adding, "I made sure that Stacey sent him a very nice bottle of scotch from the both of us, so he should still be on our side for the new few weeks."

Ash's smile grew, and he stepped in time with Elliott onto the escalator, drawing Elliott into his arms.

"I'm glad he came around when he met you. I was ready to never speak to him again."

"I would never have let you do that," Elliott argued. "No matter what he's done in the past, he's still your father. You can't just let that go. Trust me, if I knew where mine was, you know I'd be making an attempt to patch things up with him. No matter what they do, *we* have to be the bigger people."

"This is why I need you in my life." Ash grinned and kiss him. "What would I do without my wonderful, professional philanthropist to keep my big business head in line with your heart?"

"And your heart, too," Elliott said, jabbing a finger into Ash's chest. "Don't pretend like it isn't there. I *know* you, Bennett James Ashby."

Since last year, Ash had cleaned up his image and had stepped up to become an active part of the board of trustees, and now he was directing the business alongside his father. Not that they didn't still have their differences.

Ash smirked, capturing Elliott's finger against his chest. "My full name? Am I in trouble?"

"Not yet." Elliott pressed his lips together, trying to hold in a laugh. Then he leaned in and whispered a suggestive, "But later tonight, if the homeowners' association has anything to say about it, you just might be. You know they get fussy when we get... energetic."

A year with Ash had brought out Elliott's confidence and raised his self-esteem, and Elliott had learned a thing or two about flirting. No more was he the shy boy who hid behind Trevor, trying to dodge attention.

Ash had taught him his worth, and Elliott reveled in it.

"If you keep talking like that, we'll have another public sex scandal on our hands," Ash whispered into Elliott's ear, and Elliott's cheeks instantly heated.

Just because he was confident didn't mean that he wasn't still easily flustered.

They arrived at the second floor and took no more than two steps forward when a streak of black and electric blue bolted out from the North Pole and launched itself in their direction. Elliott only had a second to think before Grace swept him up in her arms, laughing.

"Oh my God, Elliott!"

"Grace!" Elliott hugged her back, grinning like a lunatic. She held onto him tight. "Has it really been that long? When did you dye your hair blue?"

"Three weeks ago, for the first time," Grace said. She released him and took a step back to look Ash over. They stood to the side of the escalator, allowing other customers to disembark without issue. "AshBen," Grace said with a nod and a fist-bump.

"What's happening, Amazing?" he asked with a small, serious nod back.

Elliott grinned at their mutual nicknames, still tickled that all the people who mattered most to him genuinely liked each other, too.

"You've been keeping my Elliott from me ever since Thanksgiving," Grace complained to Ash, crossing her arms in front of her chest and doing a piss-poor job of looking put out. "Not cool."

"Hey, I can't fault Elliott for having great taste in company," Ash said with a shit-eating grin, shrugging.

Grace rolled her eyes and snorted. "You're getting to be just as bad as Trevor, you know that?"

"Where is Trevor, anyway?" Elliott stood on his toes to peek over at the North Pole. A large group of parents obscured his view, and Elliott couldn't tell if Trevor was actually working or not. "He got to be an elf again this year, didn't he?"

"He did," she said, rolling her eyes again even though her voice was laced with affection. "And he can't shut up about being sexy. But right now he's up at the Giving Tree, handing out presents with Jose. I bit the bullet as reindeer this season, but I have tonight off, so bonus."

Elliott grinned. It looked like no matter how long Elliott spent away from Ashby's, not much changed. He loved the new life he'd created with Ash, but he'd always have a soft spot for the North Pole at Ashby's, and it did his heart good to step back into the playful banter and festive atmosphere for a bit .

"But come on," Grace insisted, grabbing his hand and giving it a tug. "There's someone else here you should say hi to. Everyone's been missing you like crazy, Elliott, but we're all so happy that you're working with the Ashby's charitable branch." She led him forward while she spoke, and Ash trailed behind them, keeping a respectful distance. "Ever since corporate transferred Martin and Kevin to the terrible Ashby's up in Skokie, everyone here has been getting along great. And the new shift manager, Krista, is a doll and a half."

Elliott didn't doubt her. On the nights he made it out for Friday night drinks at Reggie's, none of the employees could speak highly enough about Krista, and it was reassuring to know that his friends were in good hands now that their work environment wasn't so toxic anymore.

Elliott had long suspected that his boyfriend may have had a hand in that, but Ash had been evasive every time Elliott had hinted at the idea. Elliott trusted Ash completely, and knew he didn't keep secrets from him anymore. Still, he recognized the signs. The only time Ash avoided admitting the truth to Elliott, it tended to be around the issue of his constant, sneaky attempts to "spoil" him. Elliott could see how Ash might consider that having a hand in Martin and Kevin getting their just desserts could fall in that category, and he was fine with letting the issue lie.

Grace led them through the crowd of adults, and Elliott gasped with delight when he finally caught sight of just who she was taking him to see. Wrapped up in a heavy coat, looking a little thinner but healthier for it, was Nick. Beside him, smiling and rosy cheeked, was Luisa.

Even without the outfits, they were the perfect Santa and Mrs. Claus. St. Nick, in the flesh.

"Hey, kid," Nick said. Elliott swept forward and hugged him tight, and Nick held him back. "Been different without you here this year. I was half expecting you to come see me to tell me what you wanted for Christmas while I was in costume, but I hear you've been playing Santa in your day-to-day life. Congratulations on your new job."

Elliott's eyes beaded with tears, and he released Nick only so he could sniffle. After a long recovery, Nick had finally regained most of the function on his left side. There was still a little stiffness in his fingers, and sometimes the left side of his lips didn't move as fast as his right side did, but the improvement was astounding. The last time they'd visited, right at the tail end of summer, Elliott had told him that he'd been able to take the position with Ashby's Charitables.

It had been way too long since they'd caught up.

"You're looking well, Luisa," Ash said beside him, resting a hand on the small of Elliott's back as he gave Nick and Luisa a genuine smile. "Thanks for coming out tonight. You know how much Elliott loves the Children's Christmas Party."

"I wouldn't miss it for the world," Luisa said with a warm smile.

"That dog of yours still causing trouble?" Nick asked.

In the distance, Trevor was in the midst of delegating gifts. It looked like the event was already well underway.

"Donner's doing fine now. The veterinarian said he was suffering from patellar luxation, which means that his kneecap was dislocated. We brought him in for surgery and he's made a full recovery. Now he's just as happy and energetic as ever."

Donner was a remarkable dog. Once the scruffiness had been tamed and the vets had given him a clean bill of health, he'd been just as friendly as any dog Elliott had ever met. Full of love for people and other dogs, he had a habit of running after cats, but if that was his biggest issue, Elliott wasn't complaining.

"And your mom?" Nick's eyes sparkled, and Elliott couldn't tell if it was a trick of the light, or if Nick was remembering the friendship he'd forged with Anna when Elliott was young.

"She's doing well. She recently got a promotion, and she's loving it. Ash and I are going to see her tomorrow for Christmas dinner and our annual gift exchange."

Elliott smiled, already anticipating the look on her face when she saw the ugly Christmas sweater Ash had designed for her *this* year.

"I'm glad to hear it," Nick said. "Please give her my regards."

The sound of the young children's cheers and laughter was growing louder. Elliott allowed himself a moment's break from the conversation to look in that direction, his heart lifting as it always did at the sight. The gifts beneath the Giving Tree were gone—he and Ash had made sure to grant many of the wishes it had held—both here at the Chicago store and at other Ashby's locations around the country—and now the last of their kids were opening their gifts.

"I'm glad we made it in time to at least catch the tail end of the event," Elliott said. "We were lagging behind because *someone* couldn't settle on what kind of shirt to wear tonight. I kept telling him that it didn't matter, because we'd be wearing jackets, but he wouldn't listen."

"Consider it payback for all the nights you take an hour and a half to decide between Chinese takeout and Thai food," Ash shot back with a grin.

The crowds thinned further, and Trevor and Jose, officially relieved of their duties for the season now that the event was over, ambled over to join them. Jose fell in beside Grace and nodded his hello to Elliott—which wasn't unusual—but Trevor remained standing a short distance away, as though to address all of them at once.

Odd.

"Trevor?" Elliott asked, confused. "Um, what's going on? You can come over here, you know. Ash doesn't bite."

"Liar," Ash whispered under his breath. *Naughty.*

Trevor just winked at him. "Elliott G," he called out in a clear voice.

Elliott blinked, then cocked his head to the side as he looked Trevor over. Trevor just stared back, a mischievous gleam in his eye.

"Uh, yeah," Elliott finally said, laughing. "That's me."

From amongst the thinning crowd of parents, a familiar face appeared, surprising Elliott. It was his mother, and she waved at him from a short distance away. She had her cellphone out.

"Elliott G." Trevor declared, sounding for all the world like he was still on duty. Still calling children up to receive the secret wishes they'd dared to believe in when they'd whispered them in Santa's ear.

Ash parted from Elliott's side and went to stand by Trevor.

Elliott was confused.

As Ash walked away, Nick leaned over and whispered in Elliott's ear, "You might not have come to see Santa this year, but that doesn't mean that he hasn't been watching and figuring out what it is that you want. You've always been such a good kid, Elliott. And you deserve every second of this."

Elliott's thoughts were processing at a snail's pace, and he struggled to figure out what was happening. Trevor had called his name like he'd called all the children's names at the party, but now Ash had stepped forward, holding something in his hand.

A gift?

It had appeared from Trevor's back pocket. A small, black box. Unwrapped.

"What's happening?" Elliott asked, blinking.

He might have figured it out though. Excitement had begun to build in his belly, twisting up inside him in a too-good-to-be-true spiral that threatened to overwhelm him, but he pressed his lips together, holding back the smile that tried to burst out. He didn't want to commit to it until he was fully sure that he wasn't mistaken.

Ash dropped to one knee before him, and Elliott sucked in a sharp breath, daring to believe.

"Elliott Gaffney," Ash said formally. He looked up at Elliott with total adoration, a smile quirked his lips. "When you came into my life, I had no idea how much you were going to change me, or how fast that change would take place. I've become the man I am today because of you, and I *never* want to lose you again."

Ash opened the box.

Inside, partially sunken within a velvet cushion, was a simple silver band.

Elliott's knees shook. Desperately, he looked over to his mother and realized why she had her cellphone out—she was recording. And with Grace waiting nearby with bated breath and Nick and Luisa tucked against one another, smiling and hugging as they watched, Elliott knew that all of them had known what was about to happen. Even Jose, who was usually detached and inexpressive, was grinning widely.

"Elliott, will you marry me?" Ash asked.

He held the ring up to Elliott, and Elliott could barely squeak out his reply.

"Yes!"

Ash took the ring from the box and slid it onto Elliott's finger, but before he could make an attempt to rise, Elliott dropped to his knees in front of him and kissed him. Hard.

The excitement he'd been hesitant to indulge in pulsed beneath his skin and quickened his breath, and when the kiss broke, Elliott laughed with joy and buried his head against Ash's shoulder as his friends and family cheered for them.

"You're sure this is what you want?" Elliott asked in a hushed whisper. "I'm not too average or naive or unworldly?"

"You're not any of those things," Ash replied in a whisper meant for Elliott's ears alone.

He held Elliott close, and Elliott melted into his embrace, and it hit him that, now, he'd get to do so for the rest of his life.

It was exactly what he would have whispered into Santa's ear the year before—just before he'd met "Ben"—if he'd had the courage to do so. And, even if the road had been rocky for a little bit, the magic of Christmas hadn't let him down.

It never would.

Ash tipped his chin up tenderly, placing a sweet kiss on his lips, and continued. "What you are is a fantastic, loving, committed, kindhearted man who I'm proud to call my fiancé. What you are is more than I could have hoped for. More than I'd believed was possible before I met you. I love you, Elliott."

"I love you, too," Elliott said, overwhelmed with the happiness that bubbled up inside him at Ash's heartfelt words. His own heart felt full to bursting, as if the joy of it all couldn't be contained.

Ash smiled, a private one—just for the two of them—and that smile held everything that Elliott could ever wish for.

It held forever.

"Do you remember what I told you last Christmas, when we stood right here on this spot?" Ash asked tenderly.

Tears sprang to Elliott's eyes, and he nodded. How could he ever forget one of the best days of his life?

"It's still true, baby," Ash said, cupping his cheek. "And it will be, for the rest of our lives."

Elliott kissed him—the man who he'd never expected to love him, the dream that he'd dared to wish for—and Ash kissed him right back, ignoring the whistles and cheers around them as he looked into Elliott's eyes and said the words he'd first spoken the year before.

The words that made every one of Elliott's heart's wishes come true.

"Elliott, all I could ever want... is *you*."

More from Stella Starling

COMING JANUARY 2017

At Last, The Beloved Series
A spinoff series from All I Want

BE TRUE (Book One)

Trevor Rogers isn't interested in being tied down with a boyfriend, but acting the part as the public relations cover story for the once-in-a-lifetime chance he's offered by reclusive businessman Logan Carter, co-founder of the popular gay dating app *bloved*? No problem.

BE MINE (Book Two)

When Kelly Davis, co-founder of the popular gay dating app *bloved*, starts receiving death threats, he doesn't take them seriously... but to his annoyance, his business partner does. On the eve of a huge promotional push for the business that he's poured everything he has into, he finds himself whisked out of the public eye and stuck with an overbearing bodyguard who drives him crazy.

BE LOVED (Book Three)

Officer Brandon Byrne has always carried a torch for his best friend Shane. But Shane is a serial monogamist who falls out of each bad relationship directly into another, and Brandon has never had a chance to make a move. When the popular gay dating app *bloved* opens Shane's eyes to some scary truths about his current boyfriend, though, Brandon might finally get his chance... if he can keep Shane safe long enough to take it.

About the Author

Stella Starling is the storytelling team of two M/M contemporary romance authors who have far too many stories to tell on their own, so decided it would be fun to tell a few of them together.

The authors bring their love for writing, romance, and sweet, steamy "happily ever afters" to every story, and hope that "their boys" will give readers a delicious escape into a world where love always wins.

Made in the USA
Middletown, DE
22 February 2019